CALL OF THE WOLF

WOLVES OF MERCAIDA BOOK 1

MAYA RILEY

RILEY PUBLISHING LLC

BOOKS BY MAYA RILEY

STAY IN TOUCH WITH MAYA

www.mayariley.com

www.facebook.com/mayarileyauthor

www.instagram.com/mayarileyauthor

www.facebook.com/groups/mayasmaniacs

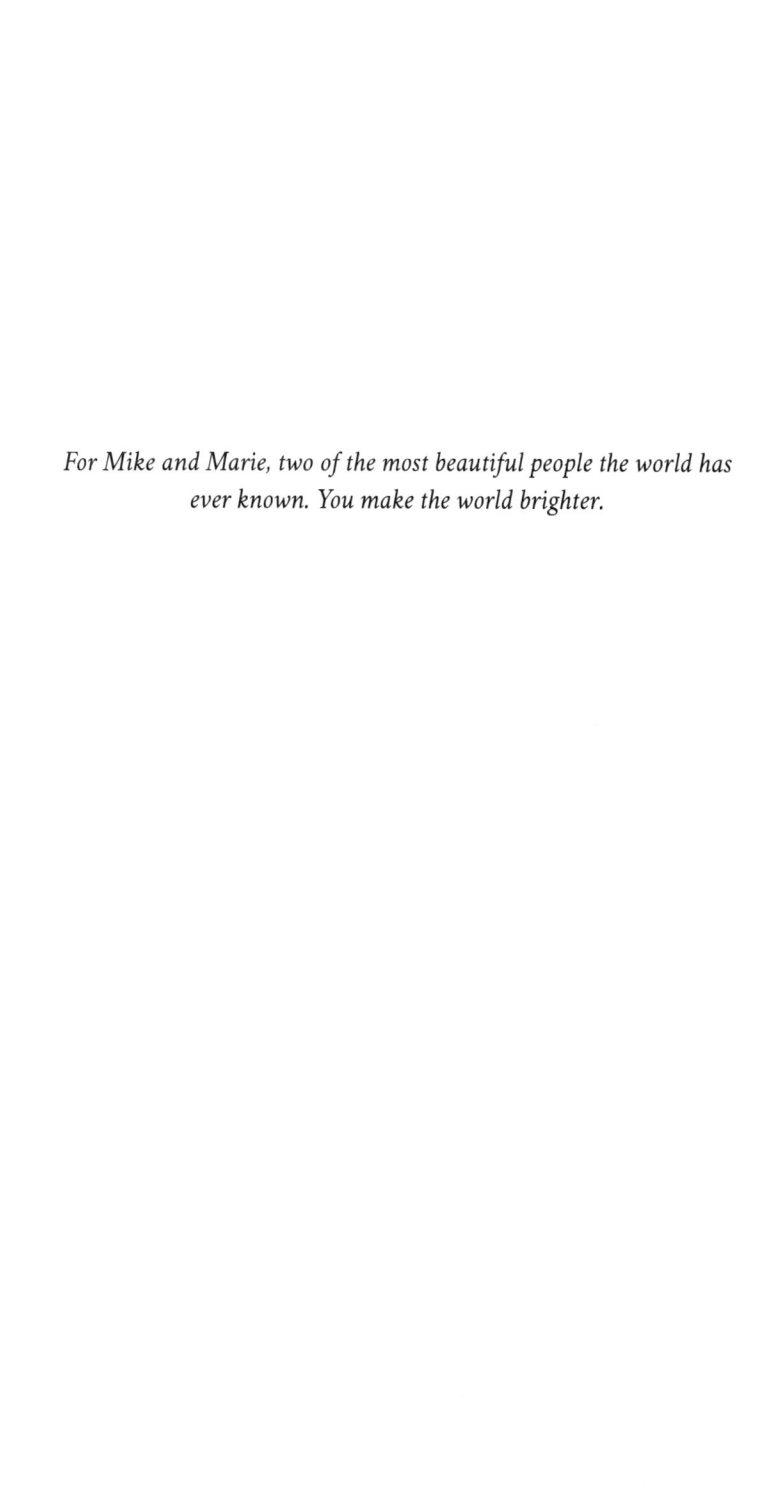

For Mike and Marie, two of the most beautiful people the world has ever known. You make the world brighter.

CALL of the WOLF

Chapter One

Makena

*R*unning naked through the woods wasn't exactly how I expected to start my day, but here I was, glowing like a Christmas tree in the early morning sun.

Using my hands and arms to cover myself as much as I could, I ran the two miles home, doing my best to ignore the glances while ducking behind bushes and trash cans as cars drove by. I wasn't fast enough when one car appeared, and the driver swung his head around so fast as he drove by, he ended up running a stop sign and the cars in the intersection only narrowly avoided hitting him.

I cringed at the loud squealing of tires as people hit their brakes, and breathed a sigh of relief when everyone made it through somewhat safely. I didn't exactly want to have this included in the police report if they would have crashed.

Memories from the night before evaded my mind. I had hoped this wouldn't keep happening, but at least this time it wasn't raining. Instead, it was just cold, really cold, as it was the start of fall in Carlisle, and I needed to get home before I froze to death.

Both the front and back doors were locked when I reached the house, and I cursed. Of course I wouldn't have been able to unlock it. I had nowhere to place the key on my stark naked body. After all these years here, why didn't we leave a spare somewhere outside? I couldn't exactly ring the doorbell like this.

Rolling my eyes in frustration, I moved back around to the front of the house and looked up.

This wasn't the first time I'd woken up in the woods, but it was one of the few times I'd woke up with no clothes in sight. I'd begun keeping a spare key on a chain around my neck specifically for times like this, but for some reason, I didn't have it on me this time and, looking up, I could see why.

There, hanging from the end of a tree limb out of my reach, was my key necklace, glinting in the early morning light. Well, at least now I knew how I got out of the house last night. Too bad I still couldn't actually remember doing it.

Looking around to make sure nobody was watching, I jumped up and wrapped my hands around the closest branch, then pulled myself up and over to hug the limb with my body. I did my best to ignore the pieces of tree bark that were cutting into my skin, deciding I'd deal with it if I could simply get inside without being caught. This wasn't something I'd want to explain to anyone.

As I reached the branch outside of my second story bedroom, I unhooked the necklace from the limb and replaced it safely around my neck. I pulled my long hair out so the chain sat comfortably around my neck, and then saw Austin standing on the sidewalk in front of my house with his hands in his pockets and a concerned look on his face.

His jaw was set in a frown, and blonde strands fell into his eyes.

Great, he was probably going to bring this up when I saw him next, and it really wasn't something I wanted to discuss in general. Even though he was one of my oldest childhood friends, we'd grown apart when we entered college. Not that we weren't still close or anything, but we'd become enthralled with our different paths in life and mostly focused on where we wanted to go and how to get there. Our conversations usually took place when we'd run into each other at the park. It was mostly my fault, as I'd fallen so hard into my work and studies that I lost sight of our friendship. I'd see him hanging out with Leah sometimes when I was out running around from one thing to the next, and would always tell myself I'd join them one day. Only, that day still hadn't come.

I felt like neither of them knew me anymore. Heck, with my mysterious sleepwalking lately, I didn't even know myself.

He probably assumed the good little college student, who focused on her work and education more than a social life, had a secret penchant for partying, and that was okay. That might even be better than the truth, depending on what exactly that truth was.

Rolling my eyes, I slid through my open window and tumbled to the floor of my bedroom. I jerked to my feet when I realized the blood from my cuts and scrapes would rub into the tan carpet and ran to the bathroom for a quick shower.

I ended up using a full box of Band-Aids to cover all the wounds. I was already running late and didn't have the luxury of washing my hair, so a horribly messy bun would have to do for today.

Rushing back into my room, I threw on the first t-shirt and pair of jeans I saw. My gaze caught on the journal sitting on the nightstand. I'd been keeping notes on all the weird things happening to me over the last several weeks. So far, all I had was a list of dates and times of when I'd woken up away from home. Which didn't help much, and I just didn't see a pattern. Looking at the clock, I decided I'd add this morning's adventure to it when I came home later tonight. I grabbed my purse, my work uniform, and then ran downstairs.

My father was sitting at the table drinking his coffee when I tossed my stuff on the floor and looked around for my shoes.

"Ah. You were so quiet, I thought you'd already gone out. Volunteering before your shift today?" He glanced over the top of his newspaper at my crumpled up uniform on the floor.

"Yeah, I'm already late."

"It would do well to set an alarm."

"Thanks, Dad, I'll remember that." I bit the inside of my cheek as I turned around to prevent myself from spilling the real reason I was running late. Setting an alarm wouldn't work if I kept waking up in the woods every other morning. This issue was becoming more frequent, and I debated whether to tell him, but I didn't want to freak him out.

"Be careful out there, Makena."

"Always am, Dad."

"More than normal. There's been something attacking and eating animals lately. Even Mrs. Monroe's cat has gone missing."

"Jenkins goes missing all the time, he'll come back when he wants to." Spotting my shoes in the laundry room, I rolled my eyes at myself for never putting them back where they belong and slipped them on.

"Normally when he goes missing, it's not during a time when a mountain lion or something is eating small animals."

"What do you mean?" I turned to him, giving him my full attention.

Laying the newspaper flat against the table, he adjusted his glasses while he ran a finger down the story he was reading to find the part he was referring to. "Ah, right here. Says there's been an increase in animal activity lately, and small bones are being found all over the place. There have been sightings of some large dog or a lion or something, but people have been too freaked out to get a good look."

"How long has this been going on for?"

"A few weeks. The sightings and incidents have happened two or three times a week since the beginning of last month."

That was strange. That was around the same time I started sleepwalking. Not wanting to consider this as more than a coincidence, I countered, "We live in Carlisle. There are a lot of animals around here. That's how life is." Mountains and water surrounded us. Wild animals shouldn't have been anything new.

He glanced at me over his spectacles. "Just be careful, kiddo."

"You got it, Dadd-o." Grabbing my stuff, I made a mad dash for the door and climbed into my beaten down car. It was enough to get me to and from where I needed to go without much hassle, except in the winter when it would need a little extra coaxing to start. That was the only downside.

Biting my lip with impatience, I checked my mirrors as the car warmed up, then flew out of the driveway like a bat out of hell. I rapped my fingers against the steering wheel as I drove, trying not to glance at the time on the clock. I'd promised the shelter I would be there by eight in the morning, and it was already twenty minutes past. If I could start taking my car when I sleepwalk, it would make things so much easier.

On second thought, that could be so much worse.

I turned onto the gravel drive toward Cara Paws, the animal shelter I spent a lot of my spare time at. It was hard to find extra time between my studies and hours at the diner, but I made it work.

Shutting off the car, I flung my purse over my head and across my body as I headed inside.

"Makena! Good to see you. We were getting worried something was wrong," Carol's shoulders relaxed when she greeted me, her cheerful tone the exact thing I needed to calm me down.

"Sorry about that, I overslept. I'll try to be better."

"No worries, dear, I'm glad you're okay. You know where everything is, and I'll be here when you get back."

Giving her a smile and a nod, I headed toward the back. She was an older lady who chose to spend her retirement years opening up a shelter. She named it after a cat she used to have before she retired, and now she spends her days— and sometimes nights—here, making sure each and every animal was properly cared for.

There were many volunteers who walked in and out of those doors, but I was one of the few who could be called long-term. I'd lived in this area my whole life. It was the only world I knew.

My dad had told me about how I was born on the side of the road, then how my mom mysteriously disappeared shortly after. He rarely talked about her, but I always yearned to learn more. Maybe someday I'd have that opportunity.

The potent smell of dog invaded my nostrils, but I was so used to it by now that it barely fazed me. I'd been volunteering here for the last four years. It started out as a requirement for a high school assignment, and I'd never left. This was the place I felt most at home. Despite how difficult it sometimes was to see the dogs leave when they'd get adopted, it was also bittersweet. I knew they were going home with families who would love them, and give them the kind of warmth a shelter was unable to provide.

"Down, boy." I grinned as I tried to hook the first leash onto Scooter's collar. His chocolate lab paws were giant for his small size. He was still growing into them, and I couldn't help but coo every time those things would press across my lap.

After hooking leashes onto the collars and harnesses of five of the dogs, I had them sit still and wait before opening the door. The last thing we needed was a stampede and for them to all get tangled up in the leashes.

"It's crazy how well they listen to you," a voice said, and I spun around and saw Tyler approaching. "They never do a single thing I say."

"You have to know how to talk to them, I guess." I shrugged. "It's all in your tone. They can tell when you're frustrated, and it frustrates them right back."

"I'll try to remember that for next time. Get out all the energy you can. I'll be taking some of them with me to sit outside the pet store later. Hopefully, it will bring in some new adopters and entice them to take a dog home." He picked up a large bag of food and walked to the nearest cage door. Tyler was a long-term volunteer like I was. He walked the dogs once a week, fed them almost every day, and was in charge of taking groups of them to certain locations to help induce adoption. Sometimes he would take a small group of short-term volunteers who were looking for some school credits, like I was in the beginning. They'd help entertain the dogs while he talked to people about the benefits of adoption. Our aim was to have as many empty cages as possible.

"I'll do the best I can," I replied, before stuffing a couple handfuls of treats into my pockets and walking outside.

Chapter Two

Makena

$\mathcal{I}$t was a short walk to the park. There were a few pathway loops, and I always took the dogs on the longest one to make the most of their time outside.

Before continuing the walk, I ran through some basic commands and rewarded them with a treat when they responded. "Sit. Shake. There's a good boy." I even gave them each an extra treat from the pocketful I'd snagged. "I don't understand why they say you never listen to anyone else. You always listen quite well to me," I cooed as I scratched behind Scooter's ears and let him gently take the treat from my palm.

Once they stopped smacking their lips and looked expectantly up at me, we got started on the loop. Pulling on the leashes, I slowed us down as we came around a bend. The hairs stood up on the back of my neck, and I clenched my fist tighter around the leashes as I pulled the dogs closer to me and looked around.

Something felt out of place, and I couldn't put my finger on it. I didn't like not knowing what was going on.

My gaze darted around to figure out what was wrong and landed on a group of five guys. They were all similar in build, but with distinct features. One of them locked eyes with me, and at that moment, the others turned around and watched me too. The dark orbs swallowed me whole, and the ground seemed to fall away as I crumbled beneath his gaze. My mouth dried, and his eyes flicked to my tongue that darted out as I licked lips.

There was something familiar about them, even though I couldn't recall having ever seen them before in my life.

We were locked in this odd staring contest, and none of us seemed to want to be the first to break eye contact. Instead, we were all standing there, watching each other as though the rest of the world didn't exist.

Until the world brought us back to reality when someone bumped into me.

"Whoa there, Makena, this is a walking path. You alright?"

I turned to look at the person who rudely ran into me and saw Austin with a wide grin. He definitely did that on purpose.

"Hey, Austin."

"Who are they?" He pointed at the group of guys I'd been entranced with. They were still standing there, watching, as though they were frozen in time.

"I have no idea. I wonder if they are new in town?" I'd lived here my entire life, and I worked at the most popular diner in town. I knew everyone who came through here, but I'd never seen them. There was something different about them. Something that said they lived a life of excitement, but there was also something familiar that I couldn't decipher.

"Hey, you guys!" Austin yelled, and I dropped my head into my palm. "Who are you?" I shouldn't have been surprised. He wasn't one to shy away from new people or experiences.

I spread my fingers enough to peek through them. The guys were still as statues, and for a moment, I could have been convinced they were. Until one of them shifted his body slightly to the side.

Their only response was to glare back. Except they weren't looking at Austin, or even at the dogs. They were looking at me. Their eyes had a curious hardness to them as they studied my face. It made me want to simultaneously hide and go over and talk to them.

I did neither. Instead, I stood there, watching the strange men and trying to figure out what they were up to.

They looked at me as though they'd been searching for me their whole lives. They didn't seem to see the ratty old jacket I'd been wearing for years or the tears in my jeans that kept growing with my determination to avoid clothes shopping for as long as I possibly could. I fell into the entrancement again. It felt as though they were looking into my very being.

"Weirdos," Austin commented, as he took a step back toward me without taking his eyes off of the mysterious men. His shoulder bumped into me as he did so, knocking me out of my stupor once again.

"Maybe they're new in town and don't know proper customs," I supplied, but he shook his head.

"Even people outside of this town know how to at least wave back. Maybe I should go talk to them."

"No, don't." I grabbed his arm before he could take off, and I pulled him back. Looping my arm through his, I guided us down the path. I tugged on the leashes, startling the dogs out of their state of hypnosis. All they wanted to do was stay and watch the newcomers.

"Strange," I muttered, "we get someone new in town and

all the animals want to interact." Austin too, but that was just the kind of person he was. No one passed through Carlisle without at least shaking his hand.

"Are you calling me an animal?" he asked, and I threw my head back in a laugh.

"You're the scariest animal of them all."

Austin and I had practically grown up together. We were friends before we could form memories, but our friendship had been off and on over the years. He used to have a crush on me, and when I turned him down, it put a strain on our friendship until we kissed at a party years ago and were both rather turned off from the idea. It erased his disappointment of my rejection and helped heal our fractured friendship. He returned to basically being my brother for all intents and purposes. I missed us hanging out. I missed my friend.

"So, about this morning…" He turned to look at me with a grin as he finally pried his eyes from the odd guys.

"I'm afraid I have no idea what you're talking about." I played it off by being cool and collected, or so I thought. Until he snickered.

"Come on, I saw your butt all the time when we were kids. Even now I'd recognize it if I saw it hanging from a tree. I know I wasn't mistaken, unless people periodically break into your house naked. In which case, I might have to stop by more often."

I slapped his chest lightly before regaining my hold on his arm. "You shouldn't go around town saying crazy things like that."

He could have easily fought to get out of my hold against his arm, but he didn't. Instead, he cupped his hand over mine and his voice turned serious. "I won't. But Makena, if there's something I can help you with, you know you can always ask me."

"I'll try to remember that." I coughed. "Changing the subject, how's Trischa?"

He shook his head. "She's good. Ever since she started working at the news station on the side, she's discovered a whole new world and decided to change career paths. She's been working with Leah for months now and is really excited about it. I'm excited for her too."

"That's good." Trischa was his girlfriend. They'd been going out for a little over a year now. She seemed like a nice girl and made him happy, but I hadn't taken the time to get to know her yet. It appeared to be getting serious, especially since he couldn't stop that stupid grin from stretching over his face every time she was mentioned. Except for this time.

"Trischa and I broke up."

"What?" My steps faltered and I tightened my grip on the leashes. "What do you mean? For the longest time, she was all you could talk about."

He shrugged. "Maybe. It was good for a while, but neither of us were into it as much as we should've been. It's been a few months now." Before I could pry further, he changed the subject again. "How about you, how are your classes going?"

I sighed. "They're going well enough. They said I could use my shelter volunteer work to meet most of their animal volunteer requirements."

"But that's not good enough for you," he noted, and he was right.

I shook my head. "I love doing this, I really do, but I just want…I don't know what I want."

"You want more." The words tumbled from his mouth with such ease, I sort of admired him for it. I couldn't always find the right words to portray what it was I wanted to say, but he always made it look so easy, and I envied him for that.

"Not really."

His head snapped around to look at me as we rounded

another bend and headed back into the main park area. He pushed his glasses up the bridge of his nose when they started to slide. "What do you mean, 'not really?' You're headed for bigger and better things."

I shrugged out of his arm and used both hands to hold the leashes. Not that I needed to since the dogs were behaving rather well anyway. They always did with me. "I was thinking of working at the zoo. The animals need more help and protection there than anywhere else."

"The zoo? So, a step up from Cara Paws?"

I nodded. "Different animals. Cara Paws deals with domestic animals like cats and dogs. I want to help wildlife."

His eyes grew big.

"Everyone wants to help the furry animals who sleep in your bed, but no one wants to help the birds who fly into your window or the poor bear cub who lost its mama."

"Probably because they'll most likely eat you before you can get close enough to help them," he remarked, and I scoffed.

"Can't hurt to try."

"Makena, nothing against what you're doing, but why not open your own wildlife rehabilitation center or something? You love animals more than anyone else on the planet. You're so good with them, not to mention you're wicked smart."

I averted my gaze. This wasn't the first time someone advised me to look beyond this little town, or even outside of the state. I just couldn't leave, this was where I belonged. Even if I didn't always feel like it.

"Don't worry, I'm not giving up on you. Join me and Leah for dinner sometime, we'll talk you into some greatness."

I laughed. "Well, you're welcome to show up to the diner whenever you want. I'm always there."

"Except when you're studying or helping animals."

"Pretty much."

"Don't take this the wrong way, but you should probably get out more. See what the world has to offer." He watched the dogs as he spoke, who were trotting along without issue.

"What does the world have to offer me? My future is right here. It always has been."

"It doesn't have to be."

Annoyed, I stopped walking and turned to face him. "What do you want, Austin?"

"Nothing."

"You've always been a terrible liar."

Blowing out a breath, he looked at me. "I'm not going to be here forever. I've been thinking about leaving Carlisle."

I raised an eyebrow. "Oh? Are there no teaching jobs you're interested in?"

"There are, but I've lived here my entire life. I want out, and I've felt that way for a long time. I want to travel and see what all there is to do. It's a big world out there." He looked down at his hands as he picked at the dirt beneath his thumbnail.

"What aren't you telling me?"

"I leave in two weeks."

"What?"

"And I don't know if I'm coming back."

"Where, exactly, are you going?" Not that he needed to answer me, because he didn't. Austin was still a pretty big constant in my life, even when we weren't talking.

"I'm planning to go backpacking across the country until I find a place I want to stay. I still have no idea what I want to do. Carlisle is beautiful and all, but this can't be the only place in the world to see. I want to travel and experience all there is. Find the hidden worlds."

Forcing a smile on my face, I looked at him. "Well, I'm excited for you."

"You can come too."

I laughed. "No thanks. I belong right here. Do you think you'll ever come back for a visit?"

His eyes turned distant as he answered, "I honestly don't know."

The silence stretched between us as we completed the loop, and a familiar ball of short, dark curly hair appeared as Austin's mom closed the door to her car and looked around.

"I gotta go, I have a lot of preparation to do." Austin squeezed my arm before heading off toward the parking lot.

I watched as he disappeared into the car and they drove away.

How strange it would be to leave everything behind like that and go somewhere new. This was where we'd spent our entire lives—this was home. Why would anyone want to leave and go somewhere they never knew?

Shaking my head from the overwhelming thoughts of the unknown, I felt a strange shiver roll down my spine. I turned around to look for the source of it and spotted the same guys from before staring at me, watching. They'd moved from their spot, only far enough to be able to peek out from the part of the loop that disappeared under the trees.

I should have felt scared, I should be running away, but there was something enticing about their gazes. They held me in place and I had to force myself to look away.

Deciding this day was already weird enough as it was, I checked the time and turned back in the direction of the shelter.

Chapter Three

Makena

The atmosphere was vibrant as I made my way through the diner, trying to get to every table in a timely manner. We were overwhelmed with the lunch rush and understaffed as three waitstaff and two cooks decided to quit this morning. Well, the waitstaff quit. The cooks were simply nowhere to be found and had gone missing a couple of days ago.

As if today couldn't get any more chaotic.

We were drowning in customers. So when a guy named Rodge walked in carrying the help wanted sign, Justine threw him into the kitchen with a spatula, hiring him on the spot without bothering to ask about his employment background. Greg was glad to have some help back there, since he was overwhelmed by orders, and we were just about to close the restaurant down to new arrivals.

"Excuse me, we'd like a refill." A woman with her mouth set in a hard line glared my way, and I did my best to keep my eyes from rolling as I approached her table with a smile and grabbed the three cups she was indicating. Two of them were still nearly half full, while the third one was barely even a third of the way gone, but I took them all anyway and brought them back their refills in record time, despite the dozens of hands in the air vying for my attention.

"Is anyone coming in to help, or is it only us?" I asked Justine in passing. She was struggling to keep up as well. Bits of food and sweat bedazzled her normally clean hair. Bunches of strands were popping out of the braid that hung over her shoulders. Somehow, her radiance still shone through the grime. "You look almost awful," I said as I reached out to wipe a spot of grease from her cheek.

Right now, we were the only two waiting tables, and while getting tips from more tables would be nice, neither of us would be getting any if we couldn't even keep up with a single table.

"Nathan should be on his way. I hope he is because we can't afford to lose anyone else," she responded, cleaning up another table right as more people were sitting down. "Here are some menus, and I'll be back in a few minutes. Are there any drinks I can start you out with?"

Writing down their drink orders, she slid her notepad into her apron pocket and carried the tub of dirty dishes to the back.

Seeing a new group of people sitting at a table in my section, I went over to do the same. My body froze a few inches from the table when I saw a pair of familiar dark eyes looking back at me, and I gulped. I managed to recover myself after a few beats, and I cleared my throat. "Are there some drinks I can start you off with?"

The man with dark eyes that pulled me into oblivion was the first to speak. Without breaking eye contact he said, "We will all start with some waters."

His voice was smooth and confident, like he had experience being a leader. I glanced around to the others to see if there was any objection to his drink of choice for them, but they only watched me. It was only when the one with hazel eyes sitting next to him nodded that I scribbled down five waters, smiled, and took off to go get them.

They were the same five guys from the park, and now they were here, sitting in my section. This was a fairly small town, though, so it could all be a coincidence. Regardless, should I tell someone? If I were to go missing tonight...

I let out a small, dark chuckle as I stuck the first glass under the nozzle for water. Of course I would most likely go missing tonight. It was what had been happening for the last couple months now. Regardless of whether or not these guys were going to do something, I probably wouldn't have control anyway.

Shaking the darkening thoughts from my head, I carried the tray of five waters back to the table and pulled out my notepad. All ten eyes watched me, and I swore they could even see every drop of sweat on the back of my neck. With a brief glance, I had them all seared into my mind.

The one who looked calm but exuded a strong power had dark eyes void of all color. I had to tear my own gaze away for fear I'd fall in and be lost forever. His back was straight and his hands had paused from fumbling with his napkin as he studied me. The next one had hazel eyes that pierced my soul as he watched me behind messy onyx hair. A shiver ran down my spine when he looked at me, his hand clenching so tightly around the menu—despite his relaxed posture—that I thought the laminated cardboard would tear. Next to him sat a man whose stunning blue eyes darted around the diner with the excitement of a new place, a new experience. He drank it all in like it was the water he needed to live, and his fingers tapped against the table to the rhythm of the growing chatter. The next one had stubble surrounding plump lips and he watched me with curiosity. His tongue darted out to lick his lips when I clicked my pen. Then the final one had green eyes that brightened when he looked at me, his arm draped protectively over what looked to be a camera bag.

"Are you ready to order, or is there an appetizer you want me to put in for you?" I held the pen ready, hoping they would order and get this over with. Instead, they all surveyed me as though they'd never seen a girl before, and I raised an eyebrow.

Finally, the one who ordered the waters opened his mouth, and the same smooth voice glided over me, calming the nerves that were threatening to go haywire.

"We're ready to order." He rattled off meal choices for himself and each of his friends, all of whom observed my every move as he spoke. They were each getting various burgers, one of them with avocado.

Nodding, I smiled and turned back toward the kitchen to put their order in. As I stuck the page with orders to the line above for the chefs to see, I breathed a sigh of relief when I saw Nathan arrive, and wondered if I could pawn their table off on him.

Not that I was super uncomfortable or anything, but... actually, yeah, that was precisely the reason. Strangely enough, I also didn't want to give up that table, despite the bizarre feelings I had toward it.

Taking a deep breath as Nathan took over some of my and Justine's tables, I leaned my head against the wall for a moment while I looked out at the diner. It was unusually crowded today, with a line turning down the sidewalk, but that should have been expected because judging by the dresses and tuxedos of half the diners, it must have been homecoming weekend.

Normally I would have known, but I'd been so caught up in my own little world that I'd barely even noticed school had started back up again. I was a year-round student, taking classes even in the summer and putting in extra hours studying over winter break so I could become as knowledge-able as possible. I didn't even care if I graduated early, I just wanted to learn everything I could get my hands on.

My summer internship at the zoo recently ended, and I couldn't wait to start up with another one. Excitement fled through me when I thought about all the new areas of study to explore. While I had my mind made up that working at a zoo was in my future, it was also important to get as much experience as I could manage. The next thing on my list was wildlife rehabilitation.

Someone bumped into my shoulder, which jolted me back into my surroundings.

"No time for daydreaming, Makena, there are tables looking for you." Justine rushed by, hurrying to each table to apologize for the delay.

I grumbled and refilled everyone's drink orders and brought out food when it was ready. I was doing a decent job keeping up with everything and constantly eyeing the table in the corner with the five guys. They were deep in conversation this whole time and spared occasional glances at me. I itched to know what they were discussing, but I could only go over to their table so many times before it became extra weird.

Steam wafted up from their food as I carried the tray of plates over to their table. I wanted to know what it was that had their heads tilted forward to close the space between them as they whispered. I couldn't help but think it had something to do with me, and I didn't think that was only paranoia. There was something going on and I was going to figure out what it was. I strained my ears to try and pick up on what they were saying, but then one of them noticed my arrival and nudged the others.

Their faces lit up as I set each dish in front of the one who ordered. "I'll grab some refills for you. Is there anything else I can help you with?"

I began adding their nearly empty glasses to the tray on my hand, but when I reached for the one in front of the guy with the dark eyes, his back went ramrod straight as my hand brushed against his.

Okay, maybe he wasn't one for touching, but that was alright. It happened occasionally. I bit back the smirk that threatened to appear at his reaction. Something in me was glad I could get a reaction from mister tall, dark, and mysterious. Something else in me wanted my hand to reach out and touch him again. "Sorry about that, let me grab those refills for you." I hurried off carrying the tray, and as the water was pouring down into their glasses, I chanced another glance at the table.

Sure enough, the guys were communicating, but not by words. They seemed to be conversing by glances, and I wished so much that I could tell what it was they were saying.

"Crap!" I snatched the nearest rag and rushed to wipe up the outside of the glass as the water overflowed, and quickly filled up the other glasses. With quick movements, I returned the waters to the guys, and they all looked at me with the same expression that sent chills down my spine.

"Thank you, Makena." His dark eyes softened when they reached mine, and I gave him a smile.

"You're welcome. Enjoy your food."

"My name is Denver." His words reached my ears before I could turn around.

"Nice to meet you, Denver. Let me know if there's anything I can do for you." When I was met with silence, I hurried off toward the break room and took a seat. I didn't care that we were incredibly slammed today, I needed a break, even if only for a moment. There was something off that I couldn't quite describe, and I needed to get my breathing in order.

I should've been more wary of them. Possibly even alert Justine to help keep an eye on the strange group of guys. Something changed in the last several minutes and I found myself stealing glances at Denver the rest of the night. Why was it, despite my own cautiousness, I found myself wanting to find excuses to run my hands through the hair of a stranger?

Denver

MY EYES FOLLOWED the strange girl as she hustled around the diner, tending to the customers. She was obviously one of us, a wolf shifter. Even more so, she was a Mercai. The scent was everywhere. Her skin. Her blood. Her soul. It was sweet like the way she greeted her customers and infused with fresh pine and lilac. We could always recognize one of our own.

She noticed us, but her eyes never lit up with the recognition they should have had. Her nose didn't even twitch in the slightest. She should know who, or what, we were, but she acted as though she had no clue. Was she really that oblivious?

My eyes followed her around the diner as my mind tried to put her puzzle pieces together. I was so engulfed in the curly-blonde mystery, I almost forgot my pack was with me. Then Julian's words brought me back to the conversation.

"If she isn't aware, then it's only a matter of time before she is. I can sense it, she should be turning twenty soon." Julian's eyes followed her around as intensely as the rest of ours did, and he was right. If she was brought up without knowing about who she was, then the change should already be taking place.

It wasn't common to be raised without knowledge of wolf society, but there were stories about it happening. It was always under extreme circumstances, so what reasons did she have?

The most worrisome was if she was entirely clueless, then she would have no idea what was happening to her. A newborn wolf in an unprepared human civilization would be dangerous. That meant it was up to us to help her.

"I'm pretty positive she doesn't know," Liam, the beta wolf and my second in command, commented as he observed her. "She's acting like a full human. Otherwise, she would've recognized us for what we are."

"We'll keep an eye on her. Maybe pick up her scent when she leaves and find out where she lives." My eyes were glued to her as we talked.

"Here she comes," Julian warned, and sure enough, she strolled through the maze of people and tables as she carried a tray of steaming food. I could smell the food in the air, mixed in with some small injuries on her body that she'd hastily tried to cover up in a rush. She'd been hurt.

She set the tray down with a forced smile, but when she picked up our glasses to grab some refills, her hand brushed mine.

My whole body froze, but my mind was whirling. Possibilities of what my future might hold flitted through my mind so fast, I could barely see any of them.

The crazy thing was, she was in all of those images. I had a connection to her and felt the need to hover over her and snarl at anyone who dared to even look her way.

She was *mine*.

I shivered as the realization hit me. This girl, who seemed to have no idea what she even was, was going to mean more

24

to me than I could have ever realized. I tilted my head up to look her in the eyes, but her face didn't show a reaction. She was completely oblivious to the spark that zapped through me like lightning. Unaware of the bond we'd just begun to form. My heart beat rapidly, and I tugged at the hem of my shirt to keep it from being too noticeable that it was most likely vibrating my chest.

"Thank you, Makena." The words left my mouth before I knew what I was saying, but I watched her face for a response.

"You're welcome. Enjoy your food."

"My name is Denver." I no longer had control over my mouth, and only shock kept me from reaching out and pulling her into my arms just now.

She bit her lower lip as she decided how to reply, and I wanted to bite it for her. Perhaps her customers didn't normally introduce themselves to her. "Nice to meet you, Denver. Let me know if there's anything else I can do for you."

All I saw next was her messy bun as she turned around and disappeared into the kitchen.

"What was that about?" Liam gave me a knowing look, his brow raised as he searched for confirmation, and I didn't even need to respond. They could sense what had happened through the pack bond and knew what this meant for us.

We were only passing through in search of other packs to plead our cause to, but this unexpected encounter created the first step to changing our lives forever.

"It looks like we're going to be staying here a little while," I whispered to the others without taking my eyes off of the swinging doors she'd disappeared through. Our mission was going to have to wait.

Chapter Four

Makena

*M*y paws pounded the ground, shaking frost from the blades of grass as I ran through the forest. This was my favorite time. At night, the darkness hid me, and I could be free. It was the one time I didn't feel tethered to the world and to all my responsibilities. Instead, I flew across the ground, driven by the pure exhilaration of exploring my land with a new set of eyes.

The cool night air was crisp, but my fur coat kept me warm. A couple of months ago it was still hot enough that I had to quickly learn how to keep myself cool. I was built for the cold, a climate chillier even beyond this, and this was my time to thrive.

Frost coated the tips of the grass, and dried leaves shattered as I ran over them. I didn't know where I was going, but I felt the urge that I was supposed to be somewhere. If only I could figure out where that was.

A gentle pitter-patter of little paws crumpled the fallen autumn leaves as they ran away from me, and my ears perked. My body stilled as I tried to catch the direction they were going, and then I took off at a sprint.

Branches broke as my strong body rushed past, searching for the critters I wanted to play with even though instinct told me I was supposed to hunt them. I didn't want to hurt them, though, I didn't want to harm anyone. I've been fighting to keep those instincts pushed deep down, giving over to my curiosity. All the new sights, sounds, and smells made me want to explore and figure everything out in this new world that I had only been able to experience in short bursts on some nights.

I reached a fence with horizontal wooden planks that allowed me to see more animals beyond. Their scents drifted to me, and I put my nose in the air to get a whiff. A moment later, I jumped the fence, and the goats all scattered when my paws hit the ground. I watched as they ran in fear, wondering what could be so terrifying about me. I only wanted to play.

A loud bang rang out and something shot past me, grazing my fur as the small object became embedded in the wood behind me. Wisps of steam rose from the hole, the object still hot from being fired.

I jumped back over the fence right as another bullet pelted the wooden frame, and I ran at full speed. Shouts could be heard in the distance as someone hollered after me, chasing me. I heard another bullet click into place, and I urged my legs to move faster.

Zigzagging through the trees and brush, I took refuge behind a large fallen tree trunk. There was barely enough space for me to squeeze down into the area where the trunk met the ground. I used my nose to move some of the leaf piles in front of me in an attempt at camouflage, ignoring the maggots whose meal I'd interrupted.

My body stiffened when I heard the crunch of fallen leaves beneath old boots as the harmful humans approached.

All was quiet aside from the crunching leaves, and I tried my hardest not to breathe. My lungs were full with the air I'd inhaled in a rush, and I only hoped it would be enough. Every moment counted, and the smallest mishap could end very badly.

I remained in my hiding spot long after the humans with the loud objects had left. I was afraid they might come back, so I stayed throughout the rest of the night. It would be safer for my human self to leave during the daytime. I only hoped she would remember enough to be cautious of her surroundings when she did leave.

THE BRIGHT YELLOW and orange blob in the sky was blinding through my cracked eyelids, and I immediately shut them again. Leaves crumpled beneath my hands when I rolled over, shivering under the chilly autumn air.

It happened again. This made for two nights in a row, only this time I could recall parts of my dream more vividly, and I wondered if it had anything to do with how I ended up here.

I cringed when something hard grazed my shoulder as I stood up, and then froze when I saw it was a large, fallen tree trunk I'd been sleeping under. There was something familiar about it, but after cringing at the sight of maggots feasting, I shook the strange feeling from my head. I had things to do today.

Running from tree to tree and hiding behind bushes to prevent being seen, I made my way home. I knew every path in these woods better than anyone by now. There wouldn't be a single spot of dirt untouched by my frantic footsteps with all the time I'd spent running them.

I was about to turn onto my street when something caused me to stop. The same new guys from yesterday were at the corner of where this street connected with mine, and the one who had been tightly clutching the diner menu the day before turned to look at me as though he could sense my presence. A shiver ran down my spine as his hazel eyes locked on me, but only for a split second. I ducked behind a car before the others could see.

"Oh, come on. Does everyone have to be near my house every time this happens?" My frustrated words were whispered as I edged my way to the front of the car.

If I had any luck, the one who saw me wouldn't tell the others. If my luck went in the direction it normally did, they would come over and find me, and awkwardness would ensue.

Approaching footsteps told me it was going to be option two, and I groaned internally. The asphalt was frosted over, turning my bare feet blue as I crouched low. I couldn't hide out in this spot forever, I'd freeze to death by the time I could move. Gravel rolled underneath the shoes of those approaching me as they reached my hiding spot.

My feet burned from the sharpness of the cold. So, throwing my arms across myself to cover my body as best as I could, I stood up and was met with five pairs of eyes that all widened in surprise at my abrupt appearance.

"Hey, guys," I said casually. Before they could respond, I darted around them, barely registering the jolt that went through me as I brushed by the one with hazel eyes. I hurried over to take cover behind the tree by my window, glad it was wide enough to hide my body from view. Bark scraped my skin as I leaned my back against the trunk.

Reaching up to grab the key from around my neck, I

winced as my fingers brushed against a wound on the side of my neck. I looked at my fingers as I pulled my hand away, and the tips had a small amount of blood on them.

That was strange. Maybe I scraped it against that log when I stood up. I looked up at the overcast sky as though it would have the answers, but an engine roaring to life pulled my attention back down to the car in my driveway. My dad was getting ready to head to work. I took another step so that my whole body was hidden by the tree as he backed down the driveway. Once he rounded the end of the street and was out of sight, I ran to unlock the front door. I frowned as I shoved the bent piece of metal into the lock. Somehow it had gotten damaged overnight, the bend right above the teeth. I'd need to get a new one made. Relief filled me as the lock turned, feeling grateful I wouldn't have to climb the tree again. Although, somehow, my wounds from climbing the previous morning were already healed, which I only noticed because the Band-Aids had fallen off at some point overnight.

Shutting the door behind me, I dropped the key onto the table and ran straight for the bathroom. I stared at myself in the mirror, smoothing my hair with my hands and rubbing a singed section in between two fingers, wondering how that had happened.

That was strange. A vague memory of the dream flashed through my mind, and I recalled the bullets flying around me, but I shook it from my head. That was too out there to be real, there had to be another explanation. If I'd been shot at while I was sleepwalking, I was certain I wouldn't be alive and unharmed the next morning. I must have been having some wild dreams.

A brief flash of fur appeared in the mirror, but then it was gone before my eyes could really register it. I brushed it off as not having a proper night's sleep and turned on the water to wash my face.

After showering and getting ready for the day, I whipped up some breakfast and sat down in front of my computer with a plate full of food and a mug of steaming hot coffee. I was going to need all the caffeine I could get my hands on to make it through this day. The assignments I had to complete were piling up, and if I spent all day working on them, I might possibly be able to make a dent in the long list.

My body was tired, and my muscles ached. I wanted nothing more than to crawl into my unused bed, but I had too many things to get through today, as well as some virtual lectures. I looked longingly in the direction of my bed, but my gaze stopped at the window. The tree outside was calm, there wasn't a breeze or the usual flapping of wings from birds flying by. Abandoning my work before I could get started, I walked over.

The area outside was void of any movement. It was cold and still with a hint of whispering secrets. It felt like someone was watching me and I looked around, but all I saw was dried leaves on the ground twitching in a faint breeze.

My gaze snapped over to nearby bushes. There was something there, watching. Waiting.

The hair on the back of my neck stood up and I scanned the area. There was more out there, and I couldn't pull myself away until I knew what it was. Right when my gaze was about to fall on the bushes again, a large animal shot out from another direction. No, it wasn't a normal animal. It was larger than a dog and I watched in awe as it's body, covered in dark fur, disappeared down the street.

There was no denying it was a wolf. Power rolled off of it in waves in the brief moments I could see it, and I got the sudden sensation to run my fingers through the coarse fur.

After a few more moments had passed and nothing else

happened, I shut the window and returned to my desk. Thoughts about the beautiful beast flitted through my mind, energizing me for the work ahead.

I took a bite of my omelet as I scrolled through to catch up on my emails, then pulled up the assignment page and looked at what was due first. Picking out my animal behavior class to start with, I was pleased to see we were moving on to learning about wolves, and a grin crossed my face. Gluing my eyes to the screen, I dug in.

The research I came across was so fascinating, I found myself easily getting lost in it, inhaling the information like I needed it to survive. "The alpha female of the pack is the glue to keeping the pack together. In small packs, human-caused mortality of the alpha female or both leaders could cause the entire pack to dissolve. Next in line are the betas, followed by mid-ranking wolves, and then ending with the omegas. Wolves cared for each other as individuals, forming relationships and nurturing their own when sick or injured." I found myself reading out loud and scribbling down more notes than necessary.

I went on to read more about the bond, wolf packs, and their lives. My pen nearly broke from scribbling notes so quickly. It was only when I paused to nurse my cramping hand that I noticed the time. I'd been fully entranced and cursed at myself when I realized I'd missed the entire online lecture because I couldn't pull myself away. I crossed my fingers in hopes it was recorded since they weren't always available to play back.

Deciding I would follow up on that later, I shook out my hand and returned my attention to the research. I'd already taken more notes on wolves than I had on any other animal or topic, but I still needed to know more.

Chapter Five

Liam

"Did we just…" Casen trailed off.

"Yeah, we did. And she was," Julian confirmed.

Denver was as still as a statue, looking off in the direction where she'd disappeared. One of his hands even left his pants pocket to run through his hair as he stared off into space, lost in thought. He was the first one to get the bond confirmation with her, and now I got it too. Much like the one with Denver, she didn't even seem to realize it. She made no indication that she felt the moment our lives were changed forever. There was no mistaking the spark that happened when you met someone you knew you were supposed to spend the rest of your life with, but she acted as though she didn't feel a thing. She could be the first wolf in history to not feel the jolt of electricity that racks your body when you find your mate.

"She's mine too," I whispered, and the others turned their attention to me. "When she brushed against me. She's meant for all of us, I'm sure of it, but she didn't even seem to notice. Fascinating, that one."

My mind whirled as memories of her brief touch enveloped me. Truth was, the reason we were here this early was to see her. After a failed night of patrol due to being distracted with the little blonde enigma, we decided to sniff her out. Her scent took us to her house but when we arrived, there was another path of her scent leading away. We barely had time to begin following it when she seemingly popped up out of nowhere. The brief glimpse I'd gotten of her bare body was already emblazoned in my head.

"That's how it was at the diner," Denver supplied. "She has no idea what she is, but judging by what just happened, she might be shifting at night and not remembering."

"I can still smell her wolf on her," Axel murmured with his nose twitching in the faint breeze. "She's definitely a Mercai, there's no mistaking it."

"How can that be?" I asked, trying to piece it all together. "We know everyone in the Mercai world. How is it possible that one has slipped through undetected? For all these years, no less." I spared a glance at her window, half expecting all the answers to come tumbling through the glass.

"I don't know, but I intend to find out." Denver slid his hand back into his pocket and began to stroll with a casual step as though he walked this street every day. He appeared so in place, even those who have lived here their whole lives probably wouldn't bat an eye.

The rest of us followed, and I hurried into step beside him. "We'll need to keep an eye on her. Find out everything we can."

He stepped off of the sidewalk and looked up at the tall tree outside of a window. "She's in there." He tilted his head to listen to something, and I did the same.

"She's on her computer, typing," I shared. The keys gave

way as her fingers moved frantically across her keyboard. Whatever she was doing up there, it must have been important.

Before I could register what was happening, Julian was already standing on the lowest branch and was reaching up for the next one. He was the fastest wolf back home, and none of us would've been able to stop him if we'd tried.

"What are you doing?" I hissed at him. It didn't matter if we were fated mates, she didn't know who we were. Seeing us watching her from the tree right outside her second-story window wouldn't do us any favors. She was still able to reject the bond if she really wanted to, and this was a sure way to make that happen before anything even had a chance to begin. This could be detrimental to us all.

"It's okay. There's enough tree coverage if I need it." He reached the large branch that had a direct view of her window and ducked back so he was hidden by the trunk. He stared down at us with large eyes that could only mean one thing—hide. So much for that plan.

"Shit," Casen cursed, as the other four of us scattered. I managed to jump into the next yard over and hide in the neatly trimmed hedges. I looked up as I crouched down.

A shadow appeared at the window, and the distinct sound of it sliding open cut through the air and turned my blood cold.

She was looking out, studying the area. Specifically the tree. I could barely make her out through the thick branches, and when I shuffled to get a better stance, her eyes shot in my direction.

I gulped hard as I waited in silence, mentally cursing myself for hiding from my mate instead of climbing up to her window and taking her in my arms. I hated myself for choosing the cowardly route.

Then a thought crossed my mind. She knew we were

here, she could sense us. How else would she know to look out the window when she did, or exactly where I was hiding? Julian had managed to get up the tree without even making a branch sway. She shouldn't have suspected anything otherwise.

A kernel of hope popped inside of me as I realized that even if she wasn't aware of it, somewhere deep down she still knew something. Still felt something.

As her gaze roamed around, I took the opportunity to study her. One hand gripped the windowsill while the other clutched a wad of her shirt, her knuckles whitening from the death grip she had. Her refusal to let the situation go was written in her wide eyes as they searched out the source of the sound that drew her there. Despite our good last-minute hiding spots, she was agonizingly patient as she sought out the truth.

Her blonde curls fell forward as she tilted her head out the window to get a better view. Drops of water fell onto the windowsill from the ends of her hair—she must have gotten out of the shower not that long ago. The cold air was already frosting her damp curls and would dry in a hard, tangled mess as she hadn't taken the time to brush the golden strands.

She suspected something, I could tell by the faint twitch of her nose as she scanned the area, but she didn't see any of us. Right as her eyes were about to rest on the bush I was hiding in, a flash of dark gray fur mixed with white ran across the lawn, diverting her attention.

She raised a hand to her mouth, but not quick enough to cover her gasp, and I sucked in some air, waiting for the scream. But it never came.

Instead, her eyes sparkled with awe as she watched Denver's wolf form prance across the street and disappear around the corner of the next house.

She was entranced by the animal sighting, and I was mesmerized by her. This was the first time someone didn't scream at the sight of us in our wolf form. Maybe somewhere in her mind, she suspected she was one too.

A smile curved her lips and she disappeared back inside the room, leaving the window open.

We would no longer be able to stand beneath it and talk about her like we were. I looked around and saw Casen and Axel emerging from their hiding spot on the other side of the house. Julian fell to the ground and, despite the two-story drop, still landed lightly on his feet.

A high-pitched scream erupted from across the street before I saw Denver's large wolf form appear from around the other house and sprint down the road. I nodded to the others, and we took off running after him before Makena could reappear in her window.

Chapter Six

Makena

My stomach grumbled loudly, pulling me away from my research. I'd managed to get caught up on all of my assignments today, and even watched the missed lesson which was luckily recorded, but now all of a sudden I needed food, and a lot of it.

Stretching my arms above my head, I leaned back in my chair when a second grumble erupted from my stomach. "Well okay then, sounds like it's time for a break."

Leaving the wolf research tabs open on my computer, I collected my purse, slid into my shoes, and climbed into my car. I was pulling out of the driveway at record speed before my windshield had even fully defogged.

I could've simply ordered delivery, but going and getting it myself would be much faster and more productive than pacing back and forth waiting for them to arrive. Otherwise, I probably would have eaten my notebook.

I pulled into the drive-thru of the first fast food restaurant I came across and tapped my fingers along the steering wheel as I waited for the car in front of me to order. When it was finally my turn, I'd already added more food to my list.

"Three double patties and large fries. Surprise me with the sodas." I got my order out before the guy on the microphone could even finish asking me what I'd like to eat. "Actually, make that four of each," I corrected, and then pulled up to the window to pay.

I continued my impatient tapping on the steering wheel as I waited for my food to be ready, wondering why in the world I even ordered so much. I'd never had a double-sized burger before in my life, yet suddenly I was craving it all.

Surely these weird dreams and cravings couldn't be…no, it had been a few months since the last time. I had thrown myself into my work and studies and hadn't been able to juggle a relationship too. Not that I really cared to have one right now, aside from not finding anyone worth the hassle.

"Here you go." The smiling teen handed me my bags and a drink tray, which I took from him with excitement.

"Oh, great!" I breathed a sigh of relief. "Thank you very much."

"You're welco—" His words were cut off as I slammed my foot on the gas and headed home.

Grease dribbled down my chin as I finished off the third burger. I couldn't seem to wait until I'd at least shut off the engine, but I was famished. The only thing I could think about was getting food in me, and as I looked at the fourth burger, I barely let myself wonder why that was before I demolished that one as well. Then all that was left were the fries, and I had no idea what I was going to do with four large sodas.

Locking the door behind me, I sipped on one of the drinks as I deposited the evidence in the kitchen trash can, burying it beneath empty grocery bags. I didn't feel like having to explain why I devoured four double cheeseburgers in one sitting. Heck, even I didn't know why. I supposed I could say it was from being out with friends, then I snorted. The most socializing I did lately was walking the shelter dogs. I briefly wondered if I could pin the great burger fiasco on them.

I was getting ready to carry the tray of sodas up to my room, grumbling about how I would be drinking nothing else this week, when a knock at the door made me jump. I barely managed to keep from spilling the sticky liquid all over me, and juggled the tray between my forearm and my hip as I went over to answer the door. I checked the clock on the way. My dad shouldn't be home for at least another two hours. I still had time to figure something out.

I flung open the door and was surprised to see a some-what familiar face. The palest blue eyes—nearly level to my own—widened as they took in my face. He was so close, I could see razor blade marks from where he tried to trim the scruff around his face, giving him a more ragged look that was absolutely adorable. I was pretty sure he was one of the new guys in town—no, I was certain he was. Why were they suddenly popping up everywhere? And at my front door, no less?

"Uh, hi," I greeted.

His lips tilted into a sweet smile. "Hello."

There was an awkward silence. Well, this was getting off to a great start.

I shuffled the drink tray to my other hand. This thing was getting heavy. "Is there something I can help you with?"

He noticed the drink tray and then held up a plastic bag. "I didn't mean to bother you when you had company."

"No company," I replied, and his eyes narrowed.

"Those are all for you?" He had a hint of knowing in his tone, which only confused me. Unless he assumed I was lying, which wouldn't bother me at all since I didn't even know the guy. I had too much going on already to worry about what these strange men thought of me.

Although, a small part of me told me I did care, for some reason I couldn't figure out. I shrugged. "I got thirsty. Here, have one." I held the tray out to him, and he held up a hand to resist, but if he could help me get rid of some of these, I wasn't going to take no for an answer. With a look that told him so, I thrust the tray forward some more until he gave in and grabbed a soda. Something zapped my skin as his hand brushed against mine, that dang static electricity again, but I kept myself from jumping back.

I remained standing there like that as I moved my eyes between his and the pile of straws in the middle of the tray, and he finally got the hint and took a straw.

In slow motion, he freed the straw from the wrapper, stuck it through the plastic lid, and took a long drink, eyeing me the whole time as though he was afraid of doing something wrong. He watched my every movement, and I didn't know what he was waiting for me to do next. I had about as much of a handle on this than I did my mysterious nighttime sleepwalking.

I had no idea what was coming over me lately, but if this was how I was going to answer the door from now on, by forcing a stranger to drink my drink before he could even tell me why he was there, then I was going to spend the rest of my days hiding in my room and finishing my studies. No one would be allowed to trick-or-treat here anymore. I wanted to throw my hands up to hide my face, but the tray was keeping me from doing that. Instead, I shifted around, wanting to hurry this along.

"My name is Casen."

"Uh, Makena," I replied. He nodded, as though my name was the only thing he needed. I glanced at the clock on the entertainment stand. What an odd time for introductions.

Wherever these guys were from, it must be filled with polite people, if this was the only reason he was here.

I waited for him to say something more, but when he didn't, I decided it was time to call it a night. "Well, nice seeing you. Want one for the road?" I nodded to indicate the tray with more drinks still in it.

He pulled his lips from the straw and held up the plastic grocery bag again that he'd tried to show me earlier. "I believe these are yours."

Confused, I passed him the whole tray, forcing him to juggle it with his own drink as we did an awkward exchange of items. I opened the bag and was surprised to see my clothing from yesterday inside. I looked back up at him, barely able to keep my jaw from hitting the floor.

"I haven't met too many people around here yet, but I was sure I'd seen you wearing this yesterday. If it's not yours, then I don't know what else to do with it." He took a long sip from his straw and eyed me, waiting for me to say something next.

"Thank you." My voice was low as shock coursed through me. Each time I woke up in the woods, I always wondered what happened to my clothes. I could never find them and chalked it up to being some sort of freak accident type thing where they merely vanished from existence. It was one of the many recent problems I haven't been able to solve. But here in this bag was not only my full outfit from yesterday, but also scraps of clothing from the other times.

I shuffled through them with one hand, turning over piece after piece of familiar material. They all had a healthy coating of mud with some leaves and twigs stuck to the fabric through the holes. The most surprising part, however, was how shredded each article was. It was as though something ripped them all to pieces. But my only questions were what could do such a thing, and how did they get off my body first?

"Everything okay?"

My head snapped up, and I remembered he was still there. "Yeah, all good," I answered meekly. "Just wondering how this happened." I couldn't keep my shock from him even if I wanted to. It didn't matter if I kept the words to myself, I couldn't seem to keep the disbelief from my expression, and he knew exactly what I was talking about.

"You don't know how the clothing got like that?" he questioned, and raised an eyebrow, studying me as he waited for a response.

I shook my head. "Not a clue. I mean…" I tied the bag shut as I rushed to make this all look as casual as possible. This kind of thing didn't normally happen in Carlisle, and I didn't want to cause a scene, at least not until after I figured it out myself first. "I was hiking, climbing trees, playing around. I do that a lot. My clothes got torn up."

"And the only solution was to tear them from your body in ratted strips, and leave them around in public places?" He raised an eyebrow, and I gulped. I didn't know how I was going to get out of this one. I needed space to think, to figure this out, and I couldn't do that while being confronted for an immediate answer.

"That's precisely it. Now, if you'll excuse me, I need to get back to my studies." I took a step back to close the door, but he lifted the drink tray toward me, and I held up my hand. "Keep them. I don't know why I bought so many in the first place."

As the door clicked shut, I turned around and leaned my back against the solid oak, breathing out. He must have still been standing in the same spot because it was several seconds before I heard his shoes on the concrete as his footsteps receded.

I came really close to someone figuring out…well, I don't know what, but I didn't like it. He was too close to knowing that something was up with me, something not normal. I needed to figure this out before someone else did. The loss of control was getting to me, and I was becoming desperate to get a grasp on whatever this was. I needed to know.

My mind whirled with all the possibilities, but none of them stood out to me as a place to start. I should have been grateful that more hints to my nighttime whereabouts happened to drop into my lap, but instead, I was even more lost than before. Several thousand new pieces just got added to this jigsaw puzzle, and I couldn't even find the dang starting piece.

After running up to my room, I spread the contents of the bag onto the floor. The mud was dried now, and the tears in the fabric were so jagged, it was as though they were literally ripped from my body. How could that happen without me remembering anything? I couldn't even find a bruise on my body to go with that.

I thought back to the dream from last night and laughed out loud.

Right, like I could be a wolf. How would that even happen?

However, something had obviously happened, and when I tucked my hair behind my ear, I was reminded about the frayed ends, much like when the bullet grazed my fur in my dream.

I heard the sound of the front door shutting, and I shoved the pieces of clothing into my wastebasket and covered them up with the plastic bag. I'd get rid of them tomorrow on my way to class. As footsteps sounded on the stairs, I jumped into my chair and clicked on my computer, pretending like it was another normal night with nothing out of the ordinary.

"Hey, kiddo, you doing alright?" My dad leaned in with his fist resting against the doorframe.

"Yeah, never been better."

"I was trying to decide what to have for dinner. Any preferences?"

Crap. "I'm not too hungry right now," I hedged.

"You've been studying all day, I thought you would be starving." He eyed me, knowing sometimes I would get too into my studies and forget to eat. But I also didn't want to tell him I'd demolished enough food to last us a weekend practically minutes ago.

Before I could open my mouth or even think of a response, my stomach growled, and I clenched my mouth shut. He smiled and pushed off from the doorframe. "I thought so. How about I put in a frozen pizza? Maybe two."

I nodded. "Sounds good. Thanks, Dad."

"Welcome, kiddo." He shut the door, and I waited until his footsteps were retreating down the stairs before I let out a breath and looked at the wastebasket with a hand over my growling stomach.

I had no idea what was going on with me, but I was going to find out.

Chapter Seven

Casen

The air was alive with the sounds of the night as I walked down the driveway, sipping from one of the sodas. She seemed rather eager to get rid of a tray full of them. If she had all of these, then she must have gotten food to go with it. Which meant her wolf was rising to the surface whether she was ready or not. It was calling to her, unable to remain hidden any longer. It was only a matter of time before she'd be forced to face the truth, and we'd be here, ready to guide her.

As I reached the street, I stopped and looked up at the window by the big oak tree. A light flickered on, and I saw her shadow in the window as she went through the contents of the bag I'd given her. She would, without a doubt, be looking at the remains of her clothing with confusion and a look of shock on her face as she'd frantically try to put the pieces together. Only, the truth she was seeking most likely wasn't the one she'd be expecting.

I wanted to march back up to her door and explain everything, tell her exactly what she was going through and why those clothes were in the condition they were, but before I could take the first step, a car turned onto the street. Without spilling a drop, I ran to the other side and tried to look like it was completely normal for me to be walking down the street at night carrying a tray full of drinks.

The car passed me and turned into the driveway, and I watched as her dad got out of the car and headed into the house.

Strange. I couldn't sense any wolf in him at all. Makena was no doubt a wolf, so she must have gotten it from her mother. Which, if her mother wasn't in the picture, could explain why she was unaware of the full truth of who she was. Some things were beginning to make some sense now.

I looked up at the window to her room, tempted to climb the tree, knock on the pane, and explain everything if she'd give me the chance. She had no idea how much I was fighting that pull. Or the desire to simply wrap her in my arms and forget the rest of the world.

Rather than acting on anything, I clenched one of the drinks too tightly and a sticky sweet liquid pooled around the top of the lid. I didn't like her being in the dark when I had so many of the answers she was searching for.

"What do you have there?"

I spun around, nearly spilling the tray of drinks across the asphalt, and saw Axel walking up to me. "I gave her the clothes."

"And she gave you a tray of drinks in return?"

I nodded. "That's literally what happened."

He arched a brow. "Alright. I'm curious, but I'll let it slide."

"There's no wolf in the old man. He's pure human."

"You sure?" Axel asked, sparing a glance at her house. His eyes softened as he spotted her silhouette.

"He just came home. She has to get it from her mom's side." I looked up at the window again, but the light shut off. "Which would explain a lot if she wasn't around to teach her about who she is."

"The others will be eager to hear about that." He toed off his shoes and pulled his shirt over his head. "I'm going to watch things from out here. Denver, Liam, and Julian are out scouting. They're going to see if there are any packs nearby who can help us. Or at least, find out more about what's going on around here. Something feels off. Denver wants you to take the south side."

I held out a drink for him. "Want one?"

Axel chuckled and jumped behind a bush to undo his pants. "Nah, man, I'm good. My wolf isn't a fan of that overly sweet stuff. Drop it off at the house if you want." After setting his clothes in a neat little pile and hiding them in a nearby bush, he got down on all fours until a gray and white wolf was standing before me. He huffed until I started moving and, with one last glance at the dark window, I began walking in the direction of the house we were staying in, sipping from one of the drinks the whole way.

Chapter Eight

Makena

"Yes!" After a lot of time spent scouring the internet and fighting with my computer, I finally had a motion detector app downloaded to my laptop. I turned my computer screen to where it would be able to catch both my bed and the window, pressed a button, and sat back in the chair to let out a nervous breath of relief and admire my accomplishment.

According to what I could find, this app was supposed to detect movement, and when it did, the camera would turn on and begin recording. Then when I woke up the next day, I could check it and find out what was happening during the nights where I'd wake up outside of my bedroom. The truth about my nighttime disappearances would finally be within my grasp.

Feeling accomplished, I got ready for bed, shut off the lights, and double-checked that the night mode for the camera was activated before crawling under the covers. I was brimming with so much hope and excitement that I might finally find something out, that I found myself lying awake in bed until well after midnight.

Howling filled the space between the crickets chirping, and I found it more calming than I'd expected. There was something more familiar about them than the typical neighborhood dogs. They made me feel safe and almost willing to drift off to sleep to their lullaby, but I couldn't tear my eyes away from my computer long enough to shut them. Sleep continued to elude me.

I tossed and turned, getting frustrated that I couldn't find sleep. The hope that something would happen tonight drained from me by the time six in the morning came around, and I placed a pillow over my head in annoyance when the most annoying sound in the world signaled the end to the night. It cut through my pillow and invaded my mind, the ringing knocking around the walls of my head.

"Oh well, it's not like it happens every night anyway." Groaning, I slammed my palm onto the screen of my phone to shut off the alarm and ended up knocking it between the nightstand and the wall. "Crap." Grumbling, I rolled out of bed and tilted the nightstand forward to fish it out.

A glint from outside the window caught my eye, and I paused. There was what looked to be a rather large dog sitting on the sidewalk across the street, watching me. It was a beautiful animal with clean gray and white fur.

Blinking away the sleep from my eyes, I squinted and blocked the sun with a hand above my brow. My gaze locked with glowing orbs, and a feeling of familiarity ran through me.

I felt as though I'd seen this dog before, but I couldn't place it. If I wasn't so exhausted, I'd even say it was a wolf, but I shook that thought from my head. What would a wolf be doing in Carlisle, watching me through my bedroom window from across the street? I needed to get myself together.

What about the wolf I saw running down the street after my shower?

My dad's words repeated in my mind. There was something out there. Attacks were becoming more frequent. Nowhere was safe.

Using the palm of my hand to rub the sleep from my eyes, I blinked and looked again, but the animal was gone. I pressed my nose to the cool glass, ignoring the numbness that swept through my cheek before the sun could warm it. The creature was nowhere to be found.

Shivering, I pulled the curtains closed, fished out my phone, and proceeded to get ready for the day. I didn't have time to ponder my hallucinations, there was too much to do.

SHOULDERING MY BACKPACK, I stepped onto campus and pushed my way through the slow moving students as I headed toward my class. While some of the animal behavior class was online, we still had to meet in person twice a week on Tuesdays and Fridays. It was the only class I stepped foot on campus for. Everything else I could complete online, which worked out well, allowing me to have such a flexible schedule.

I gave the obligatory smile at people I recognized as I passed and even stopped to pick up another coffee on the way. It was going to be a long day, and I needed to keep my yawns at bay long enough to make it through.

Mr. Morrison was writing the agenda for today on the board when I walked in and took my seat. Students piled in after me, each sporting a matching yawn. The room would shortly fill up with steam from all the coffees they carried.

To my surprise, two familiar guys piled in not long after and situated themselves in the empty desks to my right. I glanced at them and my cheeks heated when they noticed, so I turned my attention forward and shoved the memory of yesterday morning to the back of my mind while I brought my cup of coffee to my lips. I turned my attention to the front of the room, not flinching from the hot liquid that poured over my tongue and burned my mouth.

"Let's get started." Mr. Morrison dropped the dry erase marker and clasped his hands together. "As you already know if you've been following the online assignments, we've started learning about wolves. What makes them different from your typical domestic dog? What are their habits, lifestyles, and different subsystems? We will answer these questions and more as we go through."

Pausing, he held out a hand to indicate the newcomers. "We have some additions to the class. Would you like to introduce yourselves? What brings you here?"

The one with the dark hair stood up and smoothed hands down his faded green shirt which looked like it had spent more time rolling around in the dirt than I did most mornings. He was taller than I'd expected, and his hazel eyes flashed to me before he answered, "I'm Liam. I recently moved to the area from far enough away that I doubt anyone has heard of it, so I won't bother with those boring details." He gave a slight chuckle as though he'd made a joke and waved a hand in the air before moving on. "I'm here because animals are my life, I guess you could say. I enjoy learning and this seems like the place to do it."

"You're interested in pursuing a career in animal studies?" Mr. Morrison asked.

"I am. It's convenient you're starting on wolves, they're my favorite."

"I'm glad you could join us, and I hope you get a lot out of it. And you?" He indicated to the second man who stood up as Liam sat down.

The man averted his gaze from me as he cleared his throat and faced the front. "I'm Axel. I came here with Liam and a few others. We've been looking for something new, and there's something about this town that made us want to stay for a little while." He pointed to the camera around his neck. "I'm aiming to be a photographer, specifically with animals. I'm most interested in wildlife."

"Is that your wildlife camera?" Mr. Morrison raised an eyebrow and Axel shook his head.

"This is my backup. I can't go anywhere without a camera, you never know when you'd need to take a picture. I keep the giant lens one at home most days." He gave the teacher a giant grin as he patted his camera. "I like to be able to document anything at all times. The camera is a powerful tool. It reveals the things that most people prefer to remain hidden, and there's some treasured truths hiding in this town."

"Glad to have you," Mr. Morrison said, ignoring that last odd statement as Axel sat down. "Both of you. It's not too often we get newcomers who really want to stay here. Can I ask what drove you to that decision?"

"Can't really say," Liam replied with a grin. "There's just something different here that we didn't know we were looking for." As if on cue, his eyes flicked to me again and a shiver ran down my spine.

"And you?"

I looked toward where Mr. Morrison was pointing, expecting to see another familiar face, but the one that smiled back as he stood up and faced the class was unknown to me.

"I'm Griffin. I moved here with my family and thought I would enroll in some classes. I've always been fascinated with animal studies, and am still discovering what I want to do with my life." Griffin sat down with a smile and a nod then his gaze flashed over to me. It was so brief, I almost thought I'd imagined the cold depths of his gaze, but I brushed it off as stress and busied myself in my notebook.

The lesson continued as I sipped my coffee. Halfway through, my stomach started to growl. It began as a small pang, and then rose in urgency in response to ignoring it. At first, I thought I only needed to grab an early lunch as soon as class let out, but then it growled louder. I braced my arm across my body, but it did nothing to silence the raging storm inside me that was beginning to garner attention. What was going on with me?

The clock at the front of the classroom showed there was still about forty minutes of class left. I checked my bag and frowned when I realized I hadn't packed any snacks. My stomach growled again in matched disapproval. I chewed dangerously on my bottom lip as I debated running to the vending machine when a granola bar and two sticks of beef jerky appeared in my vision.

I looked up to see Axel holding them out to me, his green gaze sharp as he watched me wrap my hand around the offering and accept it with a pitiful smile. My stomach let out a long growl, and I snapped my back to the chair and tore into the food.

The meat sticks were the first to be demolished before I slouched in my seat, licked my fingers, and casually nibbled away at the granola bar.

Silence surrounded me, so thick it would need a chainsaw to cut through it, and I looked around to find every eye in the room locked on me.

I swallowed the bite in my mouth and gave a single wave. "No worries here. I scavenged." I held up the half eaten granola bar for added effect.

"Come on, guys, there are notes to take." Mr. Morrison brought the attention back to the whiteboard, and the students snickered as they faced the front again. All except for Liam and Axel, who remained watching me with a stern stare as though they weren't finding this remotely funny. Rather, they seemed concerned more than anything. The protectiveness in their gaze was penetrating and I swallowed down the final bite.

Uncomfortable with the amount of attention I was getting today, I slouched down in my chair and rested my forehead in the palm of my hand while I took notes in an attempt to block the guys out. I wanted nothing more than to disappear right now. To shrivel into something else and run away. I spared a glance at the clock: twenty-seven minutes.

The moment class let out, I packed my belongings and rushed out of the room before Mr. Morrison could even set the marker down.

As I hurried down the hall, a second and third set of footsteps followed behind me, keeping pace. Curious, I looked back. Both Liam and Axel were hot on my tail, and they caught up to me with some sort of super speed, jumping in front of me and forcing me to a stop.

"Can I help you?" I inquired. Really, though, I wanted to grab lunch, drop my stuff off at home, and head to the diner. If my appetite was going to continue down this path, I'd need to get a second job to afford all the food I'd be eating. Maybe even a third job.

"We only wanted to get to know you better," Liam replied in his smooth timbre that rolled over me like honey. His voice was surprisingly even after their sprint. He must have the lungs of a runner.

Neither of them was out of breath from practically chasing me down the hall, but I was panting as though I'd been running for my life.

"Why me? There are plenty of other students here. They're much more interesting to get to know, I'm sure."

"Doubtful," Axel retorted, as he took a step inward, his finger grazing over the side of the camera that dangled from around his neck. My shoulder brushed against his chest, bumping against the camera, and a small zap of electricity coursed through me. What was up with all the electric shocks lately? I wasn't even pulling back like I normally would have, because normal shocks hurt. These ones, though, they felt right. They felt like home. Whatever that was supposed to mean.

His body tensed as he felt it too.

"Sorry, all this static electricity is out of control lately." Grazing my thumb over my shoulder, I brushed it off and tried to take a step back, but my feet wouldn't move.

"You felt it too?" His voice was breathy and full of surprise. Hope lit up his gaze as he watched me in awe.

"Of course I felt it. It seems to be everywhere now, I'm shocking everyone I touch."

"I don't think you understand." He tilted his head low, his eyes boring into mine as they tried to tell a secret I didn't quite understand. I swallowed hard and tightened my grip on the shoulder strap of my bag.

I didn't know what he wanted, but for a moment there I was ready to hand him the world. Or at least, what little bit of it I had. I blinked. What a strange thought to have.

Clearing my throat to distract myself, I took a forced step away, only to bump into Liam's chest.

"Do you know what you are?" he asked as I jumped back again.

"I don't know what that's supposed to mean, but I'm going to take it as an insult." Because that was the only thing that made sense in my world right now. I didn't know these guys even though I felt like I should, but for them to rush up to me and question my very being was more than I could take.

Liam's eyes widened as he reached out for me, his fingers brushing against my arm as I pulled away from his grasp. "That's not what I meant. Please, allow us to explain."

"I'll see you next class." I spun around, and my fingers tightened around the straps of my backpack as I ran. At that moment, I didn't know if I would be in the next class as long as they were there. I didn't know what happened just now, but for the first time in my life, I wasn't sure I wanted to find out. I ran the interaction through my mind, but nothing really made sense. They seemed to know something that I didn't, and they were certain of it. Could it be possible the truth might be more than I could handle?

Chapter Nine

Axel

"We scared her away." My shoulders slumped. I watched the blonde curls of her ponytail bounce in the air as she ran away from us. She'd showed up to class looking like she pulled her outfit straight from the hamper. They were wrinkled and mismatched, as though she had more important things on her mind than what to wear to school.

I didn't know what to do. That look of fear on her face made me want to rip apart whatever had caused it, but that was made more difficult since I knew it was us who'd put it there. It became evident that she was my mate as much as she was to the others, and the first thing I'd done was scare her away.

"I think it has more to do with what she's dealing with than with us. It would've helped her out tremendously if we could have explained, but we'll need to find another way to do so. Something that isn't cornering her in a hallway after class," Liam said. His eyes held the same storm that raged inside me at our blunder.

She was already skittish. She did eat our food, but I thought it had more to do with her wolf calling to be let out than trust. I could practically hear the begging going on inside her as she ached for freedom. No wonder she was shifting without remembering anything. She was so far disconnected from half of who she was, it was as though she was two completely different entities. The unknown split was running her ragged.

"She's working tonight, I saw it on the calendar. Do you think it would be a bad idea to tell her while at work?"

"It might be. If they're that busy again, then yeah, it would be a terrible idea to corner her and drop this bomb on her while at work and surrounded by regular humans. She'll already be stressed enough. Wait, how did you manage to see her schedule?" Liam asked.

"With my camera. When the swinging doors opened, I zoomed in as far as I could, snapped a shot, and managed to catch a picture of things hanging in the hallway back there, including the schedule." I tugged at the camera that was dangling around my neck. It didn't give as clear of a picture as the big boy back at the house, but it did what I needed. It was the best backup camera I could have.

"That thing can get some good focus."

"That's why I got it. Only the best."

"Come on, let's report back to Denver and see what the others are up to." Liam led the way out of the school, and we walked back to the house we were staying at.

We were lucky to find this one when we did. It was pretty much abandoned, and I doubted anyone would realize there were people there now. It was hidden behind overgrown trees, and since we didn't travel by car, there was nothing to draw attention to us. It did take us some time to clear it out so it could be a livable space. It still had the odor from being abandoned for months, and the trash that was left behind had drawn quite the collection of insects and animals alike. The effort it took to clean it up was worth having a bed at night, at least when I wasn't spying on Makena while she slept.

We didn't spend much time there anyway. If we weren't observing, then we were either scouting the area for information on these attacks we kept hearing about, or searching the surrounding areas outside of Carlisle for other wolves. As soon as we realized a more important reason for staying here, Makena became our central focus.

She walked around with her head held high and confidence in her step to hide the raging storm inside her. With all that was going on, which she somehow managed to hide from the world, I had to admit I was rather impressed. Most people couldn't deal with the cards they were dealt as well as she did, let alone throwing a wolf identity into their deck.

Chapter Ten

Makena

As I passed a trash can, I dumped the remains of my lunch that should've been enough to feed a family of four and headed inside. The bell dinged above the door, signaling my entry, and Justine ran up to me in a hurry.

"I'm so glad you're here. We can barely keep up." She rushed to get the words out as she shoved a pile of menus into my hand. "Hurry up and clock in, we need you." Her ponytail bounced in the air as she zipped around from table to table, taking care of customers.

"We?" I questioned, but she was already out of earshot. Last I knew, it was only the two of us left.

Being understaffed was beginning to become a daily thing. If we didn't get some new help soon, everyone on staff was going to crumble into an unending abyss of despair. One person could only handle so much before they cracked under the pressure, and Justine was already bursting at the seams. She rushed around with her battle apron and her pen and notepad as her chosen weapons. Her barked commands and the way she forced a smile for the customers were barely enough to get her through the day. The pang of sympathy I felt for her evaporated when she widened her eyes in my direction as an indication to start moving and get to work.

I clocked in, and when I looked through the window of the swinging doors, I spotted a new guy taking orders at a table farthest from my section. He looked to be high school age, and his smile exhibited confidence. If this was his first day, then I never would've guessed.

"He's only here for tonight, but if it works out, then he'll be back," Justine explained as she bustled by me to drop her orders off at the kitchen and grab a pitcher of water. "His name's Mack. Don't scare him away."

"*Me* scare *him?*" I questioned, but she was already through the doors and back out into the diner area. I knew she was beyond stressed and most likely didn't realize how I would take her warning, so I let it slide.

As I reappeared through the doors to handle my first table, I noticed one of the tables was occupied by five very familiar looking men.

You have got to be kidding me. They are everywhere now.

I marched straight up to them and dropped a pile of menus onto the middle of the table, drawing all their eyes to me as I crossed my arms, getting ready to scold them. First the park, then the diner, then my school. They were everywhere I turned, invading my space before I could even take a breath.

"Look, I don't know what's going on here or why you're following me, but this is getting ridiculous."

The one with the dark eyes, who'd spoken to me the last time they were here, I believed his name was Denver, was the first to speak this time. "This is one of the few places with decent food. We've tried others, but there's nothing like the avocado burger you serve here. It's my favorite in town." As he shifted in his seat, his shirt sleeve rode up, exposing a sliver of a tattoo on his bicep. My eyes flicked to it, but I couldn't make out what it was.

The one who'd brought me my clothes yesterday piped up next. "It's true. It's his favorite meal in town."

They looked up at me with such innocence in their eyes, that for a moment I almost apologized. Only for a moment, though, then it was gone. Instead, I blew out a breath and uncrossed my arms to place a hand against my lower back.

"Are you doing alright there?" Liam frowned, his brows creasing with concern.

"I'm fine, just tired. So that's one avocado burger for you." I scribbled on my notepad. "Care to make it a meal with fries and a drink?" When Denver nodded, I wrote it down. Tired was an understatement, but I wasn't about to spill all my secrets to the first guy who showed me some concern. "What can I get for the rest of you?"

They listed off their orders, and I wrote them down before running the ticket off to the kitchen and taking care of the other tables in my section. I could barely hear the other people giving their food orders over the sounds of dishware clanking together and the overabundance of chatter in the diner. My throat hurt from constantly speaking loud enough to be heard over the growing volume of the diners. At this rate, my voice was going to grow hoarse by the time my shift was up.

I stopped by the guys' table to refill their drinks before their food was ready.

"Makena, can I ask you something?" Denver's words were so soft, I nearly missed them.

"Your food will be out shortly," I rasped out, then cleared my throat. My response was curt as I fought the urge to get a closer look at his tattoo. It was hidden by his shirt sleeve again, warm and snug from the cooling Fall weather.

His eyes widened a fraction then went back to normal. "That's not what I—"

"Can you take a couple more tables?" Justine appeared at my side in a flash and pointed to an additional two tables where people had just been seated. "Thanks." She whizzed off before I could answer, and I let out a frustrated breath.

"Where are the other waiters?" the unnamed guy with blond hair and stunning blue eyes asked. He scanned the area looking for more staff. His brows furrowed deep in thought.

I held my arms out from my sides with my palms up. "This is it." My throat was dry and the words struggled to come out. The man slid his full water glass over to me, a small amount of the liquid spilling over the edge of the glass as he did so, but I held up my hand to decline. Axel pulled a mini bottle of water from a separate compartment of his camera bag and tossed it to me, so I'd have no choice but to catch it.

"Drink it or we're leaving," Denver ordered. For a moment I considered tossing it back. If they did leave, that would mean one less table I'd have to worry about for the night. I pushed the thought away. I didn't want them to leave quite yet.

Giving way to his stare, I downed the water, crushed the empty bottle, and slid it into my apron pocket. "There's also some new guy who's only here for tonight. Aside from that, it's only us two until we can get more help." While my voice didn't have the same strong tone it normally did, the words came out more clearly. "Most people who work here use it as a job to get through school, and once they graduate, they disappear in favor of something better. I can't blame them, honestly. I intend to do the same when I'm able to."

If I could. I didn't plan to venture too far away, and I might not even fully leave Carlisle. All I had was my dad, and all he had was me. Carlisle was where I'd spent my whole life, I didn't belong anywhere else. Sometimes I wished it was as easy for me to up and leave like Austin was doing, but most of the time I wanted to work hard to improve things here. There were animals that needed to be taken care of and helped, and they needed someone who understood them and took the time to care. I intended to be that person.

My name carried around the room as customers called out for me. I was about to answer them and tend to each person when a, "Hey, bitch! We're starving here!" rang out along with my name, and each one of the guys tensed and turned their attention to a man who had just been seated and was apparently done with looking at the menu. The woman he was with gaped at him in disbelief, but with the way the guys next to me glared at him, I was glad I wasn't on the wrong end of that glare. I briefly wondered if I should be worried for his life.

I held my hand out, turning their attention back to me. I was flattered that they turned a heated glare on the man in my defense—Liam's fingers were digging into the worn wooden tabletop as his eyes swirled with something greater —but I already had enough problems to deal with and didn't want to add any more. "Down, boys."

"He shouldn't talk to you like that," Denver growled without taking his eyes off the man.

"I agree, but it happens. He isn't from here, so hopefully he's only passing through." I held a finger up before the rude man could say another word, signaling I'd heard him and was on my way over.

I piled their glasses onto a tray to grab refills. "I'll be back with your food in a minute." I turned around and continued my rush around to take care of everyone I possibly could after dropping off their refills. They barely noticed I'd set filled glasses in front of them, as they were casting intense glances around the diner, taking everything in, particularly the rude man.

Chatter rose in volume as the diners demanded food and refills, and I did my best to cater to each table in a timely fashion. Sweat dripped onto my notepad as I wrote down more orders, my hips bruising as they bumped into the backs of chairs on my way to the kitchen to fulfill those same orders. The room shrank at an alarming rate and I found myself struggling to breathe. As soon as one table got up to leave, more people were sitting down before I could even finish clearing it off.

Tugging at the band of my apron around my waist, my gaze met Axel's. There was something calming in his forest green eyes. The way his fingers clenched at the camera that I realized was becoming a permanent feature of his appearance. How, unlike the storms that threatened to break loose in the face of his companions, his eyes transferred a calmness to me I so desperately needed.

Tuning out the rest of the diner, I closed my mouth and took in a deep breath through my nose. The noise I blocked out was exactly that, noise. Allowing myself to get lost in the demands of others was a sure-fire way to drown. I needed a solution.

Breaking eye contact, I scanned the area, looking for Mack, and saw him calmly taking care of another table. His posture was relaxed and he seemed oblivious to the torment going on around us. The rising tide as more customers demanded attention.

I was grateful he was there and taking some of the load off, but I wished he'd work faster. He was spending a lot of time smiling and chatting with people it looked like he knew. Socializing on the job could get you tips, but it wouldn't guarantee you could come back. I gulped when he glanced at me, and for a moment I felt a pang of coldness travel down my spine before he turned away and continued his chatter.

As I spun around to make sure each one of my tables was taken care of before I disappeared into the kitchen to grab whatever food was ready, I saw Denver and Casen standing over the rude man. Their faces were calm as they spoke, but the color gradually drained from the rude man's face with each word they spoke until he was slouched so far down in his chair that I feared he was going to be forever embedded into the dated diner tile.

"Everything alright here?" I inquired as I approached, and the man jumped, nearly falling out of his chair at my presence. I placed a hand on my hip and forced a smile on my face, which wasn't easy considering all I wanted to do was scream at the top of my lungs and storm out of here. "Please play nice. This night is already insane enough as it is, the last thing I need is to drag a mop and bucket out here and clean up your remains."

I didn't think it was possible, but the last bit of color drained from the man's face at my words. What had they said to him?

His mouth opened and closed, but whatever he was trying to say never came out. Instead, he pulled out his wallet and threw a large wad of bills on the table that, at first glance, would clearly be more than enough to cover his meal and a decent tip.

Denver and Casen returned to their table with a nod, satisfied.

"Something came up and I have to head out. Keep the change, and enjoy my food for yourself if it's already been made." His words came out as squeaks while he slipped into his jacket and practically ran out of the door. It was only then that I realized the woman he was with was nowhere to be seen. I wouldn't be surprised if he'd scared her away. But what had scared him?

Sighing, I carried the money to the back where I used it to pay for his order, and my eyes widened at the extra that was left over. I slid the rest into my apron for the tip before anyone else could see it. At least it was one less jerk to deal with. Now to survive the last few hours of the night.

I balanced a large tray with five meals on one hand above my head as I maneuvered through the busy diner, and deposited each plate in front of each of the guys, watching Denver as I placed the avocado burger in front of him, but his focus was elsewhere. They were silent as I did so, and I would have thought they weren't even paying attention if I hadn't caught the appreciative grins on their faces. The blond one took his seat as I finished setting their food down. I didn't even notice he'd gotten up.

With a hand resting on my hip and the tray tucked under my arm, I looked at them all. "Anything else I can get you?"

Each of them shook their head in response and gave their thanks before digging in, but then Casen paused with his burger halfway to his mouth and looked up at me. "When you bring the check, could you also bring some hot tea in a to-go cup?"

"Of course I can. Anything else?"

He shook his head and blushed as he bit into his burger.

"Holler if you need anything," I told them before I sped back to the kitchen to grab meals for some of the other tables that were piling up on the counter in the kitchen.

Some customers were understanding and appreciative, which they showed in the tips they left behind. My apron was brimming with various types of bills that I placed securely at the very bottom of my apron. I glanced over at the guys' table and noticed they'd left. Seeing more people lining up at the front, I hurried over with an empty bin to clear off the table.

As I gathered the dirty dishes and set them in the bin, I noticed a small to-go cup with steam rising from the small hole in the lid. I grabbed the sticky note and my eyes widened in surprise. In rushed handwriting was scrawled, *You could use this more than us. Hope you like tea. Don't lose your voice.*

It wasn't until I saw a fifty-dollar bill placed securely beneath each one of their plates that I nearly broke down sobbing, but I bit back the tears.

I'd been so hesitant about them before, and then they go and do this. Maybe there was some good in these strange new people after all.

Chapter Eleven

Makena

Groaning when I saw the nighttime footage revealed nothing out of the ordinary, I shut off my computer and got ready for the day. I dressed up my disappointment in old jeans and a t-shirt as I tried to convince myself this was a good thing. Maybe whatever was going on with me had stopped. I made sure my key was secured around my neck, resting on top of a small bandage where the mysterious graze was, slung my purse diagonally around my torso, and headed off for the shelter.

Sounds of loud barking could be heard through the walls as I stepped through the front door. Carol rubbed at her temples, unable to do much about the increasing noise. She looked up and greeted me with a smile when I entered. "I'm so glad you're here. Maybe you can get some of them to quiet down. They've been like this the last few days."

"I'll see what I can do. Maybe they need some exercise and will calm down after a walk." I smiled brightly at her, trying to exude confidence over my own tired state.

"I sure hope so. We have some new volunteers starting in about a week, so I'm hoping that'll help." With a sigh, she returned to the computer to continue what she was working on.

The volume of the barking escalated when I entered the warehouse-like section where the dogs were kept, so I placed two fingers between my lips and whistled. By the time my whistle echoed off the farthest wall, the barking had stopped completely, and Javier froze in his tracks with giant bags of dog food on the rolling table he was pulling behind him. He was Carol's grandson and loved animals almost as much as I did. He had spent most of his time outside of school working here, and even stayed on once he started college.

"Wow. You might need to stop by more often," he commented, as he looked around with disbelief. "Or at least teach me how to whistle like that. They ignore mine."

I barely registered his words as I stopped in the middle of the space between the large cages and spun around in a circle. Each dog I could see was sitting on their haunches facing me, their gazes pointing forward as though they were waiting for some sort of command. It was the weirdest thing I'd ever seen, and I was pretty certain they'd never done that before.

"I guess you're leader of the pack, huh?" Javier observed, as he looked around at the sight in awe. He rubbed a hand down his arm as though he was rubbing away a shiver.

"Sure?" My voice was meek, and I swallowed my next words. No lie, this freaked me out a little. A lot, maybe. There were a lot of strange things going on lately.

Shivering as a weird feeling ran down my spine, telling me to accept it, I grabbed the leashes hanging up on a hook on the outside of some of the cages and connected them to the collars and harnesses.

Normally they would fight for my attention, each one of

them wanting to go on a walk all at once, but this time they were more patient than anything I'd ever seen.

With my fist clenched around the wad of leashes, I left the shelter with five dogs leading the way, and Javier scratching his head as I disappeared. Not a single peep could be heard from the shelter even after I left.

Shuddering in the cool autumn air, I banded an arm across my body to keep my heat from escaping. The dogs walked with a calmness that surprised even me. They were always more well behaved with me than with any of the others, but this time it was as though they walked with a purpose of something more, with little Scooter in the lead.

As we rounded a bend in our path, something red poking out from a pile of leaves at the base of a tree caught my eye.

"Right." The dogs turned off the path and to the right with their noses stuck to the ground as they sniffed. They pawed at the leaf pile, sending the leaves flying in every direction until several large scraps of red fabric were exposed.

With the leashes grasped in one hand, I knelt down, gathered the pieces together, and laid them on the frosted ground until they nearly formed a sweatshirt. My breath froze in front of my face, blurring my vision, but I already knew what it was.

Recognition filled me. It entered my body, travelled through every crevice, to the tip of every digit, as it consumed me. A chill to rival the coldest Carlisle winter.

I tried to put together the pieces in my mind, but it was much more difficult to do than putting together the fabric like I'd done. This was one jigsaw puzzle I couldn't seem to figure out on my own, and I couldn't seem to find the lightbulb moment with the one missing piece that would put everything together. I felt as though I knew what was going on deep down, but the switch wasn't being flipped.

What was my missing hoodie, ripped to shreds, doing buried in this park? I only came here during the days when I would walk the dogs, and I'd been missing this particular hoodie for weeks.

Even more importantly, how did it get torn? I remembered wearing this on a particularly frigid night, which happened to be one of the nights I was sleepwalking. I'd gone to bed without changing out of this warm outfit and woke up nearly freezing to death in the middle of the woods, surrounded by grass kissed with frosted tips and falling leaves signaling a new season.

I shoved the strips of fabric into my oversized pockets until my jacket was bulging so much that it was obvious I had shoved an entire garment in there. Still kneeling, I looked up and saw each one of the five dogs were sitting back on their haunches and watching me as though they were waiting for their next command.

"Okay, this is beginning to get really creepy, you guys."

Eager to get home and write in my journal—where I kept notes on all my weird experiences—we completed the walk, and I ushered them back to the shelter with the promise I'd be back for another walk soon. I threw up a hand to wave at Javier on my way out, not bothering to wait for his response as I ran to my car.

My stomach growled louder than the engine when my car groaned to life, and after picking up a couple sandwiches, the grazing of a small piece of metal against my chest reminded me I still had one more errand left to run.

———

GRIPPING the cord that rested against my neck, I adjusted it so it would stop rubbing against the wound there. It was in the same area where part of my hair had been singed, and was driving me crazy. The uneven strands kept falling down each time I tried to gather my hair into a ponytail.

I pulled into the parking lot of the small store, cut the engine, grabbed the key, and headed inside. I was going to get some copies made to hide outside. I didn't know why I hadn't done this sooner, but I'd like to cut down on the amount of wounds I ended up with, and climbing that tree some mornings wasn't helping.

"How can I help you today?" the teenage boy at the key counter asked as I approached.

I held out the cord with the key hanging from the bottom. It had grown more mangled in the short amount of time, the bend now threatening to snap the piece of metal in half. "Can I get two copies of this?" I'd leave one in both the front and back of the house.

"Certainly, it'll only take a few minutes." He closed his hand around the key and took it off the cord. A frown crossed his face as he observed the bent object. "Luckily that happened right above the teeth. I should still be able to make a copy."

My shoulders sagged with relief. At least that was one thing in my life that wasn't turning into a disaster.

"Is there a certain type or design you'd like?"

I shook my head. "No preference, just any."

"It's a nice key. We have some just like it." He pulled out two blank keys that looked almost identical to what this one was made out of.

"Perfect," I said. "Yeah, that works." The short, singed strands of hair fell into my face again, and I left them there. I didn't want to explain anything right now. I wanted to get back home and dive into research.

My stomach grumbled as the seconds ticked past, and by the time my new keys were ready, I was debating how much the employees here would frown upon me raiding their break room fridge.

"Thanks." I grabbed the little envelope, took my corded key necklace back, and made it through the checkout lane in record time.

I scarfed down another two sandwiches by the time I made it home, buried the takeout bag in the kitchen trash can underneath some other garbage, and ran up to my room where I emptied the fabric scraps from my pockets out onto my bed. For good measure, I grabbed the ones that were still in my little bedroom trash can and set those on the bed next to the newly discovered ones. Soon my bedspread was covered in a mosaic of tattered clothing scraps that I laid out like a map, hoping it would guide me to the truth. It was buried somewhere, I just needed to find where the X would mark the spot.

Pulling my journal from a desk drawer, I scribbled in the notes from today, explaining about finding the clothing and even how odd the dogs from the shelter were acting. I felt like it was all connected, but the line between all the events was still invisible and I failed to figure out how to put together the jigsaw puzzle that was now my life.

With my pen hovering over the next line in my notebook, I took a closer look at the frayed edges of the red hoodie and compared it to the ones from the clothing pile that Casen had brought over. There was barely a clean spot left on any of the fabric, as they were all coated in dirt and the crumbles of fallen leaves.

They were all similar, and I believed the same thing had happened to them all. Someone—or something—tore each article of clothing as though they were a thin sheet of paper.

Getting an idea, I took pictures of the tattered edges, did some reverse image searches online, and scrolled down the page. The results all showed people and animals ripping the clothing from their bodies, but it was one image in particular that made me pause.

It was one long horizontal image with various boxes. In each box was an image, like a comic.

The images started off with a human being, and then as my gaze went right, the human gained some monster-like features until I got to the final frame, which showed a wolf on four legs howling at the moon with a pile of rags on the ground around its feet.

A door slammed below, and my dad's voice carried up to announce his arrival. I shut off the search, threw the pile of rags back into the little trash can, and headed downstairs for lunch, but my mind couldn't stop whirling with all the pieces floating around without an anchor.

* * *

Denver

THE CHANGE our female was going through was increasing as she was becoming more wolf-like. She should be able to feel it, trying to claw its way to the surface during the day and succeeding at night. I watched her in the park when she discovered scraps of fabric I was certain had belonged to her. Dark circles underlined her eyes, no doubt from the sleepless nights as she underwent the change. It shouldn't be too much longer now before she understood, and we'd be right there to help her through it.

A pang in my heart kept me rooted to the spot, observing her. I wanted to go over there and shift back into my human form right in front of her, but I worried that would shock her too much and scare her away, and I didn't think I could handle it if she did that. A rejected bond was the worst fate a shifter could endure. We had to approach this situation with caution.

Movement in the nearby bush distracted me, and I perked my ears to listen. There was something over there, but I couldn't quite make it out. Curious, I stood up and trotted over. By the time I reached the spot, whatever it was had disappeared, and more movement out of the corner of my eye caught my attention again.

This time I was on full alert. I looked back to make sure my female was okay before ambling off in the direction of the unknown creature.

I sniffed the air and paused when I caught a whiff of wolf. My body became taut as my eyes scanned the full perimeter until I saw a bushy tail disappear behind some more brush. I ran after it and kept following the sights and sounds until I saw a brown wolf running, and I sprinted after it before it disappeared from sight.

We played a game of chase and the nimble creature showed great speed. I didn't know where I was going, but I eventually lost sight of the new wolf. With my nose to the ground, I realized her scent was everywhere. She'd been in this area for a little while. This incident would need to be brought to the others' attention in case she turned out to be a foe. Enemy until proven ally. We couldn't take any chances with trusting the wrong wolf, especially one who was watching our female.

Chapter Twelve

Makena

I dug through the bags of Chinese food that my dad had spread across the table, filling my plate with deliciousness as though I hadn't finished off the sandwiches not long ago.

"You've got quite the appetite there," he commented, as he eyed my sixth spoonful of rice. "They working you hard lately?"

"Yeah," I said, as I added pieces of chicken and veggies and sat back in my chair to begin eating. Steam drifted from the takeout containers and I nearly salivated at the smell. It was as though I hadn't eaten a bite of food all day. Before my stomach could start growling, I shoveled the first bite into my mouth.

"I barely ever see you in the mornings anymore."

Still chewing the first bite, I paused with my fork halfway to my mouth and then set it down against the side of my plate and swallowed. The food fell like a rock down my throat. His statement reminded me of something that had been in my head, and I couldn't get past the idea that all of this might have to do with her. "Can I ask you something?"

"Of course, kiddo, anything."

"It's about Mom."

His cheek bulged when he stopped chewing as he thought over how to respond. He'd never liked talking about her before, always deflecting my questions, so I stopped bringing it up. The last time I asked about her was at least seven years ago, if not longer. I had asked what she looked like and he told me I had the same long golden hair that she did, then he had me help hang a painting that had been collecting dust until that moment. We had a mutual, unspoken understanding that while we both missed her, she wouldn't be brought up in conversation.

"You know I don't like talking about her," he replied solemnly.

"I know, but this is important."

He thought it over for a moment as he watched my face, and I tried to convey the utter importance of how badly I needed to talk about this. If I didn't get information, then I would quite literally go mad. My eyes stung as I stared at him, unblinking. Then he swallowed his bite of food. "What do you want to know?"

"Everything. Who was she and where was she from?" A simple question that had the potential to change my life.

He sighed. "This is really that important?"

"It is," I answered with conviction and an unbroken gaze.

Setting his fork down on his plate, he laced his fingers together on the tabletop and leaned in, his eyes slightly blocked from the glare of his glasses.

He gave a nod and began. "We were young and going through life without much thought. I didn't know her very well, but one time, when I went away on a trip, I saw her running through the forest, laughing. I couldn't take my eyes off her."

"Where was this trip?" I smacked my mouth shut and mentally chastised myself for interrupting when I was finally getting the story I needed.

Instead of scolding me, he smiled at the memory. "A cabin in the woods. It was north, and just outside Carlisle."

"Sounds romantic," I whispered, thinking of cold nights and warm fireplaces. They probably enjoyed hot cocoa together.

"We were both in that forest to get away from our lives. I was stressing about getting through school and finding a job to make my family proud. But her, I never did find out exactly what it was she was running from." His eyes had a faraway look to them as he recalled the past.

I frowned. "She was running from something?" In my made-up version of her, she was perfect and loved by all.

He continued on, plowing over my question. "We ended up spending the better part of the week with each other. We were inseparable, making the most of the short amount of time we were granted together. We still kept in touch even when we both had to return to our normal lives, with daily emails and late-night phone calls." His finger drew a pattern on the tabletop as he stared absentmindedly into the past.

"We managed to sneak away from our families and our lives and met up every weekend. The time passed the quickest when we were together, but we made the most of it. We talked about dreams, goals, and what ifs. Trying to put together what would happen if we didn't have to be apart." His last words came out strangled and he took a drink of his water. "We even planned out our lives together, counting down the days until we could get started. She ended up pregnant, which really set things into motion. We were both ecstatic to meet the bright little bundle that would make our family complete. She was going to come here when you were born, convinced it wouldn't be safe for me to live where she was. I never did find out exactly what or where that was. For all I knew, she could've been trying to escape a cult."

Pausing, he took another long drink of his water before setting the glass gently on the tabletop. He didn't make eye contact and was lost in his own little world. The world that only existed in his head where my mother was. How I wished I could be in that world right now too. To be able to bathe in what was and listen to the truths of the past.

His fingers tangled in the knots at the ends of his hair as he ran them through for the hundredth time, helping pull the memories from his head. "She called me one night in a panic and asked me to come and get her, so I did. I was out the door before she could even finish the question. I met her outside of where I believed she'd been staying—she wouldn't let me go any farther. There were these guys who came after her and they looked pretty scary. Even I was concerned. They had these frowns and lines on their faces that said they weren't up to any good."

He coughed to clear his throat when his fingers began to curl into his palm as he spoke. "I put her in my car, and we came back here. She had you on the way here." His eyes were faraway, but that part of the story I knew. I was aware I was born on the side of the road, and it never occurred to me it could have been because they were running from something. "A bit earlier than we expected, but it worked out. You were as healthy as could be despite my concern over your timing, but she wasn't worried in the slightest. We had a lovely few weeks together, but there were nights when I would find her outside or at the window always looking in the same direction, toward the northeast. She had nightmares nearly every night, and the more time that passed, the worse they would get. It got to the point where she began injuring herself in her sleep as a result. She said she had to go back, and that it would help the nightmares or else they would only keep getting worse, and I let her."

His voice cracked, and he cleared his throat before taking another long drink from his water. He placed the empty glass back onto the table and ran his hand through the top of his black and graying hair, as though he wanted to brush the memories away.

"I knew better. I had strong feelings against it, but I let her go back."

"How is it bad you let her go back?" I asked when he didn't continue.

"Because she never returned. For weeks, months, and years, I've waited for her." He let out a strangled laugh. "Heck, I'm still waiting for her. I suppose I always will be."

I studied his face. He'd become more aged in the last ten minutes, years of dark circles appearing more prominent underneath his eyes.

"Everyone told me she was never coming back, that she found a new life and had no intention of returning. But I knew better. The only reason she wouldn't have come back was if she wasn't able to. No one knew her like I did."

"Did you try to find her?" I pressed.

"I tried everything I could think of. I hung flyers, posted online, set up search parties with anyone who was willing to help, called her number until it was picked up by new people, and anything else I could think of. Many times I went out to where I'd picked her up and searched every last inch of it in every direction, but I still couldn't find any trace of her. It was as though she'd vanished off the face of the Earth." He looked toward the door. "I still half expect to see her walk through that door as though nothing happened, but it's been two decades now. I know she's not coming back, but I still want to know what happened to her and why."

Wiping a stray tear from my eye, I reached across the table and placed my hand over his. "I'm sorry you went through all of that alone. I wish I could remember her."

He smiled. "So do I. You're almost exactly like her. You're a spitting image of her in nearly every way. Plus, she cared a great deal about animals too, you get that from her."

"Do you have any theory about what could have happened? If she's—" I couldn't get myself to finish the sentence. I'd always thought she'd run off and he didn't want to talk about her, and I occasionally wondered if she was even still alive.

He shook his head. "If she is still alive, then someone is keeping her from coming back. It's why we've never moved from here, from this house. Some part of me always hoped she would come home, even though most of me knows it won't ever happen. Not that I've completely given up, I just don't feel her anymore and haven't since a few days after the last time I saw her."

"What about who, how, and what she was? Do you know anything more about her?"

He squinted his eyes. "It was so long ago, but as far as what she was? I'm not sure I'm following."

I sighed. "I don't know either, I'm just trying to understand her more."

"I get that. I don't know much about where she came from. The only other people I'd seen from there were those scary looking guys who were searching for her. If I hadn't known any better, I'd say they were even growling."

"What about her likes and dislikes, anything strange you noticed or weird quirks?"

"She loved the nighttime and could never get enough of staring at the moon. She used to love to run, and she loved meat in any form. She could out eat anyone in this town. It was rather impressive."

"Interesting."

"Anything else I could help with?"

"Not that I can think of."

We continued our meal in silence while thoughts and theories swirled around in my head. My dad remained hunched over the table, his gaze glued to his plate as he ate. With how reluctant he's been to talk about her all these years, this couldn't have been easy for him, and now he was blocking out the world while he relieved the memories. He had no idea how much I appreciated every lit bit of information he gave.

"I love you, Dad."

THOUGHTS INVADED my mind as I tossed and turned in bed. Sleep was futile, I didn't know why I even tried anymore. I couldn't stop thinking about what my dad had said. Where was she from and where did she go?

There was something in my mind that wanted to give me the answers I craved, but no matter how hard I tried, I couldn't seem to connect to it.

The light on my computer kept blinking. Every time I tossed around in bed, it came on to record the movement.

"This isn't what you're supposed to record," I mumbled, as I tossed the blankets aside and crawled out of bed. I grabbed the red cardigan that was draped over my dresser and wrapped it around my body as I opened the window.

The breeze was cool, and I shivered as it stung my skin, but I loved it. This was my favorite time of year, when things were turning crisp and the air made you want to cuddle up with a mug of hot cocoa in order to not literally freeze to death.

My arms tightened around my waist as the chilly night air hit my face, sending a shiver throughout my body.

The moon could be seen in the cloudless sky, so large that I could nearly make out the dark spots that peppered the surface. It was toward the northeast, and my body stilled when I realized I was doing the same thing as my mother.

As a child, I spent many nights sitting by a window and watching the moon, convinced it was trying to show me a hidden world I wasn't yet ready for.

Tonight, I was looking out the window at night in the same direction, only I didn't know what she was looking toward. All I could see were large masses where the mountains were, shrouded in clouds. I tore my eyes away from the shadows and gazed at the world around my house illuminated by the moon. So bright, and so peaceful.

Its light was so bright, I could clearly see the teenager from down the street as he walked the dog, the phone in his hand illuminating his face as much as the moonlight on the back of his tilted head. The leash wrapped around his hand as he texted was taut as the white dog's tiny legs worked overtime in its excitement.

I felt a strange urge to jump through the window, rip the leash from his hand, and tear the boy to shreds. I caught myself as I was beginning to lean out of the window and tightened my grip around the cardigan as I righted myself again.

That was weird. Maybe it was the stress from everything finally getting to me. Maybe I'd spent so much time at Cara Paws that I was beginning to think more like a dog.

I really needed to take a break once this semester was over. Maybe relax for a few days before jumping straight back into working all sorts of hours again. Then I let out a silent chuckle. I didn't relax. That wasn't something my body knew how to do.

The dog yipped as they passed, and it brought my attention back to them. The branches of a nearby bush rustled, startling the dog and drawing my attention. Whatever it was, it was enough to make the boy look up from his phone and take a step back as a pair of eyes glared at them, glowing in the glimmering moonlight.

I looked closer and spotted what appeared to be a large dog, possibly even a wolf, sitting on its haunches at the side of the house across the street. A pair of familiar bright green eyes watched me, moving slightly to catch my every move as I pressed a hand against the windowsill to lean forward and get a closer look.

That wasn't a normal dog, it was a wolf. There was silver laced throughout the white coat, its unwavering gaze watching me with a human-like quality that pierced my soul and made me want to lay it out for him to examine. The thought startled me, and where I should have been afraid, I found myself wanting to move closer.

I was certain it was the same one I'd seen watching me before. Where did it come from, and why were those entrancing eyes so familiar?

The boy and his dog were running away now, even though the creature wasn't following them. It had no interest in them, as its full attention was on me, ignoring the pounding of tennis shoes against the sidewalk as they retreated.

Questions swarmed my mind, and the longer I watched, the deeper I fell into the vast greenness of the eyes. It was mesmerizing and it felt like home. I wanted to wrap myself up in that gaze and not emerge again for a long, long time. To embrace the warmth that glowered and wrapped around me in the frigid night air.

I was vaguely aware that the boy and his dog were now gone, they'd made it back to their house and closed the door so fast the sound of the door slamming could be heard all the way down the street.

The rest of the world went out of focus as tunnel vision completely took over. The only thing that could shake me from this trance were the prickles of pain along my fingers.

Hissing at the sharp prickles, I looked down, but the hand on the windowsill was no longer my own. It was transforming. Hair sprung up along the skin and grew into a small forest as it spread across my body. My fingers shrank into padded paws with claws poking out from between the fur.

I should be scared. I should be terrified. Oddly enough, I felt no fear as the thin fabric of my cardigan split across my back.

A pang racked through my stomach, and my shoulders lurched forward. I barely managed to prevent myself from sailing through the window. If the windowsill hadn't been at hip level, I would've been tumbling straight to the ground, headfirst.

My mouth burst open in a brief scream that immediately melted into a howl. As the transformation was finished, my canine eyes locked on the green ones, and before I knew it, I was sailing through the air.

Chapter Thirteen

Makena

*E*arly morning light flashed across my vision as I opened my eyes and then immediately shut them against the harshness.

"Not again," I groaned, as I rolled over onto my stomach. I tried to remember the night before, but everything was so foggy right now.

Leaves fell from my body as I pushed myself into a kneeling position, and I shivered at the rush of the icy morning air.

"Here you go." A white sweater neatly folded over a pair of black leggings appeared in front of me, and I jumped back. Nobody had ever been there during these mornings before. My heart pounded in my chest as questions flooded my mind, wondering what transpired last night and why there was someone else here this morning. I looked over the pile of clothing and I was met with the familiar face of Denver. My breath was visible in the cold as I gasped, creating a moment of a foggy wall in front of me.

I flew back onto my butt and covered myself up with my hands and arms as best as I could. "What's going on?" I wanted to be strong and take charge of the situation, but my unsure voice betrayed me. Confusion wrapped over each syllable as panic rose in my chest.

Denver set the clothing on the ground in front of me and stood up to take a step back. His hands were raised as his gaze remained locked on mine. "You might be more comfortable once you're dressed. Then we can explain."

We? My eyes darted around, and I realized the other four guys were standing there in the woods, all watching me closely. They, at least, had some modesty. Their eyes didn't dip below my head.

"Could you turn around for a minute?" I asked in a tone that was more demanding than questioning.

They each turned so their backs were facing me, and I quickly scrambled into the clothes. The strangest part about it was these were my clothes that had been tucked away in my dresser drawers. How did they manage to get their hands on these? I shuddered to think of people being in my room when I wasn't there. However, on the bright side, at least they weren't shredded and left in the dirt.

After sliding into the leggings, I pulled the sweater over my head, glad that I wouldn't have to run home buck naked for once. "Before I ask what's going on here, I need to know how you got these clothes from my room." When no one answered, I added, "You can turn around now."

They each turned around and then looked at Denver as though they were waiting for him to answer.

"When you left last night, I had Julian grab you something. Thought you would enjoy having some clothes to put on when you changed back," Denver explained.

"What do you mean by 'change back?'"

Liam stared at me. His arms were crossed over his chest

and his jaw was set. He was studying the situation, probably analyzing everything before he responded. His eyes bore into mine, reading me like a book for the secrets I didn't let the world see, but it only took one steady look at me to confirm for him that I still had no idea what was going on. The pieces weren't coming together.

Maybe this was all a bad case of sleepwalking. Maybe I wasn't even awake yet.

"You're a wolf," Liam stated, as though it was the most obvious thing in the world.

His words echoed through my mind as I took a few shaky breaths. He watched me closely for my reaction, his back stiff as though he expected me to hurl opposition. Perhaps even laugh in his face at the ridiculous statement. But I did none of that.

After all the hours of research I'd done for my assignments, that was the theory I wouldn't let my mind entertain. I kept telling myself it was a lie, the most improbable option. The one that pushed at the edges of my mind when I was doing research for a class assignment, but then would shove back into the dusty corners of denial. It was fun to think about in books and movies, but terrifying in real life.

Something washed over me, a sudden feeling of satisfaction that I shouldn't have felt, making me want to prance around with a proud smirk on my face. Then it was gone as fast as it had appeared. It felt like it belonged to something else inside of me.

I took a step away from them as I processed this information.

Straightening my spine and pursing my lips, I looked Liam in the eye. My dark, dusty corner of denial was still fighting back with all the logic it screamed at me. There was no research I'd come across that could prove this. "That's crazy, there's no possible way."

Liam's eyebrows shot up. "You don't believe me?"

"No." I shook my head. "How could that be possible? I study animals. It's my major, it's what I'm going to college to spend my life doing. I know for a fact it's not possible."

"This is real. You wouldn't exactly find wolf shifters in your college textbook. I highly doubt there's a class to cover that."

My stomach turned as his hazel eyes pierced mine with the daggers of truth he fully believed. He was convinced, he wasn't just trying to mess with my head for the fun of it. He thought this was real. I gulped, unsure how to respond. This wasn't something I could really deal with right now. I had too much on my plate, there was no way I could add wolf shifter onto my already overflowing platter. Why couldn't I get a side of normalcy, or even an appetizer of nothing going wrong? I didn't have enough spoons for this. "The logic simply isn't there," I whispered.

"It's true," Casen affirmed. He lifted his hand as though he wanted to reach out to me, but his expression turned pained when I flinched at the movement, and he dropped his hand to the side. "Sometimes the truth is too great to even consider, and sometimes it's the only thing that can help you."

Julian took a step toward me with a calloused hand held out, dirt-filled fingernails facing me, and I jumped at the small movement. He paused, then dropped his hand and looked at me, his blue eyes crinkled with a pitiful smile. "Didn't mean to scare you. We only want to help."

"How could you possibly help me?"

The smile vanished from his face and was replaced with a confused frown. He glanced to Denver who nodded in approval, and he continued, "Because we're wolves too. We're exactly like you."

The last of his words created a whirlpool in my mind, swirling around on repeat. *We're exactly like you.*

"This is too much. I need to go." Spinning around, I ran in the direction of my home with my key pounding against my chest as I ran. At least this time it was there, and I wouldn't need to search for one of the spares I'd hidden, or even climb a tree.

Something in my chest contracted with each step I took away from them. If I were to turn around, I would slingshot straight back. I fought against the invisible force as I sought out solitude.

Flashes from last night took over my vision, and I saw the boy texting on his phone while walking his dog, the gray and white hair appearing along my arms, and the feeling of my fingers shrinking into paws while my nails grew into long claws that retracted with a simple muscle twitch.

The world closed in around me and it felt like a vacuum, sucking all the air out. I quickened my pace.

I had a strong feeling that wasn't a dream, but I wasn't about to sort that out in the woods with these guys. I didn't even know them, yet they seemed to believe they knew more about me than I did. How could that even be possible?

What seemed like memories from last night flooded my mind, and I forgot to look both ways before crossing the street. A horn blared, causing me to fly forward, and my toes banged against the side of a car as it sped past.

I hurried on with a slight limp until the tingling in my toes went away. I'd need to be more careful. I only hoped it wasn't anyone I knew, I had no idea how I would explain this. Because of course when my life was falling apart, all I could think about was how to apologize to a stranger for nearly being run over.

Then the car's tires squealed as they turned at the end of the road, and something told me they probably didn't care.

My dad was already leaving for work as I rounded the corner of the street, and I ducked behind a bush until the sound of the engine disappeared in the other direction. I blew out a breath and continued my morning crawl to the house, forgetting that I didn't need to try so hard to hide this time since I was actually clothed for once. That one small difference was already throwing a huge wrench into my normally casual morning chaos.

The first thing I did when I reached my room was fall into my chair and turn on my computer. I sped through all the windows I'd left open, clicking out of all my assignments until I found the one for the camera.

After scrolling through until I found the hours I wanted for last night, I sucked in a breath and hit play.

The video was dark and tinged green with the night camera. I saw myself getting out of bed and grabbing the red cardigan. On instinct, I spun around to check, and saw the red cardigan was draped over the windowsill in tatters. A stone fell into the pit of my stomach at the sight, and I turned back to look at my computer, equally eager and dreading to see what would happen next.

Next, I saw myself leaning out the window, mesmerized by what was going on outside. My eyes got this faraway look to them as though I'd been hypnotized.

Then I raised my hand to my mouth as I watched the camera version of me writhe around as beautiful, light colored fur erupted along my body. Straightening up, I shook the rags loose from my body and jumped over the windowsill.

The camera faded to black, then flickered. Sure enough, a blonde head of hair appeared less than a minute after I'd disappeared, reengaging the camera again. Julian crawled through the window and into my room as Denver had said. He took a moment to survey my room before shuffling through my dresser drawers. I wanted to scream when he reached the underwear drawer, but he immediately shut it without rifling through. Fighting the urge to go back and strangle them all, I leaned in closer to the screen. If these guys messed with anything, I'd...well, I didn't know what I would do, but I'd figure it out.

To my surprise, once he had an outfit in his hand, he didn't linger. He took long strides back to the window and paused, throwing a wink at the camera before disappearing into the tree.

Everything was still again and the camera shut off. It was the last thing that had been recorded until I ran into my room this morning, setting off the motion detector again.

My heart was frantic as I clicked out of the camera. It took me several tries, my trembling hands making it difficult to get the mouse to work right. My head was spinning, and my hand was shaking. I swallowed back the bile that threatened to come up as Liam's words echoed in my mind. Giving up on the computer, I pulled my hands toward me to cover my mouth as I curled up in the chair to process this information.

It was true. They weren't lying to me. I probably could have been nicer to them, but I didn't have anything other than their word to go on. The word of strange men who knew more about me than I knew of them. I'd needed to see it for myself, and now that I had, I wished I hadn't.

How did they know? They'd said they were wolves, too. Maybe they were only here to sniff out new wolves.

I felt like I'd done something wrong, even though this was outside my control. The thought of them putting down any rogue wolf they find made me curl my body tighter into a ball. I shook the thoughts free. I couldn't explain it, but I was unable to entertain the thought of them willingly wanting to hurt me. My head became crowded with questions, and I didn't even know how to form them into thoughts to be able to deal with them.

My computer dinged, bringing me out of my stupor to alert me to a new email from my professor. Clicking on it, desperate for something normal in this moment, I saw a new assignment had been added. We were now required to volunteer at a nature reserve and write up a report on the experience. Included in the email was a short list of places, complete with contact information. I scanned down the list, my eyes unseeing as I tried to force my focus onto something else that wasn't my own problems.

A breeze blew by me, and I swiveled in my chair. Perched in the window was Denver. With the sun at his back, his front was so dark, I couldn't make out the tattoos that branded his arms which were on full display thanks to his white tank.

"Holy crap," I exclaimed, as my hand flew to my chest. "Way to give a girl a heart attack. Have you ever thought of knocking?"

"That would've taken too long."

"Seriously? Climbing a tree is much faster?"

Despite how dark his eyes were, they still seemed to glow in the shadows even as he narrowed his gaze at me. "Would you have answered the door?"

My mouth fell agape as I tried to figure out how to respond. He wasn't wrong.

Straightening his posture, he was the epitome of business as he took advantage of my hesitation. "Exactly. Now, we have some things to talk about."

An awkward laugh bubbled out of me. "You're kidding, right? You can't climb a tree, break into my bedroom, and expect me to do what you want. It doesn't work like that." Deflection. That would work right now. Anything to give me some more time to organize my headspace.

"We've already wasted enough time. We tried to give you some space to figure it out for yourself since we didn't want to scare you away. That was what we were most afraid of, but it seems to have been unavoidable anyway. As you can see from that video there" —he nodded toward the computer— "you now have confirmation you're a wolf."

"What are you?" My fingers curled around the arms of my chair, bracing myself for the answer I'd already known.

"I'm a wolf as well. As are Liam—who is the beta, the next in command—Julian, Casen, and then Axel, the omega."

"What does that make you?"

His boots tracked dirt on my carpet as he walked over to me with a slowness not unlike a villain's in a horror movie, and it made me consider running. I stole a glance at my door, wondering if I could make it.

"Bolting won't work. The others are down there."

"You have my house surrounded?" My voice screeched at the end, and I gulped as his hands landed on the armrests of my chair. As if I could sense what was about to happen, my fingers ended up twisting into each other in my lap. I could smell the fresh autumn morning on him, and only now did I notice the faint scent of wild dog mixed in.

He leaned his head in, and his dark eyes swirled as they locked on mine. They carried a seriousness I could feel in my bones, wrapped up with a softness as they explored my own widening irises. "I'm the alpha."

I shivered as his warm breath brushed against me, kissing my skin.

He leaned in a fraction more, as though drawn to me. "But you…you are something different altogether."

I was so lost in his gaze, I nearly missed his last statement. My breaths turned shallow, and I licked my lips. "What's that supposed to mean?"

"I don't know. But we're going to find out." His words

were low and carried a serious note. Inhaling sharply, he hesitated for a moment before taking a step toward me. "You haven't felt anything, have you?" His voice became curious as he watched for my reaction, and then took another step.

"Like what?" For a moment, I worried he could tell how much my heart rate sped up each time he increased his proximity. The way my fingers itched to let go of the edge of my seat and run up his bare arms to explore each and every tattoo, to trace each swirl along his tanned skin. The unevenness of my breathing as I drank him in, wanting to wrap my legs around his waist and pull him toward me.

But he couldn't know that, unless he read my mind, which I hoped more than anything wasn't included in the exclusive wolf shifter package. Even I was surprised at the thoughts coursing through my head, which didn't seem to fit with how I thought I should be reacting. I should have been shoving him away, screaming in his face, and jumping out of the window. But instead I wanted to pull him closer. To listen to every word his velvet voice had to say. Rather than doing any of those things, my body struggled with the whirlwind of what I should do, what I wanted to do, and what I was going to do.

"A spark."

"I don't understand." My voice was growing breathy, and it was taking everything I had to keep my eyes on his and not flick them down to his lips. I tightened my grip on the chair as though it were the only thing that kept me from spiraling down.

His gaze lingered on my face a second longer before he nodded and closed the distance until he was standing straight before me. "It's nothing. Maybe something we can go over later after we get through more pressing matters."

He turned to face the window, adjusting his pants in a

discreet way, but I still bit back the smile that threatened to surface.

With a casual adjustment of his waistband, he slid his hands into his pockets and faced me again. "We have a lot to teach you. I know you have a busy schedule, but this is something you need to make time for. Even if you need to drop something. You don't have a choice."

"Excuse me?" I looked at him with disbelief, all the feelings of infatuation now drained from me. "I don't know who you think you are, but you can't come into my home and order me around like this." I stood from the chair to better hold my ground, and spoke over him as soon as he opened his mouth to say something else. "You have no idea how hard I've been working. I can't drop my whole life because I'm suddenly a wolf."

"You're not suddenly a wolf," he countered between my bouts of protest. "You've always been a wolf. If you're changing now and you never knew, and you can't recall being bitten, then you must be nearing your twentieth birthday."

"How did you know that?"

"When a pup is born, they are raised by the pack. When one is raised outside the pack by a human and has no idea they're a wolf, the pup will begin to transform as it nears their twentieth birthday. There are stories of this happening, and they usually end in tragedy as they have no one to help guide them. Have your parents not told you any of this?"

His accusation hit me like a truckload of bricks, and pieces began to fit together in the jigsaw I'd been struggling with. "My dad is human," I whispered, "but my mom disappeared when I was born."

"Does your dad know anything at all about wolves?" he asked.

I shook my head. He was a man of cars. He knew them

inside and out. Animals were my territory, but he'd never once shown knowledge or interest in the subject. If he knew something, I'd be thoroughly shocked.

A ringing noise sounded behind me, and I jumped. "Oh, crap, I forgot. I have a virtual class meeting starting right now." I rushed to my chair and reached for my headphones before turning back to look at Denver. "Can we pick this up later? I have something I need to do right now. And no," I cut him off as he opened his mouth to protest, "it can't wait. I can't afford to miss any of this. You had your chance to say more, and you even said yourself that you don't know much more about me." I held up a finger when he tried to object, and I fought the urge to put the headphones down and jump out of the window with him. "We can pick this up later."

He nodded, and for a moment there I was sure I'd seen what was almost a smirk. "You got it, wolf." With the ease of a wolf, he hiked a leg over the window, crawled onto the large branch next to it, and disappeared. I coughed to get my bearings and turned to face the screen.

"Present," I said into the microphone.

Julian

"WHAT HAPPENED?" I asked as Denver rejoined us, and noticed Makena wasn't with him like we'd hoped she'd be. I crossed my arms as though I could hide my disappointment.

"She's not coming. She has some other things to take care of first, but she'll come around. It's a lot to take in, and she needs to figure out how to handle it without a bunch of wolves hovering over her," he reasoned.

"But we've been hovering over her for the last week," Axel pointed out.

"Yes, but she isn't aware of that."

"I'm pretty sure she's somewhat aware. She did confront us the other day at the diner for stalking her," I reminded him.

Denver nodded. "My point is, she needs some space. Give her some time. Then we can try and talk with her again."

"How much time, and does she know about the bond?" Liam questioned.

I saw a smirk appear on Denver's face for a split second and then it was gone. "I'm pretty sure she's aware of the bond, even if she hasn't admitted it yet." He looked up at her window, but she wasn't there. She was somewhere inside though.

"As for how much time, she might have until tonight." Everyone's eyes turned to me, and I shrugged. "It's when my first shift at the diner is."

"I have a feeling she isn't aware of this?" Denver surmised.

"That would be correct."

"Don't make this any worse for us, man," Axel warned, as he rubbed at the back of his neck and looked around.

"Relax, I don't want to scare her away any more than the rest of you. We will need to talk with her at some point." Although, relaxing was the farthest thing from my mind. "I'll catch you guys up after."

Cracking my neck and stretching my shoulders, I took off jogging down the street toward our temporary home. As my first shift neared, my mind became invaded with images of her reaction when she'd see me there. Would she be angry? A part of me hoped so. That could be fun. I enjoyed watching the fire inside of her ignite.

Nearing the end of the street, I glanced back at the empty window again, hoping to see her blonde curls. Must be a habit.

Chapter Fourteen

Makena

I was grateful the Friday classes took place online, because I wasn't mentally present the entire time it was going on. The class passed in a blur, and I kept checking the little box that gave the names of those who were online, looking for Liam and Axel. I didn't want to acknowledge how badly I wanted to see their names pop up, because I simultaneously wanted this to all be a bad dream and wake up to find they'd never been here in the first place.

About ten minutes before the virtual class ended, two newcomers clicked in and my body froze when I saw their names added to the attendee list.

"For those showing up late, you can find all the materials we covered in the folder labeled with today's date. I expect better punctuality throughout the rest of the course," Mr. Morrison boomed through the microphone, but I barely registered what he was saying.

My hand hovered above my notebook, which was still blank. Everything had been such a haze, I couldn't even take notes. I would need to check out that folder later on when I got a chance.

Relief flooded me when the class ended, but when I saw all the names disappear, I felt an emptiness that was caused by the disappearance of two specific names. I didn't know what was coming over me, I wanted to yell at them to go away while also pulling them close.

I set my headphones down and chewed on my bottom lip as I looked around my room. The trash can filled with dirty and shredded clothing, my increased appetite, and the night-time trips to the woods. How could I not have seen this coming?

Pulling my feet up in my chair and curling inward, I tucked my head into my hands and screamed. I pulled at my hair and clenched my toes, my whole body shaking as I relieved the frustration that was building inside of me.

This wasn't what I asked for when I decided I wanted to find the truth. This wasn't what I imagined when I decided to spend some of my days with the dogs. I wanted to walk them, for crying out loud, not freaking become one of them.

My voice was nearly hoarse when I finally calmed down, and I reached for the water bottle on the floor, grateful it wasn't empty since I rarely remembered to refill it.

After downing the bottle, I dropped it back to the floor, stood up, and crawled underneath the blankets in my bed. I had no idea if I'd gotten any sleep last night, or if I spent the whole time exploring in my wolf form. I couldn't remember much, and it frustrated me to no end. *What kind of thing did you leave me with, Mom?* I didn't know if I could do this on my own.

Setting an alarm to wake me up in time to get ready for work at the diner, I closed my eyes and drifted off to sleep.

I SHOVED my hands into my jacket pockets to get warm as I walked briskly to the diner. After the online class session ended, I was alone with my thoughts for far too long. I didn't know how to get ahold of Denver and the others to fill in the gaps, and doing my own research about something new didn't get me anywhere. I'd exhausted every website I could find online that could give me any information about wolves, and ended up on some website that nearly convinced me I was some mutant from outer space. By the time I finally closed out of all of my research tabs, I was too annoyed at the world to even face the wolves. So, I decided to leave early and walk to work rather than sitting there pulling my hair out. The bone-chilling cold of the Autumn air was exactly what I needed to clear my chaotic head.

People nodded and smiled as I passed, but I barely paid them any attention. I finally knew what I was doing during the nights when I'd wake up outside the next morning. The veil of the unknown was now pulled back, and it revealed an even larger abyss full of secrets and questions. It was never-ending, and every answered question led to a dozen more, and the whole endeavor was getting to be overwhelming. While I was glad to finally have my truth exposed, I wasn't sure if I actually liked knowing. This wasn't the truth I thought I would get, but it was the reality I had been dealt, and I struggled against the blurring line between reality and fantasy. Knowing I was a creature that I never thought existed was wreaking havoc on my mind more than my over-whelming course load.

I was so lost in my thoughts, I didn't notice when I stepped into the street until someone grabbed a handful of my jacket and pulled me back in time to avoid being hit by a speeding car.

"Careful there. Are you alright?"

I turned to thank my rescuer, but when I saw it was

Julian, the words caught in my throat. Were they constantly watching me now? I wanted to open my mouth and chastise him. To tell him I didn't need to be watched every moment of every day. Maybe even smile up at him and thank him for saving my life. But I rarely ever did what I wanted. I only did what I always thought was best for everyone, and pushed him away.

"I'm fine," I responded curtly, before looking both ways and crossing the street.

"Hold up, I think we're going the same way." He caught up to me and kept pace at my side. "So, I heard Denver talked to you." His words were hesitant, like he was afraid of how I might respond.

"Yes. I know I'm a wolf and so are all of you."

"Shhh, you can't run around saying that. You never know who's listening."

I laughed. "I've lived in this town my whole life. The only people I didn't know here were you five. If anything, you guys are the ones I know I can trust the least. Believe me, no one here cares enough for a witch hunt. Or a wolf hunt. If anything, they'll keep to their gossip circles."

"People can always surprise you with their actions. You don't always know everyone you think you do," he warned. "Some secrets are better left as just that, secret."

"What are you doing here? Why are you here, why are you guys always around?" I threw my hands in the air for emphasis.

He grinned at me. "I'm starting a new job today."

"Congratulations, but why must you walk with me?" I turned at the next street corner, and he followed me into the diner. Oh, crap. These guys really were everywhere. School, my bedroom, the diner, they were infiltrating every place that was mine.

"Julian! So glad to have you here." Justine rushed forward

with a pile of clothing. "Here's your uniform. The bathroom to change is through the door behind the counter. I can give you a quick rundown of things before we get busy, but the most important things are don't die and don't break anything. We're down another three sets of dishware." She rushed off before I could get a word in, and I stood there in disbelief as he smiled and waltzed off to the back area with the confidence of a seasoned employee.

"What just happened?" I mumbled to myself, as I hurried to clock in. I returned Rodge's wave as he clocked in for chef duty. He opened his mouth as though he wanted to talk, but I didn't have the energy. I tied my apron around my waist and grabbed a notebook before heading back out to take care of my first table before he could say anything.

I still had my normal section, minus a couple tables that Julian was now taking over. While I was grateful for the extra hands tonight, I couldn't help but be skeptical. How could you trust someone who had one face during the day, and then become a whole new species at night?

I'd tried to ignore the wolf issue as much as I could after Denver left, but it had still been pounding on the gates of my mind where I'd tried to block it out. I knew I needed—and wanted—to know more, but I couldn't seem to deal with it at the moment. I was being dragged in opposite directions between what I knew and what I wanted to know. It was too much.

As the evening wore on, I began to soften up a little. I noticed how Julian was very observant and left no customer with anything less than half a glass full of their drink. He smiled at them and catered to them with such ease, one would think he'd been working here for far longer than a couple of hours. I even found myself easing up around him and keeping my anger and annoyance suppressed when I pointed out the empty bins to clear tables off with.

Even Justine had taken note and pulled me aside at one point to ask if I knew him. She wanted me to make sure he kept coming back, since she was ready to put him permanently on the schedule for many more shifts.

I noticed he kept throwing subtle glances my way, as though to make sure I was doing alright. His eyes were soft and found me with ease every time. I knew he wanted to talk more about the wolf thing, but there wouldn't be any time until the diner closed, and even then I had a feeling that Justine would monopolize his time until we were out the door. She was thrilled with having him here. He was so attentive to the customers, I doubted she would let him quit even if he tried to. He was in for the long run now.

As I shoved my way through the double doors with a large tray of fresh, hot burgers, their delicious smell drifted toward me, making my stomach ache in hunger. Walking toward the waiting customers, my stomach growled loud enough for Julian to notice as I passed, and he threw me a concerned look. I ignored it and kept going, but the growling grew louder with every step until I finally reached the table and set the tray down onto a small folding table so I could unload it one plate at a time.

I set the first two plates down without issue, and then paused at the third. It looked so delicious, so inviting. I could still see the steam wafting off of the food. Even the fresh cut fries were cooked to perfection, sitting on top of a large leaf of lettuce.

My stomach grumbled louder. Maybe no one would notice if I took one fry. There were still a lot more there, and no one ever finished all their fries anyway. Technically, I would be doing them a favor.

Reaching out, I bypassed the edge of the plate and grabbed onto a fry and lifted it to my mouth.

"What are you doing to my food?" a high-pitched voice exclaimed, and I paused with the fry an inch from my lips.

"Uh…" I set the fry back down with the rest and held the plate out to her. "I was checking to make sure it was done enough. Some of them didn't look quite right. You're welcome."

The woman tilted her head back, turning her nose up in the air. "I want a new plate."

"Right…" I stood there at a loss for words, still trying to process what the heck was happening with me. I'd never done something like that before.

Before I could continue on with an apology and run away to put in a new order for her, Julian was at my side. "Sorry about that. A new order for you has been placed with the kitchen and it will be out shortly. We'll take care of this for you." He placed the fourth plate of food in front of the other waiting customer, picked up the tray, and turned me around to leave.

A zing of static electricity shot through me when his hand brushed against my arm, and I felt him tense beside me. Great, now I was shocking people on top of my screw up.

I looked around to make sure Justine wasn't in sight. She was already strung up with stress over the diner in general. I doubted she would fire me over anything, since she was already short-staffed, but I didn't need any more added stress to my life as it was.

Julian placed a hand against my lower back as we walked toward the kitchen, and I found myself slightly leaning into it. The warmth radiated along my spine, easing some of the pent-up stress. I wanted to feel that hand elsewhere. My whole body needed comfort.

My stomach growled and he quickened our pace. As we disappeared through the swinging doors, he guided me all the way to the back exit door and stopped in front of a chair. "Sit," he whispered.

I did as I was told, not feeling the urge to argue. I was about to keel over from hunger anyway.

To my surprise, he placed the plate in my lap, the smell of the food stronger than ever and unbelievably enticing. He checked to make sure no one could see us before he let go of the rim and took a step back.

"Eat," he ordered, "before you chew the face off of a customer."

I looked up at him in horror. "Would that really happen?"

He gave me a serious look. "Probably. You're a wolf without the ability to control yourself. You're going to have an insatiable hunger until you learn how to handle things. As soon as I saw your reaction to the smell of the food you were carrying out, I put in an extra order for each one of those plates. Once they're all done and the lady gets hers, the other three will be yours. It should hopefully be enough to get you through the night."

"Hopefully?" I echoed, as I picked up the burger.

"Yeah, hopefully. The cravings will only get worse the more you fight it. Once you can accept the change and learn how to make it a part of who you are, you'll start remembering what happens in your wolf form. You'll be able to change at will and prevent a change when you feel it coming on."

I scarfed down the burger and licked my fingers before going in for the fries. "I should probably stop trying to push you guys away then and let you help me."

He nodded. "That would be a really good thing to do. I highly suggest that."

"Noted," I said around a mouthful of fries. "I'll see what I can do about that."

"Food's ready. I'll take out the woman's plate and be right back with more of yours. Stay here."

The fries were gone by the time he arrived with the other three plates, and my mouth began to water all over again as he neared with the glorious food.

At least now I understood why I'd been so hungry lately. I hoped it wouldn't be like this for the rest of my life, but if he was right and it would improve as I learned to embrace my wolf self, then it could be worth a shot. Otherwise, this diner wouldn't be able to sustain my appetite and we'd be facing even more trouble.

I looked up at him as I was finishing up half of the fourth burger. "Are you sure you don't want any?"

He smiled and shook his head. "I'm good. I ate before I came here, and I can control the cravings. I barely even notice them anymore. If ever."

"You were probably young when you first started to change," I said, and he nodded. "What did you crave?"

His mouth scrunched to the side as he thought. "To be honest, I don't think I ever craved one specific thing. It was always everything. I've never been one to prefer one over another, life is too short for choices."

"Oh." Suddenly the craving was fading away into an ache I didn't want to analyze, and I lowered the burger for a moment.

His eyes widened for only a second before his expression was replaced with a playful smirk. "That is, until recently."

Finishing the last couple bites, I licked the remnants of the food from my fingers as he pulled the tray away. I felt content and almost human again. "Crap, I need to get back before Justine notices. I don't even know how long I've been back here."

"Only a few minutes. Everything is fine out there, I'm pretty sure she hasn't noticed anything."

"What haven't I noticed?"

Crap.

I looked down the small hallway and saw Justine standing there with her hands on her hips, giving us a look that demanded answers.

"She was getting sick, so I forced her to take a breather back here," Julian told her, before I could get my mouth to work.

"With a tray and empty plates?" She raised an eyebrow.

He held his hands out to the side with a shy grin. "It was the first thing I could grab in case she vomited. Figured a tray could be easier to clean up than the floor."

Justine looked to me for confirmation and I nodded. The story worked for me. "How are you now?"

"Much better. I think I'm ready to get back out there."

"Good. You've been my best employee, I can't lose you now. Especially with it being so hard to get new people in here. We just lucked out with him. I'll see you out there. Let me know if you need anything." She turned and walked away, leaving us alone in the darkened hallway.

I looked up at Julian. "Why don't the others work here too? As much as I hate to admit it, we really could use the extra hands."

Moving the tray to the floor, he held his hands up and I grabbed them, letting him pull me into a standing position. "Two of them have already put themselves into one of your classes. I came here. The others have some other work they need to focus on. We'll explain it all to you once we get a chance."

"Wait. You guys did this on purpose? They signed up for that class just to, what, spy on me?"

He nodded. "Pretty much. We had to keep an eye on you, figure out what you were, and whether or not you'd be on our side, or a threat."

"What would you have done if I was a threat?" I eyed him suspiciously, and he shrugged.

"I don't know, but I'm glad neither of us had to find out."

The sound of dishes crashing to the floor and shattering carried down the hall from beyond the swinging doors.

"We should get back out there. Talk about this more later," he suggested, as he started forward.

"We have a lot to cover. Don't run away when it's time to close," I warned, as I followed him down the hall.

Chapter Fifteen

Makena

*M*y head swiveled around on my neck as I tried to keep up with all the back and forth talk going on around me. All five wolf guys were here in my living room. They came over tonight after work because I knew I wouldn't be able to sleep until I got more information about everything, and pushing them away wasn't helping clear my head. My dad was with some friends, which meant we'd pretty much have most of the night to ourselves.

Right now, they were trying to decide which piece of information to share with me first. I looked to Denver, the alpha of the group, waiting for him to make the final decision, but his shoulders were calm and he listened with interest as the others spoke, taking in all the different sides.

When the noise volume finally became too much and I was ready to claw out my temples from how vigorously I was rubbing them to ease my impending headache, he raised his hand and they quieted down. "We'll start with who we are and where we come from." His eyes smoldered when they turned to me, and I shivered beneath his stare.

"I'm Denver, alpha of this pack. We come from Mercaida, which is a large territory. It's kind of like its own state, as a way to describe it, but not nearly as large as one. It's managed to remain hidden from humans for centuries, with barriers around it to deter the curious without them realizing it. As such, we are Mercai. There are many other wolf packs around, like ours, but there have been problems recently."

"What kind of problems?" I asked.

"There are rogue wolves who have gotten out, and they've been attacking people. It's become a big enough issue to where we're now risking exposure," he responded. "And the Alpha of Mercaida encourages this dangerous behavior."

"I thought you were the alpha."

"There are separate packs, like ours here. Subpacks, if you will, all within Mercaida. We're all under Alpha Murdock."

"Who encourages this insanity," I surmised, and Denver nodded. "Because those who survive know it's something more than only a little wolf or even a big dog?" I questioned.

He shook his head. "Because they've been doing it in a way where they're turning people who weren't born to shift, which is more detrimental than anything. Not every bite makes the person a wolf shifter. Most of the time it turns them into something else—a monster, like the kind in your fairy books. It's unnatural and monstrous, a danger to shifter society, and must be put down."

"Put down?" I repeated, getting to my feet. "You're talking about people here, innocent people who are attacked. They don't deserve this."

"No, they don't," he agreed, as he got to his feet as well and faced me, "but it's the only way. If not, they go feral. It's happened every time. It's not as easy for us as it may sound.

We don't like it, but we must do what's necessary to protect both people and wolves."

I took a step toward him. "Then what's the purpose of turning them if they need to be put down?"

"The only possibility we could think of is that someone is creating an army. There has been unrest in Mercaida for a long time now, so it doesn't surprise me. We can't trust everyone."

"Then what are you doing here? Did you escape to find a better life?" I asked, as my breathing shallowed at his proximity.

He took a step closer. "We left in search of allies. The reason we're here, why we stayed, is because of you." His voice lowered as we were now practically chest to chest.

"Why me? Because I'm a new wolf?"

His gaze shot to the side of my face, and he reached out to grab the ends of my hair. The motion was so quick, I didn't have time to react. He studied me, his palm brushing lightly against my skin. My chest rose and fell as I fought the urge to sink into him. He kneaded the strands between his fingers, and his eyes softened at the frayed edges. My stomach flipped with his touch. He was rather gentle for someone who commanded his pack and threatened outsiders with the glare of death. "This happened in your wolf form," he stated, as though there was no question to it.

I stepped back and his hand fell to his side with the action. There was no denying he was right, it was yet another piece finding the perfect fit in my puzzle of chaos that was my life. I ran a hand through my hair, remembering the vivid dream. "I thought it was a dream at first. It only happened a few nights ago, but now I realize it wasn't at all. It was real."

"How did it go?" he inquired, tilting his body slightly toward me to catch my every word.

"I was a wolf, and I was exploring and chasing after a

fluffy animal to play with." I heard a few snickers from those around me, but I pushed them from my mind and focused on Denver. Studying his face, the way his ebony hair framed his dark eyes that were locked on mine with the urge to continue. "It was going fine, then someone came out with a gun and shot at me." The other four guys got to their feet, growling, and I jerked back at the suddenness. "What's wrong?"

"Someone shot at you," Denver rumbled. His jaw was clenched so tight, it could have shattered his teeth. "Whoever it was, better hope we never find out." I reeled back in surprise at the protectiveness that rolled off of them all in waves, unsure of what I did to warrant this reaction from them.

"Why?" I asked. "You guys don't even know me." There was absolutely no reason for them to feel protective of me. They could leave this place behind and continue on with their lives, never looking back. Why didn't they realize I was no one special?

"But we do," Liam answered, as he stepped up to my side. He looked at Denver for confirmation of something, and he gave him the nod he was looking for. "You're ours to protect."

"Excuse me?" I wasn't sure I'd heard him right.

"There's a lot more information to cover," he said, as he took my hand in his and brought it to his lips for a kiss. Denver let out a low warning growl, and he let go of my hand and backed away.

"You're welcome to sit down," Denver offered.

I lifted my chin up. "I'm fine. Say what you were going to say."

I expected him to tell me the next piece of information. Maybe to even tell me I'd been abducted and we were now in some sort of spaceship, or that this merely all in my mind and I'd wake up to all of this being nothing but a dream. Instead, he took a step forward and rested a hand against my neck and jaw, with his fingers wrapping around the back to cradle my head.

Lifting my chin, I leaned into his touch, seeking more of his specific brand of warmth. Butterflies fluttered in my stomach and my eyes flicked down to his lips when they turned up in a smile. "I thought so," he whispered, and his shoulders relaxed as though a great worry had been lifted.

"Thought what?" My question was so low, it was barely audible, so I cleared my throat and tried again. "Thought what?"

"You feel it too." His stomach brushed against me as he inched forward, and I had to crane my neck to look up at him. His eyes were dark and heated, with a hint of gold flecks in the irises. I gulped when he leaned his head forward so our noses were touching and tried to remind myself not to literally drool all over him, which was becoming more possible with every breath as he continued to look at me like that.

"What do I feel?" I murmured, as I tilted my head slightly closer, aching to touch my lips to his, to find out if they tasted as good as they looked, and then groaned. To my disappointment, he clenched his jaw and pulled away.

"Not yet. But at least now I know it's mutual." He returned to his chair and I looked around the room as my cheeks heated. Did they all know what I'd been thinking? *Don't tell me they can read minds too.* Judging by the satisfied smirks on their faces, I felt like I was missing out on some massive secret, and I wasn't going to let that happen.

Returning to my chair before my legs gave way from the memory of that simple touch, I questioned him again. "I want to know what I'm missing here. What exactly is it you think I feel?"

Denver kept his eyes on me and leaned forward with his

forearms on his thighs. "The bond. It's what happens when mates find each other, and you recognize it by a spark and an internal feeling. Then you simply just...know. Your whole world changes, and suddenly you'll do anything to protect that person, even abandon your mission to focus on them." He smirked. "Some might say it feels like static electricity."

Oh, crap. I remembered feeling that, but with more than only him. I could still feel each individual spark from when they each happened, as though it never stopped puncturing my skin and coursing through my body.

"I know what you're probably thinking, and yes, you did feel it with more than just me. It's not uncommon for those in a subpack like this one to find the same mate."

"Mate? I barely have any time for dating, and now I'm supposed to be the mate to five wolves I've only just met? I don't know how that's even supposed to work." I scoffed in disbelief.

"We'll make it work, don't worry too much about that. There are more important things to consider right now," Liam responded.

"Like what?" My curiosity rose, wondering what could be so dire.

There was hesitation in the air, and I found myself dreading the response and wishing I hadn't asked.

"Like the fact that you're a Mercai," Denver answered.

"That can't be." My mind was swirling with all the information they'd dumped on me today. This was too much. "I've never been to Mercaida. I've rarely even been outside of Carlisle. I've been here since the day I was born, you must be mistaken."

Liam's eyes narrowed. "We don't make mistakes."

"We're not mistaken," Denver echoed. "We can smell it in your blood. It's a part of you, very distinct. I don't know how it's possible, because we know everyone in Mercaida and have never seen you before, and we can't think of anyone who has ever been with a pup and then the pup disappeared. Believe me when I say we're going to figure this out. You're not alone in this."

"I've already let her know Liam and Axel joined her class and I got a job with her to help keep an eye on her." Julian threw his hands up when I threw him a look. "Not in a bad way, I promise. To protect you and others. You're a newborn pup with raw instincts in an adult form. You're dangerous to everyone you come across, and their reactions can be a danger to you."

"We'll need to show her how to be a wolf," Denver stated. "Starting tonight."

"Tonight?" I echoed. "I don't think you understand the amount of work I have going on. Assignments keep piling up and will continue to do so until I graduate. I simply don't have time to be a wolf."

"We can help you with that as well." Denver sounded so sure of himself that it made me want to believe every word he said.

"Fine," I agreed. I bit back a retort, knowing it wouldn't get me anywhere. "How is that going to work exactly?"

"You'll have at least one or more of us either with you or nearby at all times."

"Now I have my own bodyguard detail?" I raised an eyebrow. I could only imagine how that would go over if they were to follow me around, shadowing every step I took.

"Pretty much, yeah." He crossed his arms and leaned back in the chair. "You may have already noticed us watching you. Usually in wolf form."

I recalled the wolf with the bright green eyes and looked over to Axel, who gave a small wave and a smile. I rolled my eyes. "Of course." Another piece falling into place in this puzzle.

"The good news is, the more you shift, the more you'll begin to remember what happened during the shift. Which means your mind will become more conscious and you'll start to gain some control over your wolf form rather than running on pure instinct and waking up the next day wondering what happened." The voice surprised me, as it was the first time Casen had spoken up during all of this

"I do have a question for you guys. I want to know what causes the change. Is there a reason or something that triggers it? And if I figure out what that is, then can I maybe put this all off for a little while?" I asked, hopeful that I could get through the rest of this semester as a human and have one less thing to worry about right now, even though I knew full well I wouldn't be able to stop obsessing about this until I knew everything and had full control.

Julian shook his head. "You won't be able to control it until you learn how to *have* control. Since the change was put off until you came of age, you're going to have years of shifting and learning crammed into a matter of weeks. This is why it's advised to learn young, but you never had that option." He looked at me with pitiful eyes which I hated.

"Is there a way I could get control faster? Because frankly, I'm tired of waking up in the woods and being down yet another outfit."

"There isn't a way to rush it, but the more you fight it, the longer the whole process will take. It's best if you give in to it, let the wolf have its time, and become one with her. She's not something to fight, she's a part of you to embrace." Casen smiled at my frustrated sigh. He got up from his seat and walked over, plopping himself in my lap, and my eyes flew wide open in surprise.

I braced my hands against his chest, preparing to push him away and fight for each breath. He didn't budge, and somehow positioned himself so that he wasn't crushing me.

He placed just enough of his body weight on me to keep me from squirming.

With an arm around my shoulders, he gave me a small squeeze. "Don't worry too much, it's something we've all gone through, and we'll help you every step of the way. We'll be there when you shift and we'll make sure you stay safe."

That last part of his words jogged something in my mind, and I recalled my dad reading the morning news, and now I wished I'd paid more attention.

"Speaking of which, there have been some animal attacks in the area," I murmured, trying to recall everything the article had said.

Casen frowned then settled down so he was sitting with his butt on the cushion next to me and his legs draped over mine. His hand looped through my arm and he held onto me while he looked to the guys. Normally I would've pushed out of his grasp and crossed my arms in defiance, but I enjoyed the feeling of warmth he gave me. I settled in closer, then stopped myself from leaning my head against his arm. That would've been too much, and I wasn't ready to fully fall into...whatever this was. I caught Denver's eyes flick to where we had our arms linked, and narrowed my gaze at him.

The guys all exchanged a concerned look. "What kind of attacks are you talking about exactly?" Liam questioned with drawn out words.

"Something has been eating animals, and a neighbor's cat has gone missing." I placed a finger against my chin as I thought. "I don't know if he's come back yet. He goes off on his own a lot, so I didn't think anything about it at the time. You don't think..."

"No," Casen assured me. "You've already told us that one thing you remember about being in your wolf form was wanting to play with the fluffy animals before running from danger. That doesn't sound like a killer to me," he reasoned with a small chuckle.

I rolled my eyes. "Yeah, I would prefer not to hurt animals. Whatever."

Chuckles rose up around me.

"We'll keep both you and the animals safe," Axel promised.

"So what do you guys eat? Or, I guess, what do we eat, as wolves, I mean?"

"We sometimes eat animals if we feel the need to, but never any domestic ones." Liam shrugged. "We haven't eaten anything but human food since we've been here."

"So then I wonder who—or what—the news articles have been talking about," I mused.

Denver was surprisingly quiet. He hunched forward with his forearms perched on his thighs, but his dark eyes were unseeing as he was deep in thought over something.

"Denver?" I prompted, snapping him out of his stupor.

"If it hasn't been us, and it hasn't been you," he began, his voice low, "then there must be something else. Has anyone else new arrived in town that you know of?"

I shook my head. "Not that I'm aware of. Everyone knows everyone here, and as far as I know, it's only been you guys. I can ask around though, find out if there's someone I just haven't seen but others have."

"That would be a good place to start." He got a faraway look in his eyes as though there was something he wasn't saying. I wanted to open my mouth and demand more answers, but Casen's warmth enveloped me and I found myself fitting perfectly into his side as he ran his thumb over my knuckles.

Chapter Sixteen

Makena

The next morning started out pretty uneventful. I woke up in my own bed which was nice, and when I went to the window, I saw three pairs of glowing wolf eyes watching me from across the street. How they managed to remain unseen baffled me, since they stood out so much to me. It was like my gaze gravitated toward them every chance I got, and I wondered if that could've been because of this bond.

I shuddered at the thought. I couldn't deny I felt something, and the more time I spent around them and the more I learned about myself, the stronger the pull became. It was there, it's presence undeniable, swirling around inside of me as it grew. It began basically as invisible floss between us, but over the course of the last few days, especially with the amount of time we spent together yesterday evening, it was well on its way to becoming a steel cord.

Every time one of them was next to me, I found myself leaning into them, wanting to be closer, to touch them. I still had a lot to learn, and I hoped it wouldn't keep escalating this much every time. Shouldn't there be some sort of adjustment period for this kind of thing?

Reaching for my phone, I scrolled through my contact list, trying to decide who to ask first when I came upon Austin's name. He'd told me he was leaving here in two weeks, but that was a week ago, and I hadn't even seen him since. I knew I was going to have to face our goodbye soon, and pretending like it wasn't happening wouldn't make it delay at all. A pang of guilt ate at me, and I chewed my fingernail as I decided what to say.

Me: Hey

Austin: What's up?

I hesitated, unsure how to ask. It was a simple question, inquiring if he knew of anyone who was new in town, but I couldn't seem to get my fingers to type the words. By the time I'd settled on how to phrase it and typed in the first letter, knocking against my bedroom window made me jump, nearly jolting the phone out of my hands in the process.

My hand flew to my chest, and I saw Austin sitting on the large branch outside of my window. I hurried over to unlock it, and he tumbled inside and onto the carpet.

"Oomph," he huffed, as he landed in an awkward heap. "That seemed to go a lot smoother when we were kids." He scrambled to his feet, straightened his clothes, and grinned. "I was already on your street when I got your text. I only have a week left and wanted to spend some time with one of my favorite people. I was hoping you wouldn't be too busy for some Austin time."

I smiled. "Yeah, things have been a little crazy lately."

His face fell into a frown. "Everything okay?"

"Yeah, yeah." I waved my hand around, brushing it off.

"Between schoolwork, the shelter, and the diner, I've been swamped."

He blew out a breath of relief. "Whew. For a moment there, I thought maybe you'd found a new friend."

I laughed. "Like I have time for much of a social life. I haven't even talked with Leah in…I'm not sure how long."

"How about we have a nighttime hangout like the old days?" he suggested. "Movies, snacks, gossip, all the fun things."

"You mean a sleepover?"

He waved his hand as he walked away to sit in my chair. "Potato, potah-to. I'll text Leah and we'll get this rolling."

I sat on the edge of my bed, pulled my knees to my chest, and wrapped my arms around my shins. "I'm really going to miss you," I admitted. "I know I've been burying myself in my work and keeping as busy as possible lately, but it's still not going to be the same."

"I know, same here. But it just means I'll have to make sure I come and visit often enough. And you too. You of all people could use an adventure in your life."

I wanted to laugh at that, but I held back. He had no idea exactly how adventurous my life was becoming right now. My life was about to redefine adventure as we knew it. "I'll have to make sure I do that."

"Good. And Leah is in. You're also going to meet her for lunch today. You still like Italian, right?"

"Huh?"

"Before I go, I'm going to do my best to make sure you get properly socialized. When was the last time you've seen another human being outside of work or class?"

"Last night," I replied, but he must not have believed me since he laughed as though it was a joke.

"Funny. I'm going to miss your jokes. And no, the diner doesn't count."

I rolled my eyes and wondered if wolves counted, and then chuckled at my own internal quip.

A part of me wanted to spill my guts and tell my lifelong friend all about the wolf side of me, and what I was going through right now, at least the little bit that I was sure about, but a stronger part wanted me to clamp down on that secret until I knew more. The puzzle wasn't yet complete.

This would be easier to talk about once I knew all the facts and could control myself, otherwise it could turn into a long, drawn out conversation filled with nothing but theories, and I already had enough theories to last me a lifetime. I needed concrete answers and the truth.

"Anyway…" I cleared my throat, getting to the point of this whole discussion. "I was wondering if you knew of anyone who might be new in town?"

"You mean like those creepy guys at the park last week?"

"Well, yeah, like them, but not them."

He raised an eyebrow.

"I mean, do you know of anyone else?"

He thought really hard. "I don't recall seeing anyone else recently, but I've also been pretty busy with packing and getting ready to leave. I never knew how many people were in this town until I started saying goodbye. The goodbyes alone are eating up my time."

I sighed. This was probably going to be harder than I thought. He knew everyone in town better than I did, so he was my best bet with this. If he hadn't heard of any new arrivals, then maybe there weren't any. "Thanks, I'll ask Leah when I see her since I'm apparently meeting her for lunch now." My words were meant as sarcasm, but I couldn't hide the smile from my tone. I was looking forward to seeing her again and regretted that the only way I can see my friends now is if it's forced.

My stomach grumbled at the mention of food and I

stiffened. The last thing I needed was to eat my friend's face off or to have him witness me eating everything in the kitchen.

"Guess it's a good thing. Should I let her know you're on your way?"

If I left now, then I could stop and get something before so I could act more normal. Or I could get there early and order some things before she arrived. "Give me a head start, I might stop somewhere first."

"You got it." He paused when he started to type away on his phone, then headed for the window.

"You could walk out the front door with me," I pointed out as I shrugged on my jacket.

"Nah, this is more fun. It's almost like old times," he replied, as he disappeared out of the window and climbed down.

I shook my head, made sure my key was around my neck, and headed downstairs.

ALL THE DELICIOUS smells from the food around me and what was being prepared in the kitchen was almost more than I could handle. It assaulted my nose and sent my stomach into a rumbling frenzy, and I tapped my fingertips impatiently against the table as I waited.

I managed to make it to the restaurant before Leah did. I didn't know what Austin had said to her, so I texted her myself, saying I was going to be a little while as I was running an errand, and then I went straight to Menagio's, ordered a few appetizers, told them to bring them out as fast as they could, and waited impatiently in hopes that I could scarf them down before my old friend arrived.

"Hey, girl!"

"Oh no," I groaned quietly, as I recognized the voice. What was she doing here this early?

I checked my watch for the time. She wasn't supposed to be here for another twenty minutes at least.

"Hey," I greeted with a strained smile as she sat down, and distracted myself with sipping on my water in hopes the liquid would help curb my growling stomach.

"I'm surprised to see you here. I just happened to be walking by when I saw you. I was going to window shop for a little while, but now this works out perfectly." She ran a freshly manicured finger down the menu in front of her excitedly as she studied the contents.

"Yeah, I got done early and figured I'd get a table. I don't even know what I want yet."

"Your appetizers will be out shortly," the waiter informed me as he arrived, and then looked at Leah. "Is there anything I can get you to drink?" I could feel sweat beading on my forehead despite the chilly air.

Leah looked at me, and I shrugged like it was no big deal. "I couldn't decide, so I picked a few things to start off with." When one lie doesn't work, jump to the next. If I wasn't careful, I would soon drown in my own web.

She asked for a water, and the waiter left us to ponder over our menus for a few more minutes. Now I was going to have to figure out how to eat a wolf-size meal for lunch without raising suspicion. I knew I should have better confidence in myself, but screw it. I was going through something that was unthinkable, and I was allowed to have a moment to be anything but perfect. I would do what I needed.

Deciding it was best to keep my appetite in check, I went with the full steak with mashed potatoes and broccoli, and perked up when the appetizers came out immediately after placing the order.

"Are we celebrating something?" Leah questioned, as she

watched me pile my plate high with two of everything while she went for a single chip at a time with the dip.

"It's been awhile," I answered around a mouthful of food, then swallowed. "I've been buried so deep in work, sometimes I forget to eat." Yeah, that sounded good. Let's stick with that story. She didn't need to know I regularly ate enough per meal to restock the diner.

The waiter refilled our drinks, and Leah watched as he retreated then leaned forward to talk low enough so no one else could hear. "He's kinda cute."

I looked up and noticed the smile on her face. "Who?"

"The waiter. Geez, you definitely need to get out more. When was the last time you went on a date?"

"Uh…" I didn't know how to tell her I apparently already had five mates, which was more than enough to juggle as it was. "I have other things to focus on for now."

"Okay." She gave me an odd look as she bit into another chip. "Anyway, have you heard the news?"

"What news?" I knew she worked for a news outlet, so she knew everything that went on around here. There were a million things she could be referring to.

"The animal attacks," she whispered as she leaned in. "I got an anonymous tip that there was a big, scary dog running around. Only, they said it was more of a wolf. Can you believe that?"

I swallowed the food in my mouth and took a long drink, then let out an uncomfortable laugh. "Yeah, Leah, a wolf running around Carlisle, how crazy is that?"

"I'm not talking about a normal wolf, Makena. According to our source, this could be something entirely new. A mutant wolf, maybe."

"A mutant wolf?" I raised my eyebrow at her. "That sounds a bit out there. The caller may have been messing with you. Kids and their pranks these days. Maybe they wanted to stay anonymous for a reason."

She shook her head. "That's why I don't know how to run with the story, or if I should even try. Maybe I should push it under the rug for now. But if there's even the chance of it being true…" She trailed off and got a faraway look in her eyes as she thought it over.

"I'm just saying to be careful. You don't want to ruin your reputation," I offered. *Or mine, actually.* This only further sealed why I shouldn't tell anyone about me, even my friend. I had no idea how they would react, especially since Leah's first response to this anonymous caller was to run the story without all the facts.

We spent the rest of lunch catching up on other things in our lives. By the end, she slipped the waiter her number along with our bill and hurried out.

"How about you?" I asked before parting ways. "You asked about my love life, but we didn't touch on yours."

A shade of bubblegum pink coated her cheeks as she tucked a strand of hair behind her ear. "It's complicated, but soon I'll be dating again, so I might as well get a head start."

Before I could pry, she plastered a smile to her face and we parted ways with a hug and promised to see each other in a few days during Austin's goodbye night.

Chapter Seventeen

Makena

Pain racked through my arm as I fell hard to the ground, exhausted. My energy had been spent and my ego deflated as I failed yet again to summon my inner wolf.

They said it wouldn't be too difficult to do. They assured me that all young pups could do it right away, and I should be no different since I was still so new to this. That my inability to keep my wolf at bay, shouldn't hinder bringing her out.

Only, none of this was as it should be. They'd never known someone who didn't come into their wolf's abilities until they were turning twenty, they'd only heard stories, rumors, and didn't understand why it was so difficult. I wasn't just another story, or a mere rumor. We couldn't solve this with theories and bedtime stories.

Every nerve in my body was screaming for me to stop and relax. I was pushing myself harder than I ever had before, and my body couldn't seem to take much more of this. I bit my lip against the tingling pain as I was stuck there, unable to do anything about it or to keep my muscles from spasming, evident by how they danced beneath my skin. My brain was turning to mush, and now I lay here becoming one with the falling autumn leaves as my body took time to slowly calm down after I stopped putting stress on it.

Hours of training were merging into days. Each time I failed, I grew more obsessed with working myself past the brink of exhaustion, convinced that was where my wolf was hiding.

An idea came to me. "You guys really don't know if there's anyone currently in Mercaida who is like me? Or that they found out they were a wolf the same way I did?"

There was hesitation, and I was going to repeat my question, but then Liam responded. "Not that we know of currently. The stories and rumors are the extent of what we've heard about this."

"If you guys don't know anymore about this specifically, would I be able to go there myself and find out more? Maybe something about being in the area that half of me is a part of will jog something. I'm actually surprised you haven't tried to drag me there by now. If that's really where I belong and all."

Another pause answered me, and I was growing concerned.

"It's not safe for you there right now, Makena." Denver's voice was low and serious, and I tilted my head to the side to look at him.

"Why not? If I'm one of you, if I'm actually from Mercaida, then don't I belong there?"

"There are a lot of things going on, and it's not a safe place for you right now." Anger coursed through my aching muscles at his assumption to know what was best for me. "We touched on it last night, and we can go over it more later. But we're not bringing you back there right now. At least not until you gain full control over yourself." His tone left no room for argument, but I was about to make some room.

I pushed myself up into a sitting position, leaving a hand on the ground behind me to lean on as I turned around to face Denver. "You don't even know me. Who are you to say what is and isn't safe for me?"

"There are things going on that you don't know or understand. It isn't like Carlisle or any other fully human area. Shifter society is entirely different and isn't meant for someone who's more human than wolf."

"Then tell me," I ground out, trying to keep myself from raising my voice. The last thing we needed was for some unsuspecting person to hear us arguing about the wolf shifter world.

"You're not ready yet."

His words hit me harder than they probably should have. Here I was with a chance to find out more about who and what I was, and he was trying to keep me from it because he didn't think I was ready?

My eyes stung as I tried to process everything, and I looked away. Anger continued to build up inside me. I needed to get out of here, but first I needed to let him know I couldn't be walked on. I would become the coal that burned his feet if he tried.

Exhaling a breath to release a small amount of frustration from my tone, I turned to look at him again. "You're trying to keep me from learning about who and what I am. If there's a way to help me, then why must I avoid it? All because you don't think I'm ready, or that I'm too fragile for wolf society?" Getting to my feet, I took a step toward him, my fingers clenching and unclenching with each step. "You only recently blew into town during a time when my life was becoming upended, and now you think you can control who

I see and where I go. Fated mates or not, that isn't how this works."

I was now a mere inch from his chest, and I closed the distance. I wanted to smirk when I saw the tic in his jaw, but I kept my composure. He needed to know how upset I was. I wouldn't grit my teeth and plaster on a fake smile. Whether or not either of us thought I was ready, I was going to do whatever it took to find out the truth.

Denver leaned forward so our chests were touching, and I could feel his hot breath fan across my face. "I don't say this lightly, but you have no idea what's going on over there."

"So then tell me," I countered, locking my gaze with his and refusing to back down.

His eyes darted back and forth as they held mine, then he finally gave a single nod. "Mercaida isn't the way it used to be. It's corrupt, led by a tyrant. He has supporters who bow to him in fear, and others who carry out his wishes with glee on their faces."

"I'll fight against anyone who tries to do me harm. I'm a biter, and I'm not afraid."

He sucked in a breath of air. "We are part of the rebellion, and we set out under false pretenses with the underlying intention to build an army in our favor. It isn't often that a pack defies its alpha, but it's not unheard of either. We're in search of supporters."

"I'll help you gather those supporters." His words were intended to convince me to stay behind, but all I could see were ways I could help.

"If we brought you back there now, you would be killed on sight. He wouldn't accept someone who's only half wolf and raised by humans, even if you are Mercai. We don't know if we will even be allowed back inside, as the length of our absence has most certainly alerted him that we might be up to something."

I leaned in another inch. He was making all good points, and I was countering every last one of them. "I'll help make up a story. Tell him you found me."

His Adam's apple bobbed as he swallowed. "We haven't been in communication with them since before we arrived here, as we didn't want to leave a trail for them to follow, and I have no doubt it's made them question our loyalty. We went dark to protect you, and we'll keep you in the dark for the same reason."

"Oh." I waited for another retort to come out of my mouth, but that one word was it. No one has ever put me and my safety first like this, and I was struggling to accept it as the last line he spoke ricocheted in my head. I didn't know what to say next.

"We could explain our absence by finding our mate, but I highly doubt that would help smooth things over. He isn't a very understanding guy." Denver's words were low, and his eyes softened as he saw the hope in my face fall. With a finger under my chin, he tilted my head so my eyes were locked with his once again. "I know you don't understand everything right now, and I'm sorry for making you think you didn't need to know. But the risk isn't worth your life."

I wanted to be mad at him. I thought I was going to say my piece, stamp my foot, and storm away, but instead all I wanted to do was melt into his arms and let him protect me like he said he was trying to do. Which was surprising to me because the Makena I knew would stop at nothing to discover the truth. I felt the urge to scream my frustrations and get him to understand how badly I needed this, while also wanting to accept what he told me and wrap his arms around my body like a blanket.

Rather than stepping away and continuing to try and gain control over my wolf, my eyes caught on a vein in Denver's neck. It was taut, poking through the skin of his neck in such a way that if I wanted to, I could pinch two fingers around it.

So naturally, instead I leaned in and ran my tongue across it. His body stiffened, his hand pausing halfway to my hip. "Makena," he growled low, "what are you doing?"

"I don't know," I answered as I pulled back. "It was either rip your throat out or lick it. I went with option B."

"I'm thankful you didn't go for option A." The corner of his mouth tilted up slightly, but before I could lick that spot too, his hands appeared on my hips and pushed me out of range. "How about we get back to training, wolf? Then later on we can see what our tongues can do."

"Well, how can a girl say no to that?" I smirked as I returned to my spot, noting how the others watched on and inconspicuously adjusted the waistband of their pants. My grin was impossible to contain.

With legs crossed, I rested my palms across my knees and closed my eyes, ready to dive back into the familiar scenes. The first things I saw were piles of assignments reaching the ceiling, and tables filled with screaming people. They were waving their arms and pointing at me as they tried to be heard over one another. Everyone was yelling at me, until the space in my head became unable to hold it all.

My temple pounded. My heart rate increased. My breathing turned ragged as I dodged their clutches and pushed away one assignment after another, toppling the piles over into a sea of papers, and struggled my way past each screaming guest.

This isn't real, I reminded myself. *This is only what the inside of my head looks like. It may be suffocating, but nobody ever achieved anything great without sinking first.*

The darkness enveloped me and the only things I could see were the anchors in my life. I'd collected them until I had a graveyard of broken ships to keep me tethered in place.

After all, life was safer when you only entertained the dreams that would keep you on the ground.

I saw Austin wave goodbye as he walked away with an overflowing backpack that he carried around as though it were weightless.

Leah stood in front of a camera, dazzling the local audience with her smile as she read from a teleprompter. She was oblivious to my struggle, to how difficult it was for me to keep moving forward when all the world around me was moving faster than I could keep up with.

My father sat at the kitchen table, drinking coffee and reading the newspaper. A blurry figure sat beside him with hair as golden as mine and a face I couldn't make out. I squinted, and the figure disappeared, much like in the real world where she vanished without a trace. I bit my lip to keep from screaming out. Would I never get the answers I craved?

I looked behind me where rays of light waited to greet me with open arms, and fought the urge to turn back. Beads of sweat dripped from my hairline as I forced myself to keep facing forward. I'd given up every other time I tried reached this spot, but this time would be different.

My body ached. My muscles screamed. My jaw clenched. Still, I pushed harder.

Forced to face all the things that had been holding me back proved to be more of a struggle than I'd expected. I still wanted to accomplish all my goals, I'd been working too hard not to. What I needed to find was a balance, so I kept my eyes open as I searched for the light in the dark, despite how much easier it would have been to continue burying my head in my work.

Fatigue weighed down my body and my legs felt like they were filled with sand. *A little farther. Take one more step*, I urged myself.

A pair of dark brown orbs pierced through the fog, beckoning me closer. I moved toward them. Denver's slender frame was an outline as he waited for me, and I moved faster, my feet barely touching the ground as I glided over the frozen blades of grass. Cold wind settled in around me, biting at the spots of exposed flesh, and I quickened my pace.

The first night they were all in my living room came sailing into my mind and I remembered when Casen jumped into my lap. I grasped onto the memory with the little bit of energy I had left, latching onto the feeling of his warmth. It seeped into my bones, clearing away the fog with each step I took.

I left it all behind me to melt the frost-covered ground.

The anchors that made up my graveyard began to drift away as Julian appeared, his bright eyes sparkling as he waited. Liam stepped between them, his eyes cold as he took in the scene, then warmed when they fell on me.

They're not really here. They can't actually see this.

A camera flashed and I saw Axel's forest green eyes before he shifted into the wolf that had been watching me before I ever knew who he was. They were here, just as they'd always been.

I felt a lightness in my chest. The weight of the world on my shoulders shifted so that I was no longer bearing it alone.

Then they disappeared when the fog cleared, all except for one pair of glowing eyes which flickered in and out.

Taking a deep breath, I drained my mind of the rest of my worries and responsibilities until the human Makena was at peace and all that was left was darkness. The darkness was where the light would shine brightest if I let it.

My breathing shallowed as I blocked the world from my mind.

I looked around inside me, turning my incorporeal eyes to every corner in search of the wolf that only came out when she wanted to. This time I wanted to meet her on my terms.

This was roughly attempt number one million, and my body and mind were still exhausted. While time and space meant nothing here, I was considering calling it quits for the day when I felt my skin tingle.

It was so faint I almost missed it, but it was there. It was like muddied paws tracking across my mind. The spark grew as I focused on it and became strong enough to keep me grounded.

I squinted my eyes through the fog, willing it to clear away, until I could make out an outline that could pass as a large dog. Only, it wasn't a dog.

A smile crossed my lips as I held out a gentle hand. I wanted to speak, to coo and let her know it was safe, but words didn't seem to exist here.

Her ears were flat against her head as her nose sniffed the air. I couldn't fully see her, but I could feel her and sense everything she was feeling. She was hesitant, which I understood. I was hesitant to trust others myself, but we wouldn't have too much of a choice since we were one and the same.

The darkness turned to gray as she took a step forward, placing her front paw hesitantly in the dirt which flew up to shield her. With each step she took, the air lightened until it was a pale pink that tinged the tips of her fur, still brightening.

The wolf eased her way toward me until she was directly in front of my face, sitting down as bright white light warmed her fur. Her ears pulled forward as she eased into me, her blue eyes illuminating as they mirrored my own.

Time was fleeting, but also had no meaning here. I was unsure how long we sat like that, but my spine remained straight and our gazes locked. Energy flowed between us, and I could feel her mind relaxing and letting me in. I saw images of my wolf and I running through the woods, chasing small animals for play, and even winced when a bullet grazed my fur. My hand drifted up unconsciously to feel the frayed edges of my hair as the memories solidified.

Her eyes brightened until they were all-consuming, and I found myself back in the woods with dirt beneath my paws.

Wait...*paws?*

That wasn't right. I glanced down and saw hair covering my legs, even though I was sure I'd shaved this morning, but then I looked up and saw Liam's smiling face. He was squatting low in front of me with an expression of utmost pride, and when I looked around at the smiling faces of the others, I realized I'd accomplished the transformation. Not only that, but I was conscious during it. I was no longer in my mind, but back in the physical world.

For the first time, I had full control.

And it felt amazing.

I threw my head back in a howl, and moments later, a chorus joined me. My head fell forward at the end and I looked around to see I was no longer the only wolf in this forest.

We ran around and played without a care in the world, while Denver kept a watchful eye for threats. I nipped at him to get him to shrug off responsibility for a while and play with us, but he snapped back and took a seat at the edge, watching us with careful eyes and paying attention to the faintest turn of the wind and every snapping twig. Not even the smallest lizard skittering across the ground would get past unnoticed.

Time flew by, and it wasn't until the sun was setting that I felt the opposite transformation happen for the first time. My muscles expanded and contracted as fur disappeared into my skin, my teeth reverted to normal, and before long I was sprawled across the ground of the forest, naked once again.

"Crap," I murmured, as I realized my dilemma. I didn't think this through during the initial change. I didn't realize it would even happen. If I had, then I would have packed some clothes and been more prepared. This part was becoming a habit I really didn't like.

I wrapped my arms around my body as I shivered in the bitter cold.

"Don't worry, wolf, we have a bag for you." Denver, now back in his human form along with everyone else, nodded at Casen, who disappeared behind a tree. They were all as bare as I was, but they positioned themselves just right to not be exposed, and they seemed to each pull out a pair of sweats from nowhere.

Moments later, Casen reappeared wearing his own pair of sweats and carried a bag in his hand. His taut frame stood out in the evening light as he walked toward me, and I found myself averting my gaze.

Mate or not, I didn't want to be caught staring. We never actually established boundaries and what would be okay or not.

Regardless, he must have noticed my lingering stare because he smirked as he handed me my bag and then tossed a second bag to the others for them to sort through.

"Thanks." My voice was meek as I quickly slid a shirt over my torso, eyeing my shredded outfit on the ground nearby when my head popped out through the top. I was really going to need to up my wardrobe budget.

I slid into a pair of sweats, finding comfort in the soft material inside. Nothing I was wearing was familiar, and they must have realized the direction of my thoughts. "They're ours, but they're yours now. We like to keep an extra bag sometimes just in case. Ever since someone ran off with Axel's extra clothes, we thought it would be a good idea."

Axel glared at Julian for providing that information, but I bit back a smile and nodded, grateful for the clothing.

"We weren't expecting you to full-on shift," Liam said, as he came over and held out a hand. I placed my hand in his and let him pull me into a standing position. "Don't get me wrong, we're glad you did. We just weren't expecting it."

"This is a good sign," Denver remarked, as he shoved a second leg through his own sweats and pulled them up. "You're going to be a fast learner, and it might make everything easier."

My hand dropped from Liam's, and I did my best to avert my eyes. Five guys with chiseled chests and no shirts? It was a good thing they were at least wearing pants, because I most certainly would be late for dinner otherwise.

"Oh, crap," I muttered. "What time is it?"

"Uh…it's almost six. Everything okay?" Julian said, as he looked at his phone.

"Yeah, I'm supposed to meet my dad for dinner. I'm going to need a shower first though, I'm pretty sure I rolled in something that wasn't dirt."

Casen and Axel scrunched up their faces, and I smacked Liam's chest when I saw the judgmental wrinkles that appeared around his nose.

"Hey, I'm new to this, give me a break."

"Whatever you need," Liam retorted, as he squeezed my hip. Denver's glare turned on Liam, whose hand slid off as he took a step back.

I didn't know what that was about, but I didn't have time to think on it. With a quick wave, I took off running toward my home.

Chapter Eighteen

Makena

*A*ll was silent at the dinner table as my dad read the news he'd missed this morning and I pondered my thoughts. The creases in his forehead deepened as his gaze roamed down the page, reading up on more disappearances. All the ones listed in there were animals, but the attacks were growing more frequent and more messy.

It was a relief to finally get somewhere with my wolf, and now, as I ate dinner at home like everything was as it should be and it was any other night, I could feel her inside me, curled up and content rather than acting like a ravaging creature trying to break free and take over.

Regardless of the progress I'd made, there were still so many questions brimming beneath the surface, so many things I wanted to know and wasn't sure how to ask. So I decided to get straight to the point.

Clearing my throat, I spit it out. "Have you heard of Mercaida?"

He looked up from his reading. I thought I saw a brief

moment of recognition on his face, but then his features returned to normal and his eyes looked slightly up and to the side in thought. There was nothing more agonizing than waiting on pins and needles for the answer to a question that your entire existence basically depended on.

I was about to backtrack and change the topic to something else, but then to my surprise, he responded. "I haven't heard that term in years." His fingers rapped against the table as his mind drifted off to the past.

"Oh?" I asked, coaxing more information out of him.

"I'm pretty certain your mother mentioned something about that, but I can't recall exactly what it was. I know after she disappeared, I did what I could to figure out what that word meant, but I always turned up empty. Nobody had ever heard of it before, and I couldn't find any mention of it in my research."

My eyes widened as I dared to fill with hope.

"I want to say it's a place she didn't like, maybe the one she didn't want to return to." He turned his gaze to me with a thoughtful look. "Where did you hear that word from?"

I shrugged, ready to answer his question with a vague response. "I'm not really sure, it's just something I've been wondering."

"Interesting," he murmured, and tented his fingers beneath his chin.

I decided to take advantage of the moment and go one step further. Diving head first into the deep end, I spit out a question that has been tearing me up inside with all the possible outcomes. "What would you do if she wasn't fully human?"

Confusion swam in his eyes as he studied my serious expression and I felt my resolve waver. "What are you getting at?"

"I've been thinking, and all the signs add up to this. What

if she was a…a werewolf of some sort?" I waved my hand in the air, trying to swirl the insanity of my words into an actual possibility to consider.

"Is this a joke?" His eyes were wild as his brain tried to make sense of my theories, and I found myself slinking down into my chair.

"I only want to learn more about her. I have to consider every possibility," I murmured as I picked at my food. It wasn't the answer I wanted, but his reaction was the answer I needed in order to know how much about myself to reveal. I was going to be alone after all in my quest for the truth.

Then, instead of going back to eating his food or scrolling through the news articles, he hesitated as though he wanted to say something else. "I don't know if you've ever been up in the attic and looked around, but there's a spot up there where I have what's left of your mother's stuff packed away."

He looked at me as though he expected me to say I'd been snooping and that was where I got the term Mercaida, but now my interest was piqued. "Oh?"

"In the back underneath the large brown blanket, you'll find sealed boxes. I haven't been up there since I packed everything up nineteen years ago."

My curiosity getting the best of me, I pushed my plate to the side, abandoning my dinner. "Thanks, Dad, I'll have to take a look."

He called something after me, but his words were lost in my excitement to get to the attic. This was the first real lead I had.

I COUGHED and sputtered through the cloud of dust that flew up with the blanket and filled my lungs. I tossed it to the side and out of my way as I waited for the dust to clear.

This area hadn't been touched in years by a single living thing if the cobwebs were any indication. One benefit of the cobwebs was that I at least didn't seem to have to worry about spiders.

Reaching out for the first box, I slid it from the pile. It was so surprisingly light, I nearly lost my balance as I pulled it to my chest and sat down.

Pale light from the setting sun illuminated a pair of rusty scissors nearby, which I grabbed, thankful I didn't need to run back downstairs. I knew he'd said the boxes were sealed, but I didn't think to grab a knife on my way up. The excitement and anticipation had taken over, leaving nothing but tunnel vision until I reached this spot.

The distinctive sound of old tape being cut filled my ears and my chest tightened. What was I about to discover? Would I find out more about myself as I unveiled the past of my mother?

Fear swelled up in me. With how exciting this moment was, it was also equally terrifying. It wasn't a normal thing to find out you're a wolf and then get the chance to discover more about your missing mother, whose disappearance was likely related to her being a wolf as well. It was the only thing I had to go on.

I pushed that thought from my mind. It was something that had been bothering me greatly, and made me wonder if I would end up meeting the same fate as she did, whatever that fate might be.

Lifting the top of the cardboard box, I gazed in. My blood chilled when I saw blue, almond-shaped eyes looking back at me.

The same blue eyes I still saw every day in the mirror.

With careful movements, I lifted the top yellowing picture to get a closer look. In it was a young woman with the same long, flowing blonde hair as I had. The untamed curls flew in every direction, and her arms were held tightly over her sweater as the wind blew around her. She had a smile so bright, it was surreal to think that smile might not exist anymore. I wondered if the world would ever see that smile again. I also wondered what it was that put such a genuine smile on her face.

Mindful of the curling corners, I slid the picture into my back pocket before continuing through the pile.

I flipped through all sorts of papers, the wording too old and faded to make out. Rubbing my eyes with the back of my hand hours later, I was about to call it a night when I spotted a second photograph. I pulled it closer and saw who I thought was my mother, but she was a little older than in the first photograph, but not by much.

She lacked the smile from the first picture, the lines around her eyes were tight, and her body was stiff as a man beside her placed his hand against her back. She was pulled away enough to leave a gap between them, and it was clear she didn't want to be there.

My eyes scanned the rest of the photo, and I spotted various wolves in the background, all watching them. I felt like there was something there I should know, but it eluded me. Maybe the guys would recognize who this strange man was. Should I bother asking my dad? Does he even know about this picture?

I studied the background for recognizable clues, but this looked like it was taken nowhere near Carlisle. I wondered if this could be Mercaida.

A loud creaking sent my heart hammering, and the picture flew out of my hand as I spun around. My dad entered the attic with his hands up and an apologetic smile on his face.

"Sorry, kiddo, didn't mean to scare you." His gaze landed

on the picture that was floating down to the floor, and he bent down and picked it up before I could react. His eyes narrowed as he looked at it. "This is your mother."

"Do you know who the guy is? Or" —I swallowed— "the wolves?" I was hesitant for his response after the conversation we'd had downstairs, but he didn't chastise me for asking.

He shook his head, sighed, and handed the picture to me. "I don't know who they are, any of them. She used to have a fascination with wolves, but that's all I know. I came up here to let you know it's after midnight, but also to make sure you hadn't fallen asleep. It can get pretty chilly up here at night."

My mind swirled with a whirlpool of questions and, without realizing my lips had even moved, I blurted out my next thought. "Do you know anything about wolf shifters?" I slammed a hand over my mouth and waited for him to brush it off as another joke.

His eyes glanced at the photograph in my hand and he paused as he thought over his answer. I opened my mouth to take it back and brush it off with a tired chuckle, but he beat me to it with a sigh and rubbed his hand down his face. "There were times when she tried to tell me about people who turn into wolves, but I shrugged it off as being nothing but elaborate stories. I didn't give much thought to it. She was quite the storyteller."

"Do you think she was one?"

He smiled. "Doubtful. I still think those were just stories, and you seem to have gotten your vivid imagination from her."

"What if I was one?"

His smile faded into a frown. "Is this some kind of game I'm not aware I'm playing?"

I shook my head. "No, just thoughts and theories."

"You should probably get to bed, tomorrow is a shelter day, right?"

Rubbing my palms across the top of the worn cardboard box, I shoved my thoughts into a corner of my mind to entertain when I was alone. "Yeah, I'll do that."

Chapter Nineteen

Makena

*E*verything looked normal as I pulled up in the gravel lot of Cara Paws, but I couldn't shake the feeling that something was off.

I shivered as I felt like someone was watching me, paused with my hand on the car key still in the ignition, and looked around. The metal chain-link fence glistened in the early morning sun, and every inch I could see was still intact. A few dogs ran out into the small, fenced yard. The building was still standing, and the interior lights showed there were people inside as normal.

Then I spotted what was different. Parked on the other side of the lot was a car I'd never seen before. Sure, it could belong to someone looking to adopt, but adoption hours didn't start for at least another forty minutes. That would be quite a while for someone to sit around and wait.

I shut off the ignition, gathered my things, and headed inside. An eerie feeling crept in when Mrs. Monroe wasn't there to greet me like she normally was.

The usual barking from inside the warehouse was replaced with silence, and when I pushed my way in, I saw that the dogs were still all in their enclosures, but they all sat like statues with their attention on something outside.

"Okay, this is strange." I'd be lying if I said I wasn't creeped out in the slightest. "Javier? Tyler?" I called out the names of those who were usually in here, but no one answered. In all my time here, it had never been this quiet and empty.

Taking in every bit of my surroundings and preparing myself for the worst, I opened the door and headed outside to where I'd seen some of the dogs when I'd first arrived. I didn't know what I was expecting, but it wasn't the tall brunette with her head thrown back in a laugh at something Tyler had said.

The laughter cut off as though someone had flipped a switch, and she reeled around to face me. In one smooth motion, she crouched to the ground and *growled*.

"Uh, it's okay, this is Makena. She's helping out here," Tyler explained, as he watched the strange girl with confusion.

I barely registered he was still there. My gaze was locked on the newcomer, and my wolf bristled at the surface, wanting to break out. My hands clenched at my sides with the effort it took to keep her from surfacing, unsure of the damage that could ensue if she was set free—not only to this new girl, but to my reputation and my life in general if everyone found out about me.

About her.

Something pounded at my senses. I couldn't place it, but she wasn't fully human. She was more, and I wanted to crouch with a snarl and protect my territory from this intruder.

I'd only managed to combine with my wolf once so far and keep control with my memories intact. There was no telling what would happen next time. I needed to test that out somewhere that wasn't in public with other people around.

My phone vibrated in my pocket, providing a welcome distraction and causing us to break out of whatever weird stare off we were in. I pulled it out, and she stood back up next to Tyler.

With a quick glance, I saw it was a text from Denver. He wanted to see if I could meet up. Sliding the phone back into my pocket to respond to later, I turned my full attention back to the girl.

"Okay, I don't know what's going on here, but maybe someone can explain this to me. Do you two know each other?" Tyler looked between us with both hands up as though he expected he was going to have to physically pull us apart. I briefly thought he might have to.

"Leave us," the girl ordered with an eerie calmness that didn't match the glint of amusement in her eyes. "We have some catching up to do."

Tyler glanced at me and I nodded. As soon as the door closed behind him, the air thickened.

"Who are you?" the girl asked once we were alone.

I furrowed my eyebrows, confused. "You were the one who went all offensive attack mode on me. Who are you?"

"Name's Kira."

"Makena."

There was a brief pause as we watched each other. "Your wolf is young. Only recently started the transformation."

"How did you know?" I assumed she was a wolf, but I couldn't sense it. All I could sense was something other than human, which was an improvement for me, but not good enough to get me through these surprise encounters. I needed to be on top of my game.

"Our kind can recognize each other."

"You're a wolf," I breathed out, unsure if I should be elated or defensive. There was another wolf in town after all.

She raised an eyebrow at me. "You really are young if you didn't realize that until now. You should've known before you opened that door."

"Not everyone has the luxury of knowing exactly who and what they are their whole lives," I snapped.

She raised her hands. "Calm down, pup. Exactly how new are you?"

"Not new enough to trust a total stranger with information about myself."

She smirked and shook the hair from her eyes. "Good, you have some survival instincts after all." Dropping one hand to her side, she held out the other for me to grab. "I'm Kira. A lone wolf. I require full knowledge of everyone else before revealing too much about myself, but there's something about you that I want to give a chance. I understand the hesitation. Nice to meet you."

I took her hand and gave it a shake. "Makena. Newly transformed. I'm a long story that even I don't know. I haven't yet decided if it's nice to meet you."

She pulled her hand back and crossed her arms as she walked in a slow circle around me, looking me up and down. "I think I might like you already."

I turned my body to keep her in my sight. "Uh, is there something I can help you with? My eyes are up here."

"I know, chill out. You obviously need a lot of work. You have such a long way to go before you even have a chance of surviving on your own. You must be a lone wolf, too, if you didn't begin your shift until this late in life. Let me guess, you're nearing twenty?" Her nose twitched as she leaned in for a single sniff. "No. I smell others on you. What pack are you from?"

"I don't have a pack."

"You must know other wolves." She stopped in front of me. "I can smell them on you."

"A few."

She bit the inside of her cheek as she tilted her head to the side. "But you only recently met them. No pack would keep their cub from shifting until this late in life, no matter how sinister they might be. You're still a lone wolf regardless. Are they too?"

I held her gaze, trying to figure her out before responding. I didn't want to give away everything about myself and what I knew about the guys to someone I'd met barely minutes ago. I knew they'd be the same way with giving out information about me. We had to protect each other at all times.

She shrugged. "It's cool, I get it. I wouldn't trust myself either. Here, let's take some of the dogs to the park and we can talk some more. I hear they like to walk there."

Without waiting for a response, she headed back inside, and I followed. Tyler was standing there talking with Carol, and they both quickly shushed as we entered. "Everything okay here?" Carol asked, and I nodded.

"All good," I responded with the most sincere smile I could manage. "We're going to take some of the dogs to the park."

When they kept their quizzical eyes on us, Kira added with a grin, "We have some catching up to do. Turns out we have a lot more in common than we thought."

Grabbing a handful of leashes from their hooks on the wall, I gave a few to her and then moved to the enclosures to collect a few of the dogs for their walk. I was surprised to find they were all still so well behaved and listened to everything we both said.

"I don't know what you did to make these dogs behave so well, but I would love to know your secret," Carol remarked with a forced smile. "I don't believe they've ever been like this. It wasn't until recently that they started behaving so well. It's quite astounding."

"You just have to know how to get them to respect you. I call it a gift," Kira replied, as she leashed her fourth dog and followed me to the side door that led outside, with Scooter in the lead.

We walked in silence until we reached the park, both of us trying to figure out how to ask the millions of questions we had about one another.

"If we're not careful, they're going to suspect something is up and then start asking questions. Once people around here start asking questions, they don't stop until they get all the answers. And honestly, I don't know how they'll react to the answers they'd get," I warned her, thinking back to our little encounter earlier.

"Relax, it'll be fine. Dogs listen to us all the time, it's just ingrained in them, they can't help it and neither can we."

"Maybe so, but they didn't start acting like that until recently, and they're noticing that it might have something to do with me. Or us."

"And you don't want people sniffing around your life?" she concluded. "I get that, I'm not a fan of it either. I don't have anyone to worry about because no one cares enough, but that's the glory of it. If I freak people out, I move and then start over again."

"I'm not like you. I can't keep moving on and starting over every time someone shows up and starts messing with my life."

"Wait a minute." She slowed down and looked at me. "How long have you lived here?"

After a slight hesitation, I decided to tell her. "I was born here."

Her eyes widened in surprise. "Oh, wow. I've never met a wolf who has spent their entire life in one place that wasn't a pack. Even some packs move around. You really are quite something."

"So I'm told."

"Hey, it's not a bad thing. I'm trying to figure you out. Maybe I could help you some. What are you doing to learn? Don't tell me you're relying on the Internet for answers." She rolled her eyes. "Anything even remotely accurate isn't put on there for humans to find. We like to keep it private. You'll need a wolf to guide you if you want to learn things."

"And you ended up here how?" I questioned. I found myself easing up the more we talked, and I sensed that she felt the same. We weren't a threat to each other. If we were, we would've been fighting before even leaving the shelter.

"I like to travel around from town to town. Being around humans usually means I won't run into other wolves who think I'm intruding on their territory. They always like to show they're bigger and better, and it usually begins with confrontation. I, personally, am not a fan."

"Which is why you reacted the way you did back at the shelter," I surmised.

"Pretty much. I thought you were a wolf coming to lay claim on your territory and I'd have to fight my way out. Glad you're not."

"Uh, thanks?"

She laughed and nudged her elbow into my side. "Relax."

We walked along the loop at the park, stopping every so often for the dogs to do their business. She had a relaxed air to her, but she kept a suspicious eye on everything around us as though she was preparing for an ambush. The tightness in her shoulders worried me more than anything.

"I could say the same to you," I commented. "Don't worry, nothing ever happens in Carlisle. I'm pretty sure we're the only wolves here."

As the words left my mouth, I spotted Denver walking straight for us through the park with the others following behind him. Kira noticed too, and spun around, bracing herself. The dogs all stood protectively in front of her, shoulders drawn back and heads low with teeth bared.

"Correction, us seven are the only wolves here."

"You know them?" she gritted out.

"Yeah. It's a long story. Calm down the army, I don't want to make a scene."

"What's going on here?" Denver asked as he reached us. He stood at my side, but with a shoulder in front of me in an attempt to offer protection.

"She's like us," I told him, setting my hand against his arm to bring his attention to me.

"What pack are you with?" While he eased into my touch, he still growled out the words and kept his eyes locked on hers. They flashed with a sense of familiarity

"Who says every wolf needs a pack?" she responded, her gaze digging into him like untrimmed claws.

"Okay, hold on now." Wrangling the leashes in my fist as the dogs grew frenzied, I threw myself in between them. "Look, she had a chance to attack me. A few chances, actually, and she didn't. We were having a nice conversation before now, and I think I can learn from her."

"These are the wolves helping you," Kira stated as her nose twitched.

Denver's eyes moved to mine, and I tried to silently communicate my urge not to have a full brawl right here and to give her a chance.

"Remember the killings lately? It has to be a wolf, and if it isn't you or us, then it has to be her. I've seen her wolf once, but she got away."

"What killings?" Kira questioned, her features scrunched in confusion.

"Animals have been going missing or were eaten," I replied. "All kinds of them, wildlife and domestic."

Her eyes widened. "And you think it's me?" She let out a chuckle. "I guess now is a good time to tell you I'm a vegetarian."

"A wolf that's a vegetarian?" Liam challenged with a raised eyebrow, and I realized the guys had filed in around Denver and me, forming a small, tight half circle.

"Yeah, it's a thing." She took a step back, tugging on the leashes in her hand. "Look, I don't want any trouble. I'm alone for a reason. This is honestly the first time I've encountered so many wolves in a town like this. You win."

"Wait," I said, reaching for her, but she moved out of my grasp. "Don't go. Give us a chance." I shot a look at the others. "They'll behave."

"How she treats you depends on how well we behave," Julian commented from my other side.

I held my phone out to Kira. "Here, put your number in here and we can talk later."

"I don't have a phone."

I arched an eyebrow. "Really?"

"It's difficult to find a reason to get a phone when you have no one to call and no place to call home."

I looked around at the guys. "Can you give us a minute? I'll be right over." I waited until they dispersed to watch from a distance before turning back to Kira. "Look, I'm sorry."

"No, no, it's cool. Girl, you may not realize it, but you do have a pack, regardless of what I said earlier. I wouldn't be surprised if they were your mates with the way they're protecting you."

"Yeah, I'm still learning everything."

She grinned. "I knew it."

"Can you stop by sometime?" I searched my pockets for a pen and paper but found nothing. I really needed to get better about carrying stuff on me, but since I often awoke in the woods without anything on, it became easy to find it unnecessary. So instead, I told her where I lived and how to find me, and she promised to stop by. Regardless of my original reservations about her, I had a good feeling that she could be good to have in my life, and I wanted to learn as much as I possibly could about myself and what I could do.

We broke apart, and she headed back toward the shelter and I went over to the guys.

"She doesn't smell threatening," Axel remarked, his eyes locked on her as he waited for her to make the slightest mistake, but she disappeared toward the shelter without the slightest indication that something was off.

"Because she's not. At least I hope she's not, because I gave her my address."

"We'll scope out your house and see if she shows," Liam decided.

"Is that really necessary?" I asked.

"We do it every night anyway," Casen added. "Most days too."

"Do you guys do anything other than watch me?"

"We train you. Help you. Work with you. Study with you," Denver answered.

I rolled my eyes but smiled. "Good news is, I could sense she was something more than human."

Julian placed an arm around my shoulders. Denver noticed but didn't say anything. "Of course you could. You're improving. How many more laps are we going to do?"

"I think I'm going to drop the dogs off after another lap, then head home to get some stuff done and rest before going to the diner."

"Good call. We've got a long night ahead of us," Julian responded.

Chapter Twenty

Makena

The buzzing of my alarm clock turned into the sound of a strangled bee when it went crashing to the floor as I slapped it away in my attempts to shut it off.

"Crap," I mumbled, as I felt around the carpet and pulled the small round object to my face, squinting to try and see the time before my eyes fully adjusted. My eyes widened when I saw the neon green numbers flashing on the screen. I'd never slept in this late before.

I swallowed back the bile that rose in my throat as the realization hit me. There was nothing more sobering than finding out class was just now starting when you were only waking up.

Throwing the covers off, I jumped out of bed, grabbed my backpack, and took off running through the house. My dad had already left for work, otherwise he would've woken me up with his heavy knocks to the door.

The freezing cold was barely noticeable as I sprinted to my

car while fighting back the tears. Being this late to class was one of my worst nightmares. I'd worked too hard and come too far to let everything come crashing down now. My chest tightened as I envisioned the whole class sitting at their desks, nodding at the lecture and taking notes, glancing at the one empty desk.

I glanced around me as I forced myself to pay attention to my surroundings, searching out a wolf to calm me down, but none were there.

The adrenaline running through me was enough to warm me up. I hadn't even thought to grab a jacket, but there was no time now. Warm clothing wasn't high enough on my priority list at the moment.

A thin layer of frost coated my windshield, and it was too solid for the wipers to get, so after doing a shoddy job with the scraper, I hopped in and took off with the heater blasting to fight off the foggy windows. It might be fully thawed by the time I arrived.

As I peeled out of the driveway and raced down the street, I did my best to calm my shaking body.

I'd never been late to class before. Or work. Or to anything really. There was only that one time when I was barely a few minutes later than normal at Cara Paws, but my arrival time wasn't exactly set in stone like everything else I did in my life. Despite my occasional night time issue, I was still punctual. I didn't even have a good excuse.

My breathing sped up as the little glowing numbers on the car clock changed with every passing minute. *Did I remember to put my assignments in my backpack last night? Did I even grab the right bag? Crap, I didn't even put on pants!* With a glance at my lap, I realized I was still in my pajama shorts and a thin cotton t-shirt. Even my shoes were mismatched, and as I pressed harder on the gas pedal, I was pretty sure the one on my right foot was one of my dad's. How I didn't trip over myself on my way out of the house was a miracle. I only hoped I remembered to close the door behind me.

I reached the school in record time as the clock ticked up another minute, and I already had the door open before I even fully turned off the car. Grabbing my bag, I ran at a breakneck speed with my mismatched shoes flopping against the tiled hallway floor, bringing attention to myself from those who were hanging around in the corridors as they waited for their next classes. How I yearned to be one of them, early to class and not filled with panic.

Every eye in the room was on me when I burst through the door. I could feel the curiosity, fascination, and a coldness I couldn't place. I rushed through the room, out of breath, and pulled my hair in front of me to hide my face as I took my seat. I knew it was a pointless feat, but any effort to feel invisible was a good one, and the knotted, unbrushed strands provided the veil I needed. It gave me a false sense of security while I tried to hide behind it and bypass the stares when I looked to the board to glance at the notes and distract my mind.

Mr. Morrison cleared his throat, bringing the class's attention back to him, and continued his lecture. I hastily pulled my notebook from my bag, but when I searched for a pen, one was nowhere to be found. I searched through the bag frantically, mentally chastising myself for not keeping extras in here, when one appeared in front of my face. I looked up to see Liam extending me a pen, and I gladly took it and proceeded to scribble down the notes from the board in sloppy, rushed handwriting. I purposefully avoided his eyes. I didn't need to look him in the face to feel the concern wafting off of him in waves.

The rest of class went faster than normal, but that could have been because I missed the first half. I slowly packed up my stuff while the other students rushed out of class as Liam and Axel stayed back to wait for me.

"Maybe we could start carpooling together?" Liam suggested, as I zipped up my bag.

"That would be a good idea. I can't believe I overslept. I've never been this late before." I subconsciously grabbed at my shirt in an attempt to pull my jacket closed against the cold air now that my heart had stopped racing, but I realized I'd never grabbed one, so instead I ended up maneuvering my tank top around and accomplishing nothing. Now that my time of panic had subsided, I could feel every last one of the goosebumps that coated my skin like an oil painting.

"Here, take mine." Axel shrugged out of his jacket and passed it to me. "It's mostly for looks anyway, I actually stay rather warm. More so than others."

"Thanks." I shoved my arms through the jacket and relaxed into the warmth. "I don't even know where you guys are staying anyway."

Liam looked like he wanted to answer, but he eyed Mr. Morrison who was walking toward us and clamped his mouth shut.

"Makena, I'm glad you could join us today."

"I must've kept hitting the snooze button in my sleep, by the time I realized it was going off, class was already starting," I explained in a rush.

"In that case, I'm surprised you made it here as fast as you did."

"Me too," I replied, and he chuckled.

"You didn't miss too much, everything I covered was in the notes on the board. Email me if you have questions about any of it, but I'm glad everything is alright. You're not normally one to be late."

"Thanks, I will."

He nodded at the three of us and motioned toward the

door. "If there's nothing else to be covered, I'm sorry, but I need to be able to lock up the classroom when I leave."

We rushed out and hurried to the parking lot where the cool air turned into a biting cold, and I tugged the jacket tight around me.

"What do you say to grabbing some breakfast?" Liam proposed.

"I could use some. Maybe I should go home and change first," I said, as I looked down at my bare legs where even more goosebumps were emerging from beneath the hem of my pajama shorts.

Liam crooked a finger for me to follow as he and Axel led the way to some bushes at the edge of the parking lot. My eyes widened in surprise as he pulled out a camouflaged bag and held it out to me. "We have some of these stashed around town for backup."

I looked inside and pulled out a pair of soft yoga pants and a sweater. There were other articles of clothing that looked like they were for them, much too large for me to wear. "These are my size," I commented, as I handed the bag back to him and clutched the clothing to my body.

Liam shrugged. "We got some things you could wear and added them in with ours, so whenever an unexpected shift happens, there's usually a bag with clothes hopefully not too far away."

I guessed it wouldn't be a bad idea to do that. Now why hadn't I thought of that back when I had no idea what was going on?

"I'm impressed with your planning skills," I commented, as I hurried back to my car and ducked inside. "Make sure no one can see, this will only take a second."

Sure enough, as quickly as I'd jumped in, I was jumping back out again fully clothed with my pajama shorts tossed into the back seat and the sweater over my tank top. I threw the jacket on again since Axel refused to take it back until we got me home later, saying I still needed it more than he did.

"Alright, where are we heading?" I inquired, inching back toward my car, then I paused and looked around the parking lot. "Where's your car?"

"We don't have one," Axel said.

"How have I not noticed this before?"

Liam shrugged. "We're wolves. We move fast in both forms."

"Right. Hop in then, I'll drive."

Chapter Twenty-One

Makena

 e ended up at a nearby café and enjoyed a breakfast of omelets and pancakes with every type of syrup they had. I was relieved when I realized I hadn't had the intense cravings much the last few days. I shoveled a piece of bacon into my mouth, relishing in the fact that I could eat like normal again.

"It's because you're connecting with your wolf," Liam explained in between bites of his omelet that was filled with nearly every topping in the café. His cheeks puffed out as he shoveled in another forkful and then swallowed. "Everything will continue getting easier over time the more you connect. Speaking of which, you never responded to Denver's message yesterday, and he's gotten worried."

"Oh, crap." I recalled his text yesterday that I was going to respond to later since I was with Kira, but then I'd forgotten about it. I patted myself for my phone before realizing I'd left it at home.

"It's alright, figured I'd go ahead and ask now. How about later today?"

"I have to work tonight so the time would be limited." I looked out the window and spotted the small park. "There's a park across the street with a heavily wooded area. We could do some wolfy stuff there after we finish eating."

"Wolfy stuff?" Axel echoed with a smirk.

"Yup." I took another bite of my omelet, and once we had finished and scraped our plates clean, Liam paid for all the food despite my protest to contribute, and we took off for the park.

To my delight, it was surprisingly empty. There wasn't a single person in view, probably all hidden away inside by a warm fire. This would make concentration for shifting easier, since I wouldn't have to worry about having an accidental audience.

The air was crisp as I watched a squirrel gather fallen acorns and carry them back to its nest with puffed out cheeks. I found myself kneeling on the ground as I observed in fascination as the squirrel ran back and forth, not at all threatened as it should be. Perhaps he knew we weren't out to eat him.

A *click* cut through my curiosity, and I spun my head around in search of the noise. Wisps of dirty blond hair poked out around the camera that was blocking most of Axel's face as his finger pressed the button, making it click again as he kept it pointed at me.

"What are you doing?" I asked, suddenly feeling like a mess and not at all camera ready. I began to fidget with my hair, which was hopeless without a shower or at least a brush.

"Me? What are *you* doing? You already look perfect," he responded, as he snapped another picture and then lowered the camera to look at me with his sparkling, summer green eyes. "I was telling the truth in the first class when I said photography is a main hobby of mine. If I see something pretty, I need to take a picture. I've been holding back so much with you when all I've wanted to do was document your every move."

No matter how hard I tried, I couldn't stop the heat from creeping into my cheeks.

"She's even pretty when she blushes," Liam murmured, and I turned away to hide my smile.

I normally hid myself away in my room, buried in my studies and work. I wasn't used to being the center of attention and getting compliments like this. I'd always been the one behind the screen, not the subject in front of it.

"So…" I coughed, trying to cover up my nervousness. "Am I supposed to be channeling my wolf or something?"

"We can do whatever you want," Axel said, as he stepped toward me, his eyes bright. "But don't expect me to ever stop complimenting you."

I turned my head to look at him. His green eyes were lighter as he raised a hand to brush my hair out of my face. His touch was so gentle, I found myself leaning into it.

With a single lick of his lips, he took the final step until our toes were nearly touching. My heart hummed in my chest, filling with a calmness I didn't expect.

My skin tingled where his fingers touched, and I tilted my head forward, as did he, until our lips met. They were soft and he applied only a slight pressure. My hands gripped his waist, my fingers digging into the wrinkled fabric of his shirt wanting to pull him even closer.

He played with my hair, twisting some strands around his finger and giving a slight tug. He managed to remain cool and collected on the outside, but we were close enough to where I could feel him practically vibrating with the desire to go further.

A warm body appeared at my back, and my hair was pushed to the side so Liam's lips could reach my neck. He started at the nape and kissed his way around to the side and just below my jaw. A feeling of security spread through me, and I wanted to get closer to my wolves. I could feel the bond between us strengthening, but it felt more than that. More than some intangible thing telling us we were destined to be together, but I actually *wanted* to be with them.

The kiss was sweet and sensual. It warmed me up more than any cup of hot cocoa ever had, and I whimpered slightly when Axel's lips left mine.

A single snowflake landed on his cheek and immediately melted away before it was followed by others. "It's snowing," Liam commented, as we all looked up at the sky.

"First snowfall of the season," I said with a smile. "My favorite one." I spread my arms open wide and stepped away so I could spin around with my mouth open to catch snowflakes on my tongue.

Before getting too dizzy, I found a large rock to sit down on while the world continued spinning around me, and let the snowflakes land on my body. I watched as the little pieces of frozen water melted on my skin.

Clicking could be heard from Axel's camera, but this time it didn't bother me. The sounds of the camera faded into the background as I focused on the calming environment around me. This was my favorite time of year. Everything simply felt *right*.

I felt the strange and sudden urge to run, to crunch the leaves, weave through the trees, and see if I could dodge every snowflake.

The view in front of me morphed as my eye level lowered, and when I took a step off the large rock, the drying fallen leaves crushed under my paws as my shoes were left behind and scraps of fabric fell from my back in tatters.

I made a mental note to become better at knowing when I was going to shift. This one happened so fast, it practically took place in the blink of an eye. I didn't feel an ounce of pain or distress.

Giving the best apologetic wolfy grin that I could muster toward Axel when I realized his jacket was part of the clothing carnage, I took a step toward them.

Axel continued taking pictures as Liam knelt down to scratch behind my ears, and I tilted my head so he could get the right spot. It felt so good, my eyes drooped shut and my tongue lolled out.

"Pretty wolf," he whispered, and then chuckled when my eyes popped open.

Liam shed his clothes so fast, I didn't have time to turn around and avert my gaze out of politeness. Before I knew it, a strong and beautiful gray and white wolf had replaced the man. Even in wolf form he was larger than me. My head only reached his shoulders, I had to tilt my head back to get a better look at him.

We leaned our heads toward each other and nuzzled each other, and then Axel joined us in wolf form as we headed into the woods.

The snow felt good on my fur and my legs felt better with their much needed stretch. Our surroundings fell away as we ran and yipped at each other.

I felt free, as though nothing could touch me. Despite all my human responsibilities that still existed when I would shift back, they didn't bother me in wolf form. The crushing darkness that always watched me from afar, waiting for me to slip up, was more at bay than usual. I had control over this carefree part of myself.

Running through the dead leaves and falling snow, I was more complete than I'd ever felt in my entire life.

My head snapped back as my chest collided with the

furry butt in front of me. Once things stopped spinning, I stood back up and looked around for the source of our abrupt halt. When I tried to take a step forward, Axel and Liam nudged me back.

The wolves' bodies in front of me reverberated with their growls as their eyes remained fixed on something I couldn't see. I focused on my senses to isolate the threat until my hair stood on end and my muscles stiffened to match theirs.

There was another wolf out there, one who wasn't one of us, and from what I could tell, I didn't believe it was Kira either.

This wolf was different, dangerous even. A maliciousness wafted off of the wolf and carried through the air. Whoever this was wanted to cause hurt and undeniable pain without the chance of mercy. Such darkness sent a shiver racking through my body, and I took a step back.

Who was this?

Liam moved to keep his body in front of me, making it difficult to see. I had to bend down low in order to peek out and see what was going on. The foliage up ahead shook as the wolf moved around inside, and I braced myself for an attack, but instead what we got was a howl. A loud, long howl.

Footsteps raced toward us down the path we'd come from as humans and excited voices rushed our way in search of the source of the howl. This park had been deserted not long ago, and now it was filling up with curious eyes.

I moved with Liam and Axel until we were far enough from the area where we could see them, but they couldn't see us, and we watched.

A group of people entered the area we had been in and anxiously looked around, but when they got to the bush the other wolf had been in, it was empty. They turned up nothing and were left with confusion, as were we.

Despite the alarm bells in my head about what I'd sensed from this strange new wolf, my curiosity wasn't going to let this one go so easily. I turned to the left and ran a wide arc around the people to prevent us from being seen or getting in their way. The gentle patter of paws behind me let me know the other two were following.

With my nose to the ground, I searched out the scent again, but it took me longer to find it, and Liam was on it first.

My wolf bristled, and I felt a warning in my mind. Something wasn't right.

Liam motioned us to follow. We carefully left the park without being seen, and made it back to my car after looping around to grab the clothes they were smart enough to take off before shifting and Axel's camera bag.

We had to be careful not to draw attention to three wolves entering my car, and I was grateful I'd added my car key to the chain around my neck, which I somehow managed to maneuver with my teeth—a skill I didn't realize I had, but you could learn any skills if you were desperate enough.

"That was close," I said, as I laid across the front seat and snatched my pajama shorts from the back. Someone tossed me a shirt which I gladly pulled on.

"There are a lot more people here than I thought," Axel noted. "It's a Tuesday afternoon, why aren't these people at work?"

"It depends on what kind of job they have," I responded. "Like me, for example. I don't work until tonight."

"That was still a close one."

"We have a bigger problem," Liam interjected, pulling up his phone. "Whoever that wolf was, it wasn't a friend. We need to be more careful."

"Denver is going to have our hides for this, isn't he?" Axel asked.

"Why? Because an unknown wolf was in the area?" I questioned, turning to face him after turning on the car and cranking up the heat.

"Because we put you in danger," he replied.

"No one's responsible for me but me," I argued.

"He's very particular about keeping each other out of trouble, and now that we have you, even more so."

"We don't need to tell him about the danger part though, right?" I inquired.

Liam's hazel eyes locked on mine. "I would advise against that. If there's anything he dislikes most in this world, it's being lied to. We all deserve to be honest with each other, despite how true our intentions may be."

"Got it," I noted. Looking at the clock, I noticed the time. "I should probably get back and work on some assignments before heading to the diner. Is there somewhere I can drop you guys off at?"

They gave me the name of the place they were staying at, which was only a few blocks from my house. It was an abandoned house that never sold, and no one wanted to work on the upkeep. It was basically a place drifters stayed when passing through, and this was probably the longest anyone had ever stayed in it.

I watched them in the rearview mirror as I pulled out of my parking space. Liam smoothed the front of his shirt even though there was nothing wrong with it, and Axel was busy looking through the pictures on his camera. I wondered what other pictures were in there and how many he'd taken today, but I refocused my attention to the road and pushed the thoughts aside.

Instead, I busied myself with memories from this afternoon and let my smile show.

Chapter Twenty-Two

Makena

*C*hatter echoed around the diner as I rushed to fulfill every order in my section. We had a new girl start tonight, and she didn't seem to have the same work ethic the rest of us did, but as Justine put it, we could use all the help we could get regardless.

It had only been two hours into the shift, and I'd already caught her texting in the back three times. Justine said it was a group effort to teach her how to be a successful employee, but the blatant way the girl ignored our advice was getting to me.

"You alright there?" Julian asked, as he was passing by with a bin full of dirty dishes. More customers were already seated at the table he'd just finished clearing off, and watched him expectantly as they waited to put in their drink orders.

I sighed. "Yeah, I'm extra irritated lately." I shot a glance at the new girl, Maribel, as she pulled out her phone to respond to a text. She thought she was being discreet, keeping it low and sometimes in the pocket of her apron, but everyone could see what she was doing. A small bubble emerged from her mouth before she sucked it back in with a barely audible *pop*.

"She does know she isn't supposed to chew gum on the clock, right? She knows that," I said, as I considered marching over there and yanking the phone out of her hand, but I restrained myself.

"She doesn't care much about the job," Julian informed me. "Her parents are making her work or else she's not going to get an allowance."

"Allowance? What is she in, middle school?"

"High school, set to graduate early in the spring."

"Well, no better time to build up a work ethic than right before you're thrown out into the world."

I straightened my shoulders and walked over to her. She slid her phone into the pocket of her apron as I approached. "Hey," she greeted, trying to conceal the gum in her cheek, but the large ball on the side of her mouth was a dead giveaway.

"I wanted to let you know that being on your phone out in the open here can get you into some trouble. Now I'm not going to do anything right now, but the boss is always watching, so it's best to wait until your break time. I don't want to see you get in trouble."

"Oh, good idea." She smiled her thanks and took off through the swinging doors where she was no doubt going to spend a good chunk of her shift hiding out on her phone. I wondered how many times I could send Justine back there for something before she finally caught her for herself.

The night wore on and my feet ached. I'd been running around a lot more lately, especially with how much colder it'd been with people wanting to have nice, relaxing meals inside that they didn't have to cook themselves. Not to mention I'd worn mismatched shoes for a good part of the day. I made a mental note to keep a bag of extra clothes in the trunk of my car, along with a spare pair of shoes.

As I wiped down another table, I glanced over and saw Maribel interacting with the customers for once—until I got a closer look and realized it wasn't a customer she was interacting with.

She was standing with Julian as he spoke with his table, but for some reason, Maribel was with him and she couldn't take her eyes off of him. My gaze followed her hand as it rested on his forearm and a growl emitted in my throat. I was readying myself to march over and yank her by the hair, but he shook her off, nodded to the customers, and disappeared into the back to put in their order with the kitchen.

Maribel was looking after him, even after he disappeared through the swinging door, biting her bottom lip.

"How's it going?" I startled her and smiled when she jumped and spun to face me.

"Oh, hey, didn't realize you were there." Her hand rested against her chest as though I'd nearly given her a heart attack.

"I have that effect sometimes. People don't always realize when I'm nearby. So, how are you doing?"

"I'm good. Actually, do you know anything about Julian?" The way his name drifted off her tongue made me want to dig my wolf claws into her skin, but instead I kept calm, holding my smile in place.

"Actually, I believe he's seeing someone right now."

"Really?" She kept her eyes locked on the swinging doors as though he would reappear at any moment. "Got any dirt on her?"

"Excuse me?"

"You know, anything I could use to get her to back off?" She had a hungry look in her eye that made my blood pressure rise.

I shook my head and kept my rage in check as I answered her. "Actually, she's rather lovely, and I doubt that's going to happen. What are you, fourteen?"

"I'm eighteen," she scoffed.

"Oh, pardon me. But no, honey. I think you should get back to work."

She scrunched her eyebrows at me as though I'd grown three heads, but I kept my sweet smile locked on her until she slunk away. I didn't move until I made sure she was back over in her section, and then I stormed off to the back.

Julian's eyes narrowed when he spotted me marching toward him on his way out of the kitchen. "What happened?"

"New girl," I gritted out through clenched teeth. "That about sums it up."

"Do you want me to talk to her?"

I shot him a glare like he was insane. "No."

He reeled back, and I realized I was seething more than I should have been. His hands flew up in a defensive gesture. "What happened? I haven't seen you like this."

"She's interested in you." The words were painful to get out, but I kept my eyes on her through the windows of the swinging door before studying his face for his reaction. I knew we hadn't done much, if anything at all in terms of human relationships, but some part of me still felt as though they were mine. Bond or no bond, I couldn't stomach the idea of them realizing I wasn't the only girl in the world, but I wanted to be the only one they saw in theirs.

The thought of seeing any one of them with someone else made my skin crawl. I struggled to figure out how to lay my claim, but I would find a way.

Was it even possible for a wolf to mark who was hers to keep humans at bay?

His eyes lightened and a small smile curled his lips. Dropping his tray to the counter, he placed both hands on my arms, squeezing my biceps as he met my gaze.

"You have nothing to worry about, I promise. Your wolf has an instinct to take down any threat, and this is one of them. Everything is as it should be."

He placed a kiss on my forehead, his breath fanning my skin as he whispered. "Everything is as it should be."

He brought me in for a hug where I inhaled his scent. Despite being in the diner for the last few hours and constantly working around food, he still smelled of freshly crushed leaves.

"What you're saying is that I need to take down my threat," I said, wrapping my arms around him. He was *mine*.

"Typically, yes, that's how it goes. I wouldn't recommend you taking down this particular threat in the middle of the diner, though. No matter how great it would be to watch you fight it out covered in burgers and pudding."

My laugh was muffled by his shirt and I pulled back, feeling much better. He gave me a squeeze before letting me go. "Our shift is almost over and you're brimming with energy that you need to let loose."

Before he could continue his thought, Justine burst through the doors carrying a bin of dirty dishes. "What is this? It's not break time. Maribel is out there doing all the work while you two…" She spotted his hands on my arms, but he didn't pull back. Instead, his grip tightened protectively, only by a little. "What exactly is going on back here?"

"I was having a meltdown," I answered her. "All good now."

"Glad to hear it." She brushed some stray strands of hair

out of her face. "Look, I know the new girl has been struggling today, and it's put added stress on everyone. Break down if you need to, but please keep coming back. You two are the best I have. I also have two more coming in next week to get started, so that should help take some of the load off. They're looking for jobs to get them through their last year of high school, so I hired them on the spot."

"Hopefully they'll be good workers," I commented, and she nodded.

"Me too. One of them is at least. Mack was here before and he's coming back. I just hope he continues to work hard." She dropped off her tray of dishes, filled up the water pitcher, and disappeared back into the diner. The doors swung closed behind her, but they gave me enough of a peek to know the night was winding down.

A gentle pressure against my biceps brought my attention back to Julian. "I know it might be hard to fight your instincts, but try not to worry so much if you can help it. I couldn't break the bond even if I wanted to. And I definitely don't want to." A smirk crossed his lips and he brushed stray hair from my face. "Although I do enjoy seeing you all worked up over me. Jealousy is a pretty color on you."

I smacked his stomach with the back of my hand then pulled it toward me to cradle against my chest. "You're hard as a rock," I hissed while rubbing at the spot on my hand that would no doubt bruise.

"I can confirm that," he whispered.

"What?" The word came out so quietly, it could have passed as nothing more than an exhale.

"Come on, let's finish out this night so we can rest. Maybe run off some of that energy first." He placed a kiss on the corner of my lips, making my heart calm down a bit with the contact, but my body heated up with wanting more.

Together we pushed through the doors and took care of the last of the customers while wiping everything down. My head pounded with everyone's voices running around inside, and Maribel avoided my heated gaze.

I slipped out before anyone could talk to me. I needed to get outside and clear my head. It was too loud in there.

Chapter Twenty-Three

Makena

My car's headlights illuminated a dark figure standing underneath the tree outside my window. Before I could decide whether or not to drive past while calling the cops, I recognized Denver's gruff face as he stood there, watching me, with his hands in his pockets like this wasn't the most creepy thing ever.

Flicking the lock and shutting the door after pulling into the driveway, I strode over to him across the grass. "Way to be inconspicuous," I joked as I stepped up to him.

"I wanted to see if you were home. Liam and Axel told me about what happened." His eyes were serious as they searched for my reaction in the moonlight.

"Yeah. My guess is whatever has been attacking animals lately is a wolf."

"You don't think it's that girl from yesterday?" he questioned.

I shook my head. "No. The scent was completely different. It was male."

He nodded, but then the silence overtook us again.

"So, is that all?" I asked, unsure what to do next. Normally these guys watched my bedroom window while I was inside, not while I was down here with them. The casual normalcy of this was out of place.

"How's your shifting coming along?"

"Much better. Today I barely thought about it. As long as I don't shift while at work, or some other unsuspecting and inconvenient time, we're good."

"What about at night? Are you sleeping alright?"

"What's up with the twenty questions?" I countered.

"That was only four." He shrugged. "Trying to get some information and help you out. Get to know you more." His eyes caught on something behind me, and I turned to look over my shoulder.

The teenage boy from down the street was walking his little white dog again. The ball of glow in the dark white fluff walked fast, its little legs going a million miles per hour to match the boy's strides. The teen was too busy scrolling through his phone to pay enough attention to slow down a little.

"What's up?" I asked, but by the time I turned back around, Denver was gone. I looked around but couldn't find him anywhere in the dark.

My senses picked up that something was off, and my muscles tensed. I moved over to place my back against the brick wall as I scanned the area. Nothing seemed out of place, but at the same time everything was wrong. Horribly wrong.

A high-pitched scream sounded from down the street, and I took off running.

Beneath a streetlamp, I could see a woman who was climbing the lamppost as though her life depended on it. Her hair fell in clumps around her shoulders, pulled from the tight hair tie that fell to the ground in her haste. A dark figure loomed where the light met the shadows, and the beast's yellow eyes turned on me before the thing shot forward.

I didn't miss a step. As I neared the monster, I ripped my name tag from my shirt and lunged, digging the small, sharp pin into the side of its neck. It let out a howl that mingled with the woman's screams and then threw me off to the side where I rolled across the frozen asphalt.

Right as the yellow eyes turned to search me out, a second large figure jumped over me and locked jaws with the yellow-eyed beast.

"Crap," I hissed, as I scrambled to my feet while Denver fought off the attacker. It was a strange sight with the black and white wolves flying through the air mingled with random streaks of red.

My need to help Denver was pushed back as an over-whelming feeling came over me, telling me to run. The feeling wasn't my own.

I sprinted over to check on the woman. "Hey, they're a little preoccupied right now, so if you come down, we can run and hide inside my house. It's not far, only a few houses down on this street." I kept my voice as calm and even as I could, which was an accomplishment considering the storm that was rolling across the ground around us.

In the yellow light, I could see her white knuckles from the death grip she had on the post, but she gave a nod and slid down. I flinched as her nails grazed the metal lamppost on the way down until she landed on shaky legs. Wasting no time, I grabbed her by the wrist and pulled her along as I ran.

We made it inside, and I slammed the door shut and flicked the lock, breathing hard.

"What's going on?" my dad asked, flipping on the living room light.

"Monster," was the only thing the woman managed to get out between panting breaths, and now that I got a good look at her in a place where we had less of a chance of being mauled to death, I recognized her. She was the mother of someone I used to go to school with but didn't interact with much.

"I think whatever has been attacking those animals is now switching over to people," I said, leaning my back against the strong oak door as I focused on sounds from the outside, but all was silent beyond the door.

"Come in, sit down, I'll grab some water." He disappeared into the kitchen, and I heard the faucet turn on. "How did you get away?"

"Another animal attacked it, distracting it, and we ran," I responded, as I entered the kitchen and prepared a wet rag before returning to the living room and placing it against the woman's forehead. "Here, this will help."

She took the rag and held it in place, then took the glass of water my dad handed her with a grateful smile.

I bit my lip, wondering what was going on outside. I doubted I would be able to go back out now without either of them following me, but I needed to know what was happening to Denver.

"I'll be right back." I ran upstairs to my room and threw open the window. Looking up and down the street, I saw the coast was clear. Aside from some drops of blood spotting the pavement where the light from a streetlamp hit, it was almost as though nothing had happened. But that couldn't be right. I knew I hadn't imagined the whole thing.

My heart hammered in my chest as I worried about what might have happened to Denver. Heck, I didn't even see that teenager with the white dog anymore.

Oh, no. Don't tell me that monster got the dog.

To my partial relief, I saw the dog and teenager strolling

back down the street, the boy scrolling through his phone as though nothing had transpired, and I noticed a cord attached. He was wearing earphones, he didn't hear a thing.

The dog, on the other hand, was now looking around frantically with his little legs going even faster than ever.

"Denver?" I called out in a whisper, not sure how loud I should be. I didn't want my dad to hear me calling out a name and start asking questions I didn't know how to answer yet. "Denver?"

Right as I swung a leg over the windowsill to climb down the tree, a figure popped up, surprising me so much that I fell backward and landed with my spine slamming into the floor. This carpet wasn't anywhere near as soft as it looked.

"Shoot, sorry, Makena." Denver crawled inside, reached for my hands, and pulled me into a sitting position. "I was climbing the tree, and then when I heard you, I hurried up faster. I didn't mean to startle you. Are you alright?"

"Yeah, I'm fine." My voice squeaked, and I placed a hand against my ribs as I struggled to breathe. "Give me a minute."

Soon, air started flowing through my lungs and I took a large gulp of it. "That's better. But dang, next time warn a girl."

"Sorry." His arms cradled me while I began breathing again, his touch so gentle. "Other than right now, you weren't hurt though, right?"

I shook my head. "I'm good. I grabbed the woman from the lamppost, she's downstairs now with my dad. Speaking of which, you probably shouldn't enter the living room from the top of the stairs. That would raise more questions than I care to answer."

"No worries." He helped me to my feet, and I flipped on the light switch. The room flooded with light, and my heart clenched when I saw the blood dripping from his forehead.

"What happened?"

He frowned. "You saw what happened."

"That's not what I mean. Sit down." I guided him to my bed and ran to the bathroom to grab a wet cloth and was relieved when I saw the small bucket was still under the sink.

"Makena, are you alright up there?" My dad called from the bottom of the stairs. "You've been gone awhile."

"I'm good, Dad, just getting cleaned up. I'll be down in a minute!" I rushed back into my room with a wet rag and a bucket of water, shutting the door behind me.

"I don't even know where to start. I should've grabbed a second rag. Here." Without thinking, I placed the bucket on the nightstand beside the bed, dipped the rag in the water, and climbed up so my knees were planted on either side of his thighs as I straddled his lap to get a better angle to clean his head. His hands wrapped around my hips, holding me steady on the mattress, and I tried not to focus on how the tips of his fingers squeezed slightly.

Placing a finger under his chin, I tilted his head higher then moved my hand to cradle the back of his head. I winced when I realized his onyx hair was sticky with drying blood and would need more cleaning than this one rag could do.

His eyes were dark as could be as they watched every move I made. I lifted the rag to his forehead and applied very little pressure, expecting to hurt him with the simple touch, but he didn't even wince.

"He got away."

"What?" I was so focused on gently wiping away as much blood as I could, his words barely registered with me.

"The wolf. It was a big one, and I'm pretty sure he's a lone wolf. We haven't sensed any other packs around here."

"I'm glad it was only one," I whispered as I focused on cleaning every last drop of blood from each crease on his face.

"Stronger than I expected too. I managed to injure him,

but I have no idea who it is or where he came from." He winced as I hit a particularly rough spot, and I pulled back.

"Sorry." I set the rag in the bucket beside me, rinsed it out, and got back to work. Once I was satisfied I'd cleaned him up as best as I possibly could, I dropped the rag into the bucket and braced my palms against his shoulders as I checked him over.

He was going to have a scar above his right eye. "Do wolves possess some sort of extra healing ability?" I asked, recalling the scrapes on my legs that healed faster than normal.

"What do you mean?"

"If you get hurt, do you heal faster or scar?"

"We do heal a little faster than normal humans, but we also still scar, depending on the severity of the wound. Most wolves wear them with pride."

"Then I guess we better inflate your ego, because you're going to have one right here." I touched the area below the cut and then pressed my lips to the wound as though my simple touch could heal it. Really, though, I was just being selfish and wanted to get closer.

"All the scars are worth it if I get to let you clean me up after." His voice was growing gravelly, so I pulled back slightly. His hands slid down so his fingertips pressed into the backs of my thighs, practically creating a seat for me so I could take some of the pressure off my knees.

"I'm glad you're okay," I whispered.

"Same to you," he responded.

I knew I should get up and head back downstairs, but I couldn't seem to get off his lap and walk away right now. He held me in place with his hands on my thighs and his gaze that acted like a cord of steel. I was frozen, and the bulge straining his jeans wasn't helping much.

Static drifted through my fingertips, and I clenched my

fists in his shirt, pulling myself closer until my mouth landed on his. He banded an arm around my back, pulling me into him as his tongue met mine.

The thin fabric of his shirt began to rip at the collar as I pulled harder to keep him against me, and then I moved my hands so my fingers could tangle in his hair. My hips rolled forward and his arms turned to steel around me. I swallowed his groan, and he gulped down mine as though it was the air he needed to breathe.

My mind whirled, lost in the frenzy of needing to get closer. Of needing more.

It wasn't until I heard footsteps on the stairs that my eyes flew open and I threw a blanket over Denver as I pulled away. I tumbled from the bed and ran to the door, breathing hard.

Crap. I should have gone straight back downstairs. Now I was about to be busted.

I met my dad at the top of the staircase and shut the door behind me. He gave me a concerned look when I tried to meet him with a confident smile. "Hey. Everything alright?"

"Yeah, everything is fine. The cops are here, and they wanted to ask you some questions. I got worried since you never came back down. I thought maybe you were hurt."

Oh, crap. What was I supposed to say to the cops? I couldn't tell them two werewolves were fighting, and then prove it by shifting in front of them.

"Sure thing. I was cleaning up and lost track of time. I'm not hurt, I just fell on the ground when I tried to get away." I followed him downstairs where two police officers were waiting, each with a notebook and clipboard in hand. The woman looked like she was ready to nod off where she sat with her head propped up in her hand as she held the ice pack to it.

"We hear you were part of the attack?" one officer asked as I entered the room. "Can you describe it at all?"

I blew out a breath. "It all happened pretty fast. I saw this woman here climbing a lamppost to get away from something…big."

"Did you happen to get a look at it?"

I shook my head. "It was too big and fast. It growled and snarled. Could've been a dog. Or a rhinoceros." *Great one, Makena*. I wanted to mentally smack myself.

"How did you get away? She told us there was some sort of distraction with another animal."

Crap, I was hoping to keep Denver out of this, but maybe I could make this work. "We got lucky. Another animal showed up and they ended up battling each other, so when it was distracted, I grabbed onto her and ran straight home. It didn't seem to follow us, so if it's not out there anymore, then I guess we succeeded and it forgot about us."

"Was the other animal a rhinoceros too?" one of the cops questioned with a chuckle, and the first cop tapped his clipboard against his arm. On the plus side, that might distract them from what kind of animal they were really looking for. If I sent all the cops around here searching for a wolf, I was going to be in a lot of extra trouble every time I shifted.

I gave them all the information I could while protecting the full truth. I was rather proud of myself for keeping the shifter world a secret despite how many questions they asked. I'd lost count somewhere in the double digits.

"I think we got all the information we could get. Thanks for your cooperation, I'll go file this. You all have a lovely night."

"What about the woman, is she going to be okay?" I asked before they could leave.

"We had a paramedic here checking her out. She seems to be okay and doesn't require immediate care, nothing a little sleep can't help. She didn't want to come with us. We think she's afraid to leave the house at the moment."

"Thank you, officers." My dad closed the door behind them. "Well, I guess we could either see if she wants to stay in the guest bedroom for tonight or sleep right there."

"She looks pretty comfortable in that chair if you ask me," I noted, as her head bobbed from dozing off.

"Makena."

"I know, I'm on it." The woman startled as I rested a hand on her shoulder, and I knelt down to be eye level with her. "Hey there. You're welcome to stay the night here, but we thought you might be more comfortable in the guest bedroom."

"Are they gone?"

"Yes, the cops just left," my dad said.

"No, not them. The beasts."

"I think so. The cops couldn't find any. Do you live nearby? We can make sure you get home alright if that's what you want, or we could wait until morning." I took the ice pack from her. She was physically fine, but she seemed to be pretty shaken up still, and I didn't blame her. I wouldn't want to leave until daylight either if I were her.

"Staying here until morning would be great if it's not a problem for you guys."

I nodded and stood, helped her into a standing position, and then guided her to the guest room on the lower level. "There are extra blankets in the closet if you need any, and water bottles in the fridge in the kitchen. If you decide to leave before either one of us is awake, then please flip the bottom lock on the front door when you go. Otherwise, I'll see you tomorrow."

"Thanks." She snuggled under the covers and passed out before she even finished the word.

"What a night," my dad grumbled as I reemerged. "You sure you're okay?"

I smiled. "I promise."

"As much as I hate you being in danger, I'm still glad you were there to help. I can't imagine what would have happened to her otherwise. Or even what we would've found if no one had gone outside until morning." He shuddered.

"Yeah, it was pretty crazy. Luckily I was there." I let out a big yawn. "It's been a really long day and I'm going to call it a night. I'll see you in the morning."

"Night, kiddo."

"Night, Dad."

Denver was still huddled underneath all the blankets when I entered my room again. With a wicked grin, I ran over and leapt into the air, landing on him with an *oomph*.

"Ow, ow, injured guy here."

"Oh, sorry." I scrambled to move off the bed, but he took advantage of my distraction by snaking an arm around my waist and flipping me over so he was hovering above me.

I rested my hand against the side of his head, so my thumb was grazing along the skin where the cut ended. It was already starting to fade. "I didn't realize you were still around out there," I whispered. "I turned around and you were gone. I thought you'd left."

"I didn't leave you. Something wasn't right and I needed to shift. I left my clothes behind the tree. All it took was one moment and then *you* were gone." He tucked a few strands of hair behind my ear. "I was glad I didn't leave, I don't know what would have happened otherwise. Although I have to admit, shoving your name badge pin into him was a pretty good move."

"I used what I had. My next option would have probably been to use the strings of my apron to strangle him, but I doubt I could've held on for that long."

"Why didn't you shift?" he asked.

I shrugged. "I don't really know. It wasn't something that occurred to me at the time. Probably because I was already running with a plan to attack in human form."

I sighed, tired of talking. I was tired of thinking. Tired of being a wolf, and being human. All I wanted was to sleep, so without further words, I rested my head in the crook of his neck and fell asleep listening to the gentle thrum of his heart.

Chapter Twenty-Four

Makena

My hand began to cramp as I scribbled in my notebook. I was watching the wolves at the nature reserve I was volunteering at for a class assignment, studying their every move, but most of these notes would be for my own personal use.

Every wolf here had arrived as a rescue. Some were missing limbs while others had healed nearly back to normal, but they all had one thing in common—not a single one was able to be reintegrated back into the wild. They were now too dependent on humans in order to survive. If they were set free, they wouldn't even make it a day.

A camera clicking nearby caught my attention, and I saw Axel taking pictures. Kneeling on the ground, he was still as a statue as he snapped away. I didn't realize he was here, and with the way he was hunched over as he looked through the lens, I doubted he knew I was here either. I was at the nature reserve because of an assignment for a class he wasn't in, but

I suspected he was here for the pictures and for some discreet wolf interaction.

The wolf he was aiming at opened wide for a big yawn, and he snapped the picture when he could get a full view of teeth. That was going to turn out amazing. I made a mental note to see if he would show me some of his pictures sometime.

Careful not to disturb him, I turned to a clean page in my notebook and silently ran the pencil over the paper, creating lines that eventually met up and began to form a person.

Axel was always so busy capturing the beauty of others, he had no idea someone was doing the same to him.

I wasn't an artist by any means, but I liked to think my sketching wasn't all that bad. The lines grew and darkened as I went, and I was so engrossed in the activity and perfecting what I'd put down, I didn't notice the steady footsteps heading my way.

"It's pretty peaceful here." Axel's voice was soft as he sat down beside me, and I quickly flipped back over to my notes. "Places like these are the only ones where I'm okay with wolves being in the care of humans. They put their wellbeing first, and they're safe here."

"Do you think they like it here?" I asked. I'd been trying to figure that out, and from what I could see, the wolves looked pretty content. I hadn't seen any of them fight or lash out at me or any of the caretakers.

"I know they do, I can sense it. So can you."

"I can?"

"It's something you feel, and it will eventually become second nature and happen without you trying. Kind of like how when that girl knew you were a wolf, you'll be able to sense more as you become more in tune with your wolf. Take that one over there, for instance." He pointed at a wolf that was deep in a stretch with her butt in the air. "Put your focus on her and see what you can sense."

Attempting to do as he said, I blocked out all the rest and concentrated on her. I opened up my mind, and I thought I was doing it wrong when I realized the reason I only felt calmness was because that was what the wolf was emitting. As she sauntered over to the full-time caretaker, who entered the enclosure and ran her fingers through her fur as she scratched her back, there was nothing but contentment.

"I see what you mean," I murmured, as I continued to watch, opening myself up. Then something happened that I wasn't expecting.

My heart clenched, and I lurched forward in a way to protect my vital organs from impending doom.

Except I wasn't being attacked. There was no danger where I was, and as I lifted my head to look around, I was utterly confused by the calmness surrounding me, which was completely untouched by the terror running through every cell of my body.

I found myself gasping for air, as though invisible walls were closing in on me.

"Makena?"

I was vaguely aware of a familiar voice calling my name, but there was another voice inside of me I needed to listen to first. It sounded scared, like it was trying to warn me about something, but I couldn't figure out what. All I could think about was getting my next breath.

My fingers dug into the dirt as Axel's hand touched my arm, feeling like a million, white-hot needles piercing my skin. My nails extended, slicing the dirt as they did, before retreating back into my body.

The pressure around my head lightened and feet pounded the ground as people ran toward me, but my body returned to normal as though nothing had happened.

"Are you alright?" One of the caretakers landed next to me with her knees in the dirt, and she helped me sit up.

I looked around in confusion. "Yeah, I'm good. I think I need to take a short break to get some water." I forced a smile to prove everything was fine, but I really needed a moment to speak with Axel.

As though he could sense my thoughts, he stood up with me and guided me away from the barrage of questions as more concerned people arrived, and we headed toward a water fountain that was farther away and more private.

"What happened out there?" he inquired once we were alone, and I gulped down some water.

"I got a warning."

He lifted an eyebrow. "What kind of warning?"

"I don't really know, but it isn't good. I think my wolf was trying to tell me something. She was panicking. Absolutely terrified." I took another drink of water and wiped my mouth. "Maybe I was imagining it."

His features grew stern. "I don't think so. If something isn't right, then you should listen to it. Your wolf is trying to get your attention, and it's usually for a good reason. Either something spooked her, or there's something she wants you to know."

I chewed on the inside of my cheek, and he rubbed his hands up and down my biceps. The warmth that came from it soothed me, and he wrapped his arms around my back when I leaned into his chest.

"This is so much. Only a couple weeks ago I knew who I was. Heck, I even knew *what* I was. But now all I know is that I know nothing, and things keep getting even more confusing. I have more things to worry about than ever, and I don't know if it's even worth finishing these classes." I didn't mean to unload all my worries on him like that, but once the first words were spoken, there was nothing I could do to stop all the rest from tumbling out.

I wadded up his shirt as I fisted it, scrunching up the fabric and probably pulling a little too tightly. He responded by rubbing his hand up and down my back. I didn't like showing vulnerability, but with all these drastic changes happening in my life, I didn't know how much more I could take right now. Not to mention whatever my wolf was warning me about, would now follow me like a dark cloud until I figured it out.

A shrub outside the fence moved as a bushy tail disappeared around it, and I gripped Axel tighter. Before long, we went back out, and I smiled as though nothing was wrong. The sun was still shining, and the wolves were active and playful. As far as anyone else was concerned, it was another day much like any other.

Chapter Twenty-Five

Makena

*M*emories from this morning kept invading my mind, making it difficult to focus. After deleting words for the ten millionth time, I shoved my notebook off my desk and hung my head in my hands. Not even the light tapping against the window could pull me out of my moment of anguish and feeling like a failure.

The window slid open and light footsteps shuffled over to me. "Makena?" Casen's hand rested on my back as he knelt beside me. "Are you alright?"

I lifted my head and took in his stooped posture. "I'm okay, just tired. I need to get these assignments done, but it's hard to focus."

He glanced at the jumbled mess of open windows and tabs on my computer. Before I could object, he slid his arms behind my back and underneath my legs, lifting me up and carrying me over to the bed.

"What are you doing?" I objected, but I didn't fight him off. His hold was so comfortable, I wanted to fall asleep right there. He exuded calmness from his body. His touch. The way he held me. "I have stuff to finish."

He laid me on my bed and tucked the blanket around me. I protested, but my body remained calm as he did so. "Relax. I'll take a look at things and see how I can help you. I do know a lot about wolves, after all. Give me a few minutes to see what I can do, and then you can get back up."

His lips touched my forehead before he pulled back and sat in the chair at my desk. I watched his shoulders shrug up and down as he maneuvered the mouse and his fingers flew across my keyboard. The rapid rhythm was soothing to my overstressed brain.

I closed my eyes for a moment to ease the burning behind them, and the next thing I knew, I was opening my eyes again to bright light streaming through the window. Casen was snoring with his head on my desk, and every last one of my assignments that I currently had were completed.

Careful not to wake him, I snuck downstairs. My dad was still asleep, so I moved as carefully as I could to not make any noise as I started the coffee pot and opened the fridge. I was going to make omelets, but my hand hesitated over the eggs when I spotted the blueberries. They were so bright and blue. Changing my mind, I grabbed the berries and had three plates full of blueberry pancakes in no time. I put two plates together on a tray with butter, blueberry syrup, and two mugs of coffee, leaving the third plate behind on the counter for my dad.

A strong blueberry scent wafted off the tray of food as I ascended the stairs, and Casen jumped from the chair when I shut the door behind me with a *click*.

I smiled as he wiped the sleep from his eyes and beckoned him over to the bed. Setting the tray carefully on the night-stand, I cringed when I accidentally nudged the alarm clock too far and it fell to the floor again. Truth be told, it'd been slammed against the wall so much anyway, I was surprised it even still worked. I would worry about that later.

"How'd you sleep?" he asked, as he sat down on the bed next to me, and I handed him a mug of coffee. He accepted it without hesitation and took a sip, then scrunched his face.

"It might still be hot. I brought up some sugar, since I didn't know how you take it."

"This is perfect," he replied, as he took another awkward sip.

"There's pancakes too." I passed him a plate, and he set the mug back onto the tray. A smile took over his face and he dug in. "I was going to make omelets, but this seemed like a better idea."

"Blueberry pancakes are my favorite."

"Really?" I paused from sipping my coffee.

"There's nothing else on the planet quite like them. Whenever I make them back in Mercaida, I always make a plate for Axel too, knowing full well he doesn't like sugar and I'd have to eat it instead."

I chuckled. Picturing them all sitting in the kitchen eating breakfast and Casen eagerly sliding Axel's plate closer to himself while he glared at him, was something I'd like to see someday.

"You didn't have to do all this," he told me around a mouthful of food.

"It's the least I could do. I didn't realize you'd be up all night finishing all my assignments."

"It was the least I could do too. We've monopolized a lot of your time with wolf stuff."

I shook my head. "That isn't your fault. I'm a wolf whether or not you guys are here. If you weren't here, this would all be so much harder. I'd probably be lying in a ditch somewhere."

He paused with the fork halfway to his mouth. "Not funny."

"You're right. I'd probably be waking up in the woods right now with no idea what's happening." I placed my hand on his arm and looked him in the eye so he knew I was serious. "I mean it. I'm really glad you guys are here."

A smile crossed his face, surrounded by extra scruff. "Did you get enough sleep last night?"

"Best night's sleep I've gotten in a long time," I answered, before digging into my own pancakes. "I can't thank you enough. Honestly."

He beamed, and my heart melted as his smile grew. He was so proud of himself for helping me. I didn't know what I did to deserve so many people who genuinely cared.

Now that my assignments were caught up, and I didn't have anything else planned, we spent the rest of the day working on connecting with my wolf after a surprise visit to Cara Paws to walk some of the dogs. Casen was hesitant at first when I told him they needed to be on leashes, but he quickly warmed up to them and spent the rest of the morning playing with them in the park. He even managed to find the best sticks for playing fetch. My favorite part of fetch was watching his shirt ride up every time he threw a stick, and I'd have to quickly avert my eyes before being caught.

It felt like the world had been lifted off my shoulders. I never felt this free, I'd only wondered what it would feel like. We met up with the others to work on my wolf connection. The shift came easier, and by the end of the day, I was shifting back and forth with ease without destroying any clothing.

MY SHOULDERS RELAXED and I sank further into my chair with each assignment I submitted. I was still surprised with how much Casen got done last night, and I was so relieved I wasn't going to be far behind like I expected. He even did all the research for me so the few short assignments that were going to come through next, would be able to be completed in a breeze. I felt a pang of guilt, but I still looked over everything to make sure I wasn't missing out on any knowledge.

Once they were all turned in, I leaned back in my chair with my feet up on the seat to take a moment to relax. My teeth scraped across the plastic of the pen in my mouth as I thought about what to do next. I was tempted to text the guys to come over, even though I'd already spent the day with them. The sun was beginning to set, and I wondered what they were doing right now.

A light tapping sounded on my window behind me, and I nearly fell out of my chair as I spun around. Once I recognized the brunette hair filled with leaves and twigs, I jumped up and ran over to unlock the window and let Kira in.

"Thanks. I was halfway up the tree when I realized it might not even be the right window. Your scent is everywhere, girl." She stepped inside and shook her hair out the window until all the tree bits fell out.

"I'm so glad you're here, but holy crap you scared me."

Her face scrunched up. "I thought that's how everyone gets inside your house. That tree is covered with various scents. Does your front door even work?"

"It's becoming more common for more people to use the tree. Mostly wolves, apparently. How have you been?"

"I'm fine, but I'm mostly here to warn you."

"Uh-oh."

"Being a lone wolf, I don't actually belong anywhere. It also means I'm not normally seen as a threat, because I don't have a pack behind me to back me up, so when I see or overhear something I'm not supposed to, there's not always retaliation. They think I'll keep my mouth shut out of fear." She ran her finger along my dresser as she spoke, and I thought I caught a hint of longing in her eyes.

Turning, she composed herself before continuing.

"I overheard something, and I believe it has to do with what's been going on around here. And I'm pretty certain it's not a coincidence with what's also been going on in Mercaida."

I frowned. "How do you know about Mercaida?"

"Like I said, when I hear things that aren't meant for my ears, it gets brushed off a lot." She shook her head. "Anyway, whoever this is, I believe they're after you. That's why they're here and attacking things. I could be wrong, it happens, but I'm pretty certain someone doesn't want you to go to Mercaida."

Chapter Twenty-Six

Makena

The smile I had plastered on my face was genuine.

My shift at the diner tonight was the calmest one I'd had in a while. The two new guys were starting this evening—well, Mack and the new guy whose name I should probably learn—and while we did need to take some time away to train them, at least Maribel was spending less time hiding away on her phone in the back and more time out here around the customers, even if she couldn't stop ogling them. The best part was that she seemed to take the attention she'd been giving Julian and put it toward watching the new guys. Apparently they went to a different high school than she did.

Another benefit was that my wolf guys were all here too. Aside from Julian, who was currently on the clock, the other four were seated at their usual table with a pile of menus. After I'd told them about Kira's visit, and especially after the recent attack, they took it upon themselves to be around me more despite my protests that I didn't need a horde of bodyguards at all times. I wouldn't admit it to them, but I did kind of enjoy knowing they were always there when I needed them.

I brought out a tray of waters for them, and while it looked like they were all studying the menu intently, I noticed how their gazes continuously drifted around the diner as they watched everything. Their eyes spent more time off the menu than they did on it.

"Can I get you an appetizer to start you out?"

"We could use one. Surprise us. We may be here awhile." Axel grinned up at me, and I knew full well they had no intention of leaving before my shift was over.

I rolled my eyes to hide my budding smile. "I'll be right back out with something."

Pushing through the swinging doors, I put them in for an order of cheese sticks and chips with dip, recalling the many times they'd ordered them before. I even wrote down an addition of guacamole for Denver.

As I was on my way back out with a bin to clean off an empty table, I stopped before I turned back into the small dark hallway. There were people back there, and they were whispering.

Turning slightly to the side so I could peek out the small window in one of the swinging doors, I saw Maribel bussing a table with the new guy whose name I didn't get, but I couldn't get a better view of the rest of the area without going into the hallway.

I strained my ears as I tried to pick up on what the frantic, hushed voices were saying, but all I could make out were, "girl," "tonight," and "bad."

The swinging doors opened, and Justine entered carrying a tub of dirty dishes. I stepped out of the way and peered down the hall, but there didn't seem to be anything there other than overturned crates and a stack of extra chairs. The lightbulb still needed to be replaced and the shadows made it creepier.

Taking the chance, I walked down the hall until I got to the end and found the back door slightly ajar. I pushed it open and poked my head out, but still found nothing. Whoever it was, they were now gone. Did they work here? If not, then what were they doing here?

I headed back inside the deserted hall and nearly knocked over Justine as I ran into the main diner area. Looking around, I scanned the space to see who was missing. I saw Julian, who was watching me with a look of concern, and stepped forward as though he was debating whether or not to walk over to me. The guys were still in their booth, but Denver and Liam, sitting on either end, had their bodies turned outward and a palm pressed against the edge of the table, waiting for a signal to get up. They knew something was wrong, but they couldn't figure out what was bothering me, so they were now on high alert.

Maribel laughed at something the first new guy said, but the other new guy, Mack, wasn't anywhere to be found. I was about to go into full-on, major search mode for him, but the men's bathroom door swung open and he walked out before I had a chance to act.

If the people in that hallway weren't anyone here, then who were they? Were they customers who snuck back there for a private conversation away from prying ears?

I scanned the room again. There wasn't a single empty table, and without knowing exactly how many people were here before, I didn't have a way of knowing if any of them slipped away from their companions. At this point, I was uncertain if all the chaos had finally gotten to my head and I was being paranoid for no reason.

"Are you okay?" Justine appeared at my side, staring at me as though I'd crawled out from a lava pit.

"I'm fine."

"Okay, because you don't look it."

I brushed off her concern. "Do you know if anyone here has left?"

Her eyebrows nearly jumped through the ceiling as they rose. "Is there a reason why our customers aren't supposed to leave the restaurant after finishing their meal?"

"That's not what I meant. Did you see if anyone walked through those swinging doors who wasn't supposed to?"

She thought it over for a moment before shaking her head. "I can't recall seeing anyone, no."

My shoulders sagged as I blew out a breath, deflated.

"Do you need to take a break? It should be getting close to one," she suggested, as she looked at me with a watchful eye.

"I don't know."

"Go sit down. We've got enough staff now to be able to take proper breaks. You've been working really hard, and I see it." She squeezed my arm and walked away to her newest table, taking the pen out from the side of her hair as she reached them so she could write down their drink and appetizer orders.

"What happened?" Julian whispered as he reached me.

"I'm not sure." I motioned for him to follow me to the table where the others were already halfway out of the booth. It would be easier to only have to tell the story once rather than five separate times.

Once we were all situated in the booth with Julian standing at the end of the table—and I'd checked to make sure the people at the table behind were deep in their own conversation—I recounted the story. They listened intently as I replayed the oddness of what happened.

"It could be anything," Casen said. "Anyone, really. But why would people be back there in the first place?"

"I have no idea, but the door was open when I checked it, so if it was already open before…"

"Then they could've seen the open door and taken advantage of the privacy of an empty, deserted hallway," Julian finished.

"In that case, it could be pure coincidence," Axel mused.

"The words you heard could be anything," Liam added.

As they ran their theories by each other, I kept my gaze focused on Denver. His eyes were stern and unseeing, and I wanted to know what was going through his head. The others caught on and their voices fell until it was quiet with all eyes on him.

"Denver?" Julian prompted. "What's going through your mind right now?"

We all waited until he noticed us watching him. "I'm not sure, but I have a bad feeling about it. When I fought off the other wolf, he had his focus on Makena, completely forgetting about the girl he'd chased up the lamppost. I had to work harder to make him fight against me. I assumed he was focused on the woman climbing the lamppost."

"And now you don't think he was?" Liam asked for clarification.

Denver shook his head. "The wolf was after her at first, which made me think she was his target. But I don't know how I didn't see it until now." He rested his elbows on the tabletop as he rubbed his hands across the length of his face and then threaded his fingers through his hair before looking up again. "That woman, she looked similar to Makena in some ways. Same color and length of hair, and around the same height too. It could've been easy to mistake them as one another, especially with the shadows hiding her face and unable to notice the age difference."

"What are you getting at?" Liam growled, his voice lowering to a level that sent chills down my spine. I felt sorry for anyone who ended up on the wrong end of that growl.

"Once Makena made herself known, the wolf went after her and completely ignored the original target. It wasn't the other woman he was targeting. I believe it was Makena."

Silverware clanged against his plate as Liam slammed his fist onto the table.

"Why would someone be after her?" Casen questioned. "What would that accomplish?"

"I can't put all the pieces together yet, I need more insight about motivation, but I'm sure it has something to do with her being a Mercai, and possibly the only one who wasn't born and raised there."

"You mean…" Axel trailed off, and Denver nodded.

"If my guess is right, then yes, I do mean that."

"Does someone want to fill me in here?" I heard their words, but I couldn't piece together what they actually meant.

"We think someone might be trying to take you out," Denver answered. "If I'm right and they know of your existence, they might not want you to make it back to Mercaida. It would explain all the attacks that didn't begin until after you started to sleepwalk and shift."

"What's so bad about me going back to where I'm apparently from? I have nothing to do with the war going on."

"Right now, it's pretty evenly split, and you're an extra number. They could be thinking if you can't be swayed then you must be taken out," Axel explained without taking his eyes off of Denver. "It's only a theory though and could be wrong. We'll need some more information first."

"Well, that makes no sense at all to me."

"Don't worry too much, we won't let anything happen to you," Casen promised, as he slid an arm around my back and pulled me into his chest.

"I'm not as worried about myself as I am about all the people who'll wind up in their path as they try to get to me," I murmured. "All those senseless attacks? This means I'm responsible for them. All those poor people and animals, all because of me."

"You can't blame yourself for the actions of others, regardless of the reasoning behind it," Liam soothed. "The fact that you care more about the innocent people and animals in all of this shows exactly what kind of person you are. Those who hurt others on their path to destroy someone else aren't the ones whom you should let dictate the difference between right and wrong."

The front door opened, and Austin and Leah stepped into the diner. He shoved his hands into his pockets and looked around until he spotted me.

"I'll be right back," I said, as I got up and went over to them. "Hey," I greeted.

"I've mostly finished packing and wanted to come by and see my friend again." He looked around the nearly full diner. "Any spots open?"

"Yeah, over this way." I led them to the last available table in my section for what would likely be the final time. I swallowed past the lump in my throat, trying not to get choked up. I would have to worry about a more difficult goodbye soon enough.

I picked up the stack of plates and the tip left behind by the people who had just left. They sat down but didn't bother with menus, since they ordered the same thing they did every time they were here.

When I came back out from placing their orders, I noticed Leah scrolling through her phone while Austin had his eyes locked on the table with my guys who were, without a doubt, watching my every move.

I tended to my other tables, making sure their drinks

were filled, their orders were placed, and their food was brought out before finally sliding into the empty seat between Austin and Leah.

"Don't look now, but those guys over in the booth by the window won't stop staring at you," Austin whispered as he leaned in. "Do you want me to do something about that?"

A laugh bubbled out at the seriousness in his voice, and I waved him off. "No, it's okay, I know them. Sorta," I quickly added, realizing I hadn't breathed a word about them to either of my longtime friends. Leah had looked up from her phone and was glancing between us and the guys.

Austin reeled back with a hand over his chest in mock surprise. "I haven't even left yet, and you're already going out and making replacement friends?"

"Don't worry, no one could replace you." I grinned. "Either of you."

"Avoiding the risk of mushy feelings, I think a strawberry milkshake sounds good too," Leah interjected, providing the distraction I needed, although I knew she would be giving me the third degree about this later.

"Coming right up." Grateful for the brief distraction, I hopped up and ran to get her a milkshake.

As I approached their table again, with the glass from the shake frosting my hand, I heard troubled whispered words. My mouth turned down in a frown. Something had happened while I was gone.

"What's up?" I butted into their conversation as I reclaimed my seat, placing the shake in front of my friend.

Leah turned her serious gaze on me. "There was another attack. Except this time it was a girl."

My stomach churned as my questions spilled out, dreading the answers. "What? Where? Who?"

"Today. I just got the alert. The station already has plenty of people covering it, but I'm having them give me real time updates."

Her phone pinged nonstop with all the updates coming in. Sure enough, it was a girl about the same age and height as me with long, curly blonde hair. I knew exactly what the attack was about, and I fought the bile that threatened to rise up my throat. At least she lived, which was most likely only because of all the witnesses who helped her out, although she needed to be hospitalized.

I thought back to the voices in the hall and had an eerie feeling it was somehow connected.

Chapter Twenty-Seven

Makena

"What about a nice, quiet dinner?" I asked, as my dad jotted down more items onto his grocery list.

He was still planning a big party for my twentieth birthday tomorrow, and as the day neared, my wolf ached to run free. I could feel her beneath the surface, urging me to go outside and let her out, but that wasn't going to happen for a little while.

"You don't want to celebrate with your friends?" he asked without looking up from his list.

"Austin is moving, and Leah is busy with her career. Everyone else I barely see because I've been so busy."

"Exactly why it's a good idea to hang out with them when you get the chance," he countered. "You have your whole life to grow apart. There are a lot of people in town who want to celebrate with you."

"They all like to celebrate in general. You really don't

need a reason. Your tomato seed sprouted? Everyone will come over with cake."

The oven beeped, signaling it'd been pre-heated, but before I could put a pizza in, the doorbell rang.

"Who could that be at this hour?" I muttered, as the clock flashed seven o'clock. My dad went to answer it while I reached for the frozen pizza.

"Is Makena here?" The familiar voice drifted into the kitchen, and I nearly dropped my pizza, wondering what Denver was doing at the front door. Setting the frozen pizza in the oven and starting the timer, I ran out to see what was going on.

Out of all the surprises I'd been faced with lately, I didn't expect to find Denver and Liam standing in the living room talking with my dad as casual as could be. The sight was so mundane, I stood rooted to the spot as I watched them interact, before shaking myself into motion.

"Hey, what's going on?" I asked, as I entered the room.

Liam's hazel eyes had a tinge of seriousness as they flashed to me. "We were in the neighborhood and thought we'd say hi."

"Liam here tells me you go to school together," my dad said, as though they were now really chummy. They bonded more than I thought during the short time before my entrance.

"Yeah, they're new in town and started a little late, but they've helped me out with some things." I left out exactly how many things they'd helped me with. More than school-work, that was for sure.

"We were getting dinner ready, would you care to stay for some pizza?" my dad offered, and my heart pounded.

This couldn't be good. I racked my brain, trying to come up with some excuse for them to leave before my dad got too suspicious.

Denver nodded. "We'd love some pizza."

"Perfect. Makena, could you put in some extras?"

"Sure, Dad." I tried to catch Denver's and Liam's eyes, but they were too busy looking around. Of course they were, they'd spent a lot of time looking at the outside of the house, sometimes even the inside of my room, but this was the first time they'd ever been through the front door. I hurried to add another two pizzas to make sure we had more than enough for their wolfy appetites.

After getting the three pizzas to fit snuggly on three racks in the oven, I joined them at the table where they were chatting animatedly about school assignments, the fun things to do around Carlisle, and Colorado in general.

"It's a beautiful place," Liam commented as I sat down. "We love the outdoors, so a lot of our time is spent outside."

"Even with the cold? It's getting pretty chilly now, but if you're not used to it then you may want to get more prepared before winter really hits," My dad cautioned.

"It's good, we're used to the winter weather. It's almost always cold where we come from," Liam replied.

"Where is that?"

Denver opened his mouth to answer, but before he could get any words out, I jumped in. "It's a place pretty far away. I can't really ever remember the name myself."

Denver's eyes locked with mine and he nodded in understanding. "What kind of pizza are we having?"

"One cheese, one pepperoni, and one with basically everything on it," I answered, grateful for the distraction. Right then, the oven alarm went off. "Care to help me with it?"

I'd meant for both of them, but only Denver followed me into the kitchen. "I take it he doesn't know?" he whispered, as I opened the oven. I cried out in pain as I reached for the pan, realizing I'd forgotten to grab oven mitts. "Makena." He grabbed my wrist and pulled it toward his mouth to blow cool air on it while he guided me over to the kitchen sink.

I sighed as the cool water ran over my hand, soothing the blistering ache. "I'm a little distracted."

"I see that." He shut off the water and kissed my wrist. "Don't worry, we'll be good."

Dinner went smoothly enough, and by the time every last bite of pizza was gone, the guys had my dad and I roaring with laughter. He didn't let them leave before they accepted his invitation to my birthday tomorrow, which they promptly agreed to.

"Those are some good guys," my dad remarked after closing the door and cleaning up. "I think one of them even likes you."

I bit back a smile, knowing full well they both did, and they weren't the only ones. "They are good guys."

He shuffled around some things by the front door. "Hey, you haven't seen a missing shoe, have you? It would look like this."

I looked up and saw him holding up the shoe that went with the one I busted through during my morning of mismatched footwear.

"It's NOT that big of a deal," I grumbled as I straightened my dress.

My dad was setting up all sorts of food, both in the kitchen and in the backyard. He had various meats ready to go by the grill, and lights and streamers decorated the deck. It was a lot more than I was expecting, which actually wasn't anything at all.

"Of course it's a big deal. You're turning twenty, that has

to mean something," he replied, as he dumped another bag of ice into another cooler.

It did mean something, he was right about that. If only he knew exactly how right he was.

My wolf had been growing more restless inside of me as we struggled to coexist together. We'd made a lot of progress, and now I at least had control in wolf form, but the dreams were a whole other thing. I felt like my wolf was trying to warn me of something, and while those signs were becoming more obvious, I'd been growing more anxious and ready to figure out what was going on.

People began arriving, setting their gifts and snacks on the designated tables before coming over to give me a hug. I was over a dozen hugs deep when I spotted Austin's ex-girlfriend entering the yard and I headed for her.

"Trischa," I greeted with a grin. We hadn't hung out much at all while she was dating Austin, but every interaction I'd had with her so far had always been strained, like she didn't like being around me or Leah. I was surprised to see her here.

She set the gift on the table. "Hey, happy birthday." Her smile was bright and genuine. "Do you have any big plans?" she asked, as she set a covered tray onto the food table.

I shrugged, surprised by her friendly tone. "Not too much. Right now I'm trying to get through school, and then I don't know. Work somewhere. Maybe even travel." I thought of Mercaida as I said the last words. I knew things were kind of crazy there right now, but I had a feeling I would still be visiting at some point. I was torn up inside between my obligation to stay near Carlisle, or allow my heart to guide me to an unknown world.

"That sounds exciting. I've been looking forward to getting out of here and seeing the world for so long, but now that it's happening, I'm terrified to leave." She scratched at her forearm as she spoke. Her nerves were growing.

"What do you mean you're leaving?"

"I mean, there isn't anything for me here. I want to give traveling journalism a try. I was working with Leah for awhile, but then I realized…it's just time for me to see what else is out there. Find all the stories that are out there waiting to be discovered."

I nodded as though I understood. "The world outside is huge." I threw her a friendly smile. "You'll have an adventure as you explore it. Besides, you can always return home any time you want."

She smiled. "I hope so."

"I bet Leah will miss working with you."

She winced, but didn't acknowledge it. "I'm leaving without too much of a plan. After spending some time with a cousin, I'll be hitting the road and winging it from there."

I placed my hands on her arms and had her look me in the eye. "Look. You are a talented woman. I have no doubt that you'll find stories, and you'll rock them. Nobody can tell a story quite like you can. Regardless of what happens, you'll still have that."

She surprised the heck out of me when she threw her arms around my neck and gave me a hug. I patted her back in return, wondering why it took a goodbye to get us to have a decent conversation together. "I always liked you," she whispered, startling me with her statement.

A shout sounded out from somewhere in the distance. It was faint, but still loud enough to grab the attention of people at the party.

I pulled away and looked around, seeking out my wolves, and their eyes made contact with mine. They'd heard it too, and we knew exactly what was going on.

"If you'll excuse me, I'll be right back." I hurried through the gate, not bothering to close it behind me in my rush.

I stripped down as I ran, throwing my shoes off to the side and reaching behind my neck for my zipper. For once, I wasn't going to bust out of my clothes, but I didn't have time to stop and set them somewhere safe, so I'd have to find them again when I changed back.

Footsteps behind me told me my wolves were following, and together we ran down the street right as another scream erupted. A woman with blonde hair trailing behind her as she ran was heading straight for us, but a large animal lunged at her from the side, cutting off her scream as she hit the pavement.

My dress and bra fell to the ground at the same time my body started to shift. My back arched and my claws extended until I was running on four legs, pounding my paws against the hard concrete as I flew over the ground. To my horror, the large wolf at the end of the street grinned with recognition as he turned toward me and sprinted at full speed, leaving the crying woman on the asphalt.

We locked jaws as we clashed, and we each threw our claws about, trying to gouge one another where our teeth couldn't reach. I slipped as I tried to gain the upper hand, and the wolf pinned me to the ground with his fangs pressed against my throat. I expected him to clamp shut, but instead, he paused.

Pain erupted across my foreleg as he was thrown off me in a blur of fur. Growls sounded out around me as my wolves fought him off until he fell hard with a yelp and took off, my wolves trailing after him.

I stood up to give chase, but they were nowhere to be seen. Even with my nose to the ground, I couldn't figure out which trail to follow and ended up running in circles until I finally turned around to head back and find my discarded clothing. I froze in the middle of the road when I saw Trischa standing on the sidewalk with a phone in her hand and her jaw hanging open in shock.

I took a step toward her, expecting her to run away in a screaming fit, or at least pull out her camera and start scribbling in her notebook she kept with her at all times, but she didn't. Instead, she surprised me by doing what I least expected. She snapped her jaw shut, let out a cough to compose herself, then knelt down and picked up my discarded clothing.

Her legs shook as she stood back up, and for a moment I thought she might fall over, but she regained her balance, set the clothes behind the nearest bush, and turned her back while I sauntered over, shifted back, and quickly dressed.

"Trischa?" Her name was quiet on my lips as I let cautiousness flood through me. I didn't know what to expect, and I worried she would run back to the party and tell everyone what a freak I was.

I cringed as the word *freak* ran through my mind, and realized that was why I hadn't told anyone, not even my dad, even though this could have something to do with my mother's disappearance. Right now it was the only lead I had, but I still couldn't get myself to tell anyone. And now here I was without a choice. I could beg and plead with her all I wanted, but my fate was in her hands.

She looked like she was about to speak, then ran a hand through her hair as she hesitated. Her skin was paler than before and she took a few shaky breaths, her eyes going in and out of focus. Finally, she decided to get it over with and met my gaze. "Are you alright?"

"What?" I was taken aback by that. I didn't know what I expected her to say, but that sure wasn't it.

She stumbled over her words before she repeated herself. "Are you alright? That looked pretty intense."

"I don't understand what you're talking about. Why aren't you running away?"

She blinked. "Why would I run away? If anything, I should thank you." She looked over my shoulder. "That woman should thank you too."

I spun around, having completely forgotten about the woman who was being chased. Her body was shaky as she got to her hands and knees and looked around. She was scraped and bruised, but otherwise alright.

Her eyes locked on mine and widened. I ran over to her, half expecting her to collapse. "Do you know where it went?" Her voice was meek, but I reached down and helped her to her feet, holding onto her arm while she got her footing.

"I'm fine, I think. But what was that?" Color returned to her face as she looked around wildly for the animal that attacked her.

"It's gone now," I assured her. "Some friends managed to scare it off. Is there anything I can do for you? Anyone I can call?"

She shook her head and tucked a strand of blonde hair behind her ear. "No, I'm only the next block over. It's not far."

"Here, why don't we walk you home to make sure the animal really is gone?" Trischa offered with a renewed strength in her voice. She stepped in front of the girl, who nodded.

"Okay." Her voice was uncertain and I wanted to get her home before her questions could start tumbling out. I placed my hand against her back as we began walking in the direction she indicated, with Trischa on her other side.

We walked in silence, aside from a dog barking as we passed a house. The woman was pretty shaken up, and I was worried she would fall over before we could get her home.

She let out a shaky breath and straightened her shoulders

as we walked, trying to pull herself back together. I waited for the string of questions I was sure would come, but she didn't say a word.

We quickly made it to the woman's house. Once she was inside and assured us she didn't need anymore help, I glanced around at our surroundings, feeling the urge to get back home. Trischa and I descended the steps and headed back. Laughter from the party carried toward us as we rounded the corner onto the street, and I figured it was now or never.

"Why?" I asked, as I picked at the fabric of my dress.

"Why what?"

"You don't have to do this. I don't understand what's in it for you, for keeping my secret." Nobody did anything solely out of the goodness of their heart. There was always an endgame.

Chewing at the inside of her cheek, she mulled over her thoughts. "Secrets are a powerful thing. They can build bonds, and they can also destroy kingdoms. There are some secrets we just have to accept, no matter how hard it might be." Her eyes unfocused as she spoke, and I became more confused.

"If this is about Austin and Leah—"

She cut me off with a laugh. "It's about more than them. I'm not keeping your secret just because I broke up with my ex boyfriend."

Frustration crept into my confusion. My two friends were the only link between us. I didn't see what else there could be. "Are you aware that as a traveling journalist, you're going to be exposing more secrets out there? Here I am with a nice juicy one to land you on the front page, and you won't even entertain the thought."

"You're a good person. We all have our secrets that should be hidden from the world, and I can respect that." Neither of us said another word before we reached the party, and I had a feeling I wasn't going to get more answers from her. I didn't know what made her so pro-secret.

Chewing on vegetables, I studied her as she interacted with the other guests. She looked content, and it threw me off. I'd never paid as much attention to her as I was right now. She might be ready to keep my secret, but I wanted to know whatever she was hiding. Perhaps she was a better person than I was. Maybe she had a secret that was scarier than mine. Or maybe occasionally running around on four legs and covered in fur wasn't as newsworthy as I would have thought.

Reaching for some vegetable dip, I paused when I spotted the guacamole in a bowl next to it. Not a single growl or howl could be heard.

My wolves still weren't back, and I hadn't seen any sign of them since the attack. It worried me, because I expected them to be back by now, but I had to trust they were alright.

They had to be, there was no other choice I could possibly consider, and that thought scared me. I didn't realize how much their absence could affect me.

Chapter Twenty-Eight

Makena

*A*fter scouting the neighborhood a final time after the party was over, I headed back home. I didn't know where else to look, and my wolf wasn't picking up anything that could be useful. They'd been all over the place, as had the attacking wolf, so it was impossible for me to be able to pick up their scents. I kept disappearing from the party to look around the neighborhood with no luck.

Wherever they ended up, I hoped they were alright. I refused to believe anything else.

I dragged my tired body up the stairs after saying good-night to my dad and thanking him for the party. Even with my eyes constantly on the backyard gate when I was outside with people, it was still a great celebration and I even got closer with Trischa. I kept waiting for the veil to lift and for her to out me, but her notebook remained untouched throughout the party and she even made an effort to talk to me more throughout, as though she didn't care that she had the power of the area's largest breaking story in history. I believed she would keep my secret for now. I didn't have a choice other than to trust her, my whole existence was at her mercy.

As I swung my bedroom door open and slipped inside, something moved in the shadows. I opened my mouth to scream, but before I could get a word out, a hand was over my mouth and an arm banded across my shoulders, pinning my back to the wall, and an instant calmness swept over me.

His foot closed the door with a tap as he towered over me, and I breathed in his minty scent. As he lifted his arm from my shoulders and the lock on the door clicked, I stuck my tongue out and licked his palm.

The corners of Denver's mouth turned up in a smirk. "Not going to work with me, little wolf."

A fire heated in my belly and I stared at him, wide-eyed.

He slowly removed his hand and gripped me by my upper arms, his thumbs rubbing my skin. "Are you okay?"

"Yeah, I'm fine, but what about you and the others? I looked everywhere I could think of, but I couldn't find you." Our voices were low so as not to be heard, and I forced myself to stay calm and not squeal and throw my arms around his neck like I really wanted to.

"I'm fine, and so are the others. We chased him and fought until we had the upper hand."

"Where is he now?" My hands lifted to rest gently against his sides.

"He's gone, Makena. Took his own life before we could get anything useful out of him."

My fingers paused at the hem of his shirt. "We're back at square one then. Does this mean the attacks are over?"

"We have reason to believe he wasn't working alone. Now with the most immediate threat out of the way, we need to keep an eye out for more, especially after what you over-heard yesterday at the diner. We will figure this out." His voice grew closer as he lowered his head until his forehead was resting against mine. "I promise you."

My hands dipped beneath the hem of his shirt, gliding across smooth skin and taut muscles. I paused when my fingertips grazed over lumps of scar tissue. "Is this from today?" I whispered.

"It is. It'll continue to heal at an accelerated rate."

I bit my lip. "I'm sorry you got hurt. I should've been the one fighting."

"Don't you go around apologizing. You jumped into the line of fire to protect someone else, regardless of what would happen to you. There is absolutely nothing to apologize for, and nothing more noble than that. Just like I'm never going to apologize for helping you. We all make decisions, and we have to accept them, regardless of whether or not we like the outcome."

I continued my exploration of his body, tracing every spot with raised scar tissue, every swell and dip of muscle, until I got to another scar and paused.

"There isn't a wolf out there that doesn't bear a scar."

I pulled my hands toward me again and rubbed at the sleeve over my forearm. It was growing itchy, and I'd been so distracted earlier that I forgot to check.

"What's this?" He pulled back slightly and gripped my wrist with one hand while pulling the fabric up my arm with the other. He moved barely enough for a thin trickle of moonlight to illuminate the shallow red cut across my arm. It was already healing over and didn't look like it had even bled much. I'd told my dad it was from the rose bush along the neighbors sidewalk when I tried to smell the roses, and I didn't get any more questions about it.

There wasn't anything he could do about this. What happened was already done. We could wallow in self-pity, or we could move on while wearing our scars like our best piece of wardrobe. A permanent accessory to our everyday lives.

"It's like you said, there isn't a wolf out there who doesn't bear a scar. And now I have mine."

His thumb lightly grazed the set of claw marks on my skin with his face set in a frown, and I didn't even flinch. Anger rolled off of him, and veins were now threatening to pop out of his skin where he held himself back from going into a fit of rage. It amazed me how he could force himself to be so calm all the time, even when rage is billowing off of him in waves.

Instead, he pulled my arm to his mouth and placed a kiss to the healing wound, the gentle move odd compared to the fury that raged inside him. "Your scars look beautiful on you," he whispered.

I swallowed my next words, my brain unable to come up with a response. My eyes were glued to the spot his lips had touched as though his kiss had magical healing powers and I expected to see the area mend itself before my very eyes.

"You know, I wanted to be the first to kiss you." He lifted my arm with his fingers tangled in mine and pressed my palm against his shoulder as he stepped in to fill the gap. It was good, too, because there was too much space between us. When had that distance gotten so big?

"Are you mad?"

"No. I'll just have to make up for it now."

"We can definitely make up for it." I tilted my head up to look at him, but my lips caught on his instead. His mouth pressed gentle kisses against mine while his body flattened mine against the wall. My free hand slid under his shirt on the way to his abs, wanting to feel his skin against mine again. I should never have taken both of my hands off him.

Something pressed against my stomach, and I dug my fingers into his back to pull him closer to me. I gripped the hem of his shirt as my fingers trailed back down his body, gripped a handful of the fabric from his shoulder in the process, and swayed my hips from side to side. I fisted his shirt so tightly, I'd be surprised if I didn't puncture a hole in the fabric.

"Makena," he growled the second we broke apart for air.

I answered him by dragging my nails up his sides and scraping them along his pecs. He pressed his hips forward slightly, and I responded by pushing against him in return. Before I realized what was happening, his hands were gripping my butt and my legs were wrapping around his waist.

He held me close with his forehead resting against mine as he looked at me, the room too dark to see anything other than a sliver of the side of his face illuminated by the moonlight. I couldn't see his eyes, since they were clouded by the shadows, but I returned his gaze anyway. "I don't know if you realize what you do to me," he whispered, his voice low and unsteady as he tried to regain control.

"I do, because it's no different than what you do to me."

I urged him to carry me over to the bed, afraid of making too much noise against the wall. Our clothes fell to the floor along the way, and he paused as he hovered over me. "I don't have anything," he panted as he hung his head.

"I've got the implant, we're good." I flipped us so I was on top of him on the bed. His hips gripped my waist in protest, ready to flip us back over. "Not this time, alpha," I purred, as I kissed along his neck.

His body hardened and shuddered. His fingers pressed into a forceful grip on my hips, guiding me onto him. My breathing quickened as I rolled my hips into a steady motion and sealed my mouth against his to silence both of us.

My heart rate sped up, following the beat of his beneath my palm.

I clenched around him and moved faster. The metallic

taste filled my mouth as I bit his lip to keep from screaming his name throughout the quiet house. He pulsed beneath me, his hands bruising my skin as he came, our groans drowning out the crickets.

I rolled off, breaking the kiss, and turned to face him again as though our bodies were magnetized. His hands reached for me, wound around the back of my head, and pulled me in for one more kiss, not caring about the blood that coated his bottom lip.

We managed to stay as quiet as possible, but the silence between us just now spoke louder than any words ever could.

Chapter Twenty-Nine

Makena

A slight pressure on my lips brought me into consciousness, and I reached up, threading my fingers through the smooth hair above. "Morning," Denver rumbled as he kissed me awake. "I have to go check on some things, but I'll come back. I'll always be around. Have fun today."

With a kiss to the wound on my inner arm, he pulled away, and a cold chill hit the empty space where he was no longer curled into my side. I pulled the blanket around me, using it as a shield against the cool air that blew in as he opened the window and disappeared outside.

Holding the comforter around me, I rushed to the window in time to see him morph into a dark gray wolf with tufts of siler and white and run away to join the pack who was waiting for him across the street. Their eyes locked on mine before they turned and ran off to wherever they were going, and I fought the urge to run after them. Instead, I sat in the open window and watched the sunrise.

The morning went by quickly. I got through my new assignments and felt like I should be rising to the top of my class with the wolf knowledge I was gaining. I expected to get an A in this subject now, since everything was becoming second nature.

Austin and Leah arrived midafternoon, carrying armfuls of bags filled with enough supplies to get us through the next month. My dad left for work not long ago and was working a double shift, so we'd have the rest of the day and all night alone together.

"I hope I brought enough stuff," Leah said, as she dropped her pile onto the middle of the living room floor.

"I think we came over well prepared," Austin remarked, as he set his own pile down next to hers and began to sort through it. "What do we do first? Start out with a little horror, or ease into it with some comedy?" He held up a movie for me to see. "What about *Wolfman*? That sounds fun."

I cringed, then cleared my throat. "That does sound, uh, interesting."

He looked at me. "What, you don't like wolves anymore? I thought you used to love them."

A laugh bubbled out of my throat and became uncontrollable. Before I knew it, I was lying on the ground with my hands over my stomach, failing to stop the giggles from erupting.

If only they knew.

"Did I miss something?" Leah asked.

It took me another few minutes to get myself under control and sit up to face them, but I couldn't keep the smile from my face. I wiped my eyes with the back of my hand, not realizing that my shirt sleeve slid up as I did so, revealing the fading scar on my forearm.

Leah reached out and grabbed my wrist before I had a

chance to pull away. She studied it as she traced the claw marks with her fingertip. "What happened here? This looks like an old wound, and I never noticed it before."

Austin leaned in to get a look, and I pulled my arm free from Leah's grip.

"It's nothing. An animal scratch."

"What kind of animal? That looks pretty big. Is it the one that's been attacking all those animals and some people?" Leah questioned, her eyes widening. She reached for her bag and pulled out a notebook and pen, ready to take notes.

I rolled my eyes and groaned. "This isn't newsworthy, Leah."

She blinked as my words sunk in and then her mouth formed an "oh" and she set her notebook down. "Sorry, habit."

"I know, it's the reporter in you." I smiled at her, but on the inside I was bristling with anxiety. She was my best friend, but if she found out about me, which side would she choose—me or the story?

She looked up at me patiently, and I blew out a breath and began. I could give her a partial truth while still retaining my wolf identity. I could get through the night like this. "I think it might have been what's been attacking, but I couldn't get a good enough look at it to see what it was." Okay, that was only a partial lie. The first night I saw the wolf it had been pretty dark. "It was at night."

"When you saved that lady? Your dad told some people, and now everyone knows," Austin said.

Great, of course everyone knew. Couldn't expect something like that to happen without word getting around.

"Yeah, that's when." I looked at the piles of items on the floor nearby. "How about we change the subject?"

"Good idea," Leah chirped, as she pushed her notebook

away from her and looked at me with a giant smile. "Let's get to talking about those guys from the diner."

"I—what?"

Austin laughed. "I'm surprised it took you this long to bring it up."

"I was hoping Makena would say something first, but I couldn't wait any longer to get the ball rolling. We saw how they looked at you and how you were with them. There has to be something going on. So which one?"

"What?"

"Which one are you seeing?"

I gulped. "Well, all of them."

Her eyes widened. "There were five of them."

I nodded and bit back a grin as I waited for her response. I had to admit I was enjoying her reaction. If only she knew this wasn't anywhere near the craziest part of it all.

"How do you handle that?"

I shrugged. "Not really sure, but so far it's working out."

"Fascinating."

"I hate to interrupt this girl talk, but I have a very important question," Austin declared as he held up a box. "Popcorn now or later?"

"Now," we answered in unison, so Austin got up and headed to the microwave.

The next few hours passed with laughs and screams as we burned through one movie after another. None of us were getting tired yet, even after the clock passed midnight.

We were spread out across the floor, with cushions and pillows strewn around to make it more comfortable.

My wolf bristled underneath my skin, wanting to come out, but I fought to keep her at bay. This wasn't the best time for me to shift. I tried to remind myself that Trischa had managed to keep my secret so far, but the thing that worried me most was Leah.

The movie faded into the background as my mind wandered, and I imagined myself running through the woods again, free as could be. I could almost feel the ground beneath my paws, the soil cold and damp from the morning frost.

There was a figure in the distance I couldn't make out. It was more like a shadow that started out shaped like a wolf and then turned into a human. I watched as the mysterious shadow's head turned to look at me with blood-red eyes.

"Makena?" The strangled cry brought me out of my thoughts, and I looked over to see Leah with her hands over her chest as she looked at me with terror.

Austin crawled over and sat in front of me with his hands in the air, unsure what to do. "We might need to call an ambulance. I don't understand what's going on."

I tried to ask what was wrong with them, but the words morphed into what was almost a howl, and I looked down to see my body slowly shifting. My shirt had small tears in the fabric and my jeans had full rips in the thighs.

It was a slow enough process that you might not notice anything right away without watching, but there was no mistaking this. The growing fur and elongating claws were only the beginning.

Reeling in my thoughts and emotions, I imagined myself as a human again, sitting in my living room having a normal night, but the shift completed before I could get control of it, and soon I was on four legs, watching as one of my lifelong friends screamed bloody murder and looked as though she was going to pass out. Austin's face paled, and he looked like he was going to be sick.

I quickly shifted back and reached for the nearest blanket to cover myself. "Sorry, don't panic, it's me. I'm still trying to get the hang of this."

"You're—what?" Leah couldn't seem to form words, and

instead blurted out shrieks as she tried to wrap her mind around things.

"Is this why I've seen you running home some mornings?" Austin inquired, as he pieced things together, and I nodded. "I thought you were…well, I didn't know what, but not this. This has never crossed my mind."

Leah gaped at him, stunned with how calm he was despite the paleness of his face. He took a few deep breaths, and color began to return to his cheeks.

"Believe me when I say it's a really long story. I didn't even realize what was going on until the last couple weeks."

"Why didn't you tell us?" Leah whispered, as she lowered herself back to the floor and crossed her legs. "You've been going through this on your own? I'm your best friend."

I looked at her with a sad smile and told her the truth. "I love you, Leah, but I can't tell you things if you're going to tell the world. I know how much your job means to you, and honestly, if it came down to it, I didn't know if you would choose me or your work."

She pursed her lips and nodded. "That's fair. I have been kind of obsessed with it lately."

"Not a single other person knows?" Austin asked, and I cringed.

"Well, one person knows. Yesterday at my party, there was an issue with what's been responsible for the attacks and I had to shift in order to fight, and Trischa saw me shift. She promised she wouldn't tell anyone, but that could've been because she was too freaked out to think straight."

I looked at Leah, expecting her to be hurt, but I wasn't prepared for the anguish and betrayal that marred her beautiful face. "You two have never gotten along. The few interactions you've had only ended in argument or awkwardness."

"I don't know what to say. It wasn't planned, she just happened to be there. I can't say why she didn't run a story."

Austin nodded. "She saw you save a life. That's more important than a news story, and she probably figured it was worth protecting you over."

"Either that or she didn't think anyone would believe her, which is also a viable option." I shrugged.

He laughed. "That's true."

I turned to Leah. "She is a good person. I'm sorry she's leaving, but I must admit you have some decent taste in friends."

"Thanks, but we aren't actually friends. She doesn't like me, and hasn't for a long time." She looked down at her hands and started picking at her nails. "She loves working at the news station, but she's leaving because she needs to get away from me. There are other stations out there she wants to find."

There was silence when none of us knew what to say next. Leah and Austin exchanged looks. By the time Austin nodded, I was racking my brain for something to say when Leah spoke up.

"We've been seeing each other."

"What?" I struggled to understand her words and thought I must have heard her wrong.

"Me and Austin. We're kind of breaking up now that he's leaving, but it's complicated."

My jaw dropped as she pulled her knees to her chest. "How have I missed this?"

"You've been so busy with everything, we rarely saw you." Her words ended in a whisper and she lowered her eyes to the floor as she spoke. "I'm sorry we didn't tell you sooner."

A genuine smile lifted my lips. "I'm sorry I've been so busy and have missed out on time with my two best friends. I'm happy you got together, though."

Austin's hand was rubbing the back of his neck so hard, there was a red spot forming. "I'm sorry I didn't try harder to be in your life before now. I had no idea you were going through this…this…this thing."

The way they handled this news left me filled with awe. I felt like we'd been apart for so long and were now finally coming back together just in time to fall apart again. Our apologies and regrets closed the space between us as we lifted our burdens to make space for something new.

"Can you tell us more about it? I want to know what all has been going on with you," Leah spoke up, changing the subject back to my wolf. "I'm surprised you've been able to keep it a secret while still doing everything else, and I have no idea how." She turned the volume down on the TV and draped a blanket over herself before looking at me expectantly like she was ready to get story time started.

"I'm curious too," Austin added.

Breathing out, I started from the beginning. I even went so far as to tell them about my wolves and how they're connected to me. They listened to my story with wide eyes and gasped at all the appropriate times, even asking questions throughout to try and understand it more.

I pulled the picture of my mom with the wolves from the pocket of my shredded jeans that were lying on the floor in front of me and showed it to them. Thankfully I hadn't damaged the photo during the shift. They were as fascinated as I was and formed theories with me.

They surprised me. I didn't know what I originally expected of them, but now I realized I was foolish to doubt the people who had been there my whole life, thinking they would turn their backs over one thing that was out of my control.

"I DIDN'T REALIZE SAYING goodbye would be this hard," I said, as I wiped another tear from my eye. Leah was in much worse shape than I was as she couldn't get any words out through her sobs. She placed sad kisses on his lips which he returned with a longing.

Austin wrapped his arms around me for the thousandth hug of the morning. "I know, it's really strange to be leaving, but I'll be back. This isn't goodbye forever, only goodbye for now."

I squeezed him one last time before letting go. "Take care, my friend."

He got into the car with one final wave and drove away. Leah wrapped her arms around me and leaned her head against my shoulder as more tears fell.

Seeing my childhood friend drive off into the sunrise in search of something different in life ignited something within me that I didn't realize was there.

I looked up and down the street I'd lived on my whole life. There were the same houses and mostly the same people within them. The trees that towered over the homes had grown along with me, and I always assumed that I, like the trees, would stay here forever.

Now, however, something inside of me desired to get out. Not just for a quick vacation, but for something more. Something worth it.

"Leah," I whispered before I had even fully formed the thought. "I'm getting out of here. Maybe not right now, but someday. I'm going to go to Mercaida."

Chapter Thirty

Makena

Sweat dripped from my hair as I bustled around the diner, putting in orders, bringing out food, and trying to keep a smile plastered on my face when all I really wanted to do was break the pencil in my hand, stick my head outside the door, and inhale a deep breath of that Carlisle air. Despite the dwindling temperatures outside, the diner was packed to the brim. The sheer amount of people inside did wonders to keep this place warm, and when you were running around nonstop, it could pass as summer weather in here.

The diner was as busy as usual, if not even more so. We barely had time to communicate with one another, and I kept looking over at the clock, willing for it to go faster.

I had plans to wolf out tonight and run through the woods, and I couldn't wait to feel that freedom. Imagining the cold air blasting across my face as I ran was enough to keep me going. I also couldn't wait to talk with the guys. I didn't want to keep holding back from new experiences and from finding out more about where I came from. They originally stayed here for me, to get to know me and experience this bond between us. Now, I was ready to take it even further.

There was a lightness in my step as I flew around the diner taking orders and bringing out food. Even Justine was in a surprisingly good mood today, which was nice to see. For a moment I thought it would be a perfect night and we'd make it through quickly with how well staffed we were, until I looked over and saw Maribel walk up to Julian and rake her nails down his back.

He stiffened under her touch. He didn't need to look to know that it wasn't me behind him, but it was too late. A thin thread within me that had already been weakening throughout the night snapped, and I flew across the diner until I'd smacked her hand away and put myself between them.

Julian placed his hands on my hips as he looked over my shoulder. I could sense his amused smirk as he held me back, he was probably enjoying this—not the confrontation so much as my reaction.

I didn't have to say anything to her. My actions and my growling were enough to make her take a few steps back until she'd fully retreated into the bathroom with watering eyes.

Warm breath caressed my neck as Julian leaned in from behind to whisper into my ear. "I think we've created a little scene, love. Everyone's looking."

I looked around, and sure enough, every eye in the diner was on me as Justine wove through the tables as she headed for us. "I don't know what that was about, but take a few minutes to cool off," she demanded, before continuing on to the next table. Her forced smile never wavered.

"You heard her," Julian said, as he guided me toward the

swinging doors and pulled me toward the end of the darkened hall. We really needed to get this lightbulb replaced.

"Now I feel kind of bad. I didn't mean to make her run away and cry. But I also wanted to claw her eyes out."

Julian chuckled. "It's the bond that's making you extra defensive, regardless of whether or not you mean to be." He wrapped his arms around my waist and pushed me against the wall.

"This is a position I'm finding myself in a lot lately."

"What?"

I chuckled, thinking back to the other night with Denver, and warmth spread through my chest. Instead of answering him with words, I tilted my head up and took his lower lip between my teeth with a growl, pulling slightly. As I let go, he leaned forward and captured my lips with his, leaving no space for me to bite again.

My fingers tightened around his upper arms, pulling him closer.

We got lost in each other without bothering to search for a way out until he pulled his head back with heavy breaths. "She did say to take a few minutes to cool off, not heat up."

"We can cool off after we heat up," I replied, as I ran my tongue up the side of his neck and lifted my knee to press against his outer thigh.

With a growl, he gripped me beneath the knee and hiked my leg over his hip as he rolled into me. "You're not making it easy to hold back."

"Then don't hold back," I whispered. "Everyone's too busy to come back here. Even if they did, it would be too dark for them to see anything." I undid the top two buttons of his shirt and kissed along his chest. A rumble vibrated from within.

"I want you. All of you." His fingers dug into my thigh, and I mentally cursed myself for wearing leggings. Despite how cold it was outside, this was a rather inconvenient time for them.

"These pants though," I murmured, as I rolled my hips into him, pausing for a moment when I felt a hardness I didn't want to pull away from.

He growled and tightened his grip. "I can still make this work." In a smooth move so quick that I wasn't sure how it happened, he spun me around so I was facing the wall and his chest was pressed against my back.

With one arm banded around my middle, holding me against him, the other slid around me. He nudged my feet apart and leaned in to kiss my neck. My muscles relaxed under his touch in every spot he kissed.

My head rolled to the side, granting him access, and he peppered kisses down my neck until he got to the base above my collarbone and began to suck. "More," I demanded, and he delivered. My palms splayed against the cool cinder blocks as heat rose up inside me, fighting off the shiver of anticipation.

His hand dipped into the waistband of my leggings and continued downward, pushing them to the floor along with my underwear. He teased me until I rolled into him, and he slid a finger in, spreading my arousal before dipping farther inside. His movements were smooth and slow, the complete opposite of the impatient storm brewing inside me.

I let go of the wall, desperate for something to do, or else I'd leave finger-sized chunks in the cinder blocks. I gripped his arm that was holding me and tugged, wanting to pull him closer. Needing him like I needed air.

"Love, if I was any closer to you, I'd be inside you," he growled against my neck, before adding a second finger and pumping faster. His hand flew up to cover my mouth as I moaned, still managing to brace my body at an angle with his arm, and I nearly fell as I rearranged my grip, still desperate for something to do, some way to move.

"Ride my hand," he whispered, nibbling my earlobe.

I rolled my hips forward in time with his fingers, and he tightened his hold over my mouth as I came, my head nearly cracking his collarbone as I flung it back in the process. He milked my orgasm until I went limp in his arms, and then he pulled his fingers out, brought them to his lips, and sucked. "You taste just as amazing as you feel."

Without releasing me, he maneuvered us so he was sitting on the nearby chair and positioned me in his lap, fixing my tunic and apron over my leggings. I rested my head against his shoulder as he rubbed my back, and my eyelids drooped.

"You're next," I whispered, then glanced up when I sensed something. That was weird.

"Watching you come was more than anything I expected to experience tonight, but I look forward to it," he murmured as he pushed hair out of my face, and then frowned when he saw my eyes. "What's wrong?"

"I don't know. I thought we were being watched, but there's no one there. It was probably nothing." The hallway was still dark with the only light coming from the kitchen at the other end of the hall and the windows on the swinging doors just beyond.

He followed my gaze, came to the same conclusion that it was probably nothing, and chuckled. "Could be all the people out in the diner who missed out on dinner and a show."

I laughed and turned to kiss him when something else caught my eye. I stumbled off his lap. "No." I rushed to the door that led to the outside and pressed against it. The door was ajar. "It wasn't like this twenty minutes ago when I was back here taking trash out. I know I shut it. Someone was here after all."

My heart hammered at the thought of someone watching

us, and I wanted to recoil, to curl up in Julian's arms and have him tell me everything would be alright.

He opened the door and stepped outside. He looked around and, finding nothing, came back inside and shut the door tight. "Maybe someone came back here after you did. One of the new staff who needed a phone or smoke break."

"I didn't smell smoke out there."

He sighed. "Neither did I."

"It could have something to do with what I overheard out here a few days ago. I don't like this feeling. Something is off."

A thin stream of light illuminated us, and I turned around to see Justine standing at the end of the hall. "If you've cooled off, I could really use the help. Maribel went home for the day."

"On our way," Julian called, and Justine disappeared, leaving us in darkness again.

"I'm going to clean up, I'll see you out there." I lifted onto my toes to give him a kiss before we parted way to disappear into the bathrooms. I made a mental note to keep a better eye on that door, because something definitely wasn't right.

Chapter Thirty-One

Makena

Excitement filled me as I entered the house and rushed up the stairs. Tonight I was going to run through the woods with my wolves and let all my stress and frustrations out for the trees to swallow up. They were great at keeping secrets. After everything that had happened lately, I was so ready for this. I could practically feel the excitement bleeding out of me with every step I took.

I paused mid-step at the landing when I saw my bedroom door was ajar. That was strange, I'd gotten pretty careful with making sure it was closed every day.

Not a sound could be heard as I walked to the door and pushed it open, then my heart threatened to stop when I saw the scene inside.

My dad was sitting on my bed with a broken and forlorn expression on his face. Bloodied and shredded scraps of fabric hung from his loose hands, and the floor had a trail of the shredded clothing leading over to my overturned waste-basket that I never got around to emptying out.

"Dad?" My voice was hesitant. I didn't know what to say or even where to begin. He didn't react when I spoke, so I tried again. "Dad!"

He lifted his head slightly. "What's going on, Makena? Are you in trouble?"

My stalled heart hit the floor when I saw the look of utter helplessness on his face. I'd never seen him look so broken before, and it was because of me. Because of something I'd kept from him, and now he thought I was in over my head with trouble. Which I pretty much was, only not the kind he probably suspected.

"I promise you, it's not what you might think."

"What do I think? Because I'm at a loss for words right now. Did I do something wrong?" His eyes shot to me and my heart clenched. "Who are you?"

I wanted to hang my head and stand there without answering. It would be easier to let him come up with his own theories and for me to ask for forgiveness. But I was tired of taking the easy way out and hiding from everyone. Who I was wasn't only because of my mom, it was because of him too, because I wasn't only a wolf and he deserved to know about this.

"It's a long story, if you'll give me time to explain."

"I have nowhere else I'd rather be."

I nodded, shut the door out of habit, and walked over to the head of the bed. Once I was situated with a pillow in my lap and was contentedly picking at the end of the pillowcase, I blew out a heavy breath and began.

"It all started a few months ago."

I told him about waking up in the woods, keeping a key around my neck, and even the part about missing clothes. I shared the strange dreams that didn't make sense at the time, then watched the color leave his face when I talked about my first memory of shifting.

For a while there, I thought I might only be convincing him I was crazy, but when I got to the part about the woman on the lamppost, a light came back into his eyes.

"That makes more sense now," he uttered, and I felt a sense of relief flood through me that he might believe me after all. I hadn't realized how terrified I was of rejection by my only living family member.

I even took out the picture I'd found of my mother in the attic and showed them to him. His eyes scrunched in confusion when I pointed out the wolves. He already knew about the picture, but there was a lot more to the story behind the picture that he wasn't aware of.

After I told the story all the way through until today, including how I thought we were being watched but leaving out what all happened in that hallway tonight, he was sitting as still as a statue. I watched him as I waited for him to move, to say something, to do anything at all.

Finally, after I didn't think I could take it anymore, he spoke. "Wow."

Okay, so that wasn't the prolific kind of fatherly advice I was half expecting, but it could have been worse.

"What do you think?" I asked, begging for some kind of a reaction as I squeezed the pillow tighter and mindlessly ran my fingernail along the seam.

His fingers twisted around the shredded clothing in his hands. "It's a lot to take in. I hate to ask this, but…"

"Yeah, no problem." I set the pillow off to the side to prevent destroying it any further and sat up straight. Closing my eyes, I put all my focus into not screwing this up and, to my relief, I managed to avoid doing just that.

My eyes opened at his gasp, but this time my vision was through my wolf. I was still sitting up in the bed, but my eyes, nose, and mouth were all wolf-like features. My nails were elongated into claws with hair covering my hands, and

I'd managed to avoid busting out of yet another pair of clothes, which was a huge relief because I badly needed to go shopping for a new wardrobe.

It was a partial shift and it wasn't comfortable, so I couldn't hold it for long, but thanks to all the time I'd spent practicing, I was improving with each passing day.

His eyes widened and his mouth fell open with a squeak. I quickly shifted back to normal and pulled the pillow into my lap to put a physical barrier between us.

"It's okay, I was pretty shocked the first time too, and I didn't want to believe it or talk about it with anyone. It's okay to be surprised, but please don't be afraid of me. I'm still me, I'm still the same Makena. Just with a few…upgrades."

"I now understand why you've been climbing the tree to your room more often than using the front door."

"Wait, you knew about that?"

He smiled, sending a sense of relief rushing through me with that small action. "Many times when I'd be leaving for work, I'd see you running down the street, jumping between bushes, and then climbing the tree. I never got a close enough look to realize you weren't wearing any clothes, so I might need to start becoming more observant myself, but yeah. I noticed. And all those fast food bags in the kitchen trash can? I thought you were throwing parties, I didn't realize you ate all those yourself."

"Wait, you thought I was throwing house parties and didn't say anything to me?"

He shrugged. "You spend so much time studying and working, I was glad you might be having a social life."

I laughed. "Now my social life is with wolves."

"So those young men from out of town who were here for dinner the other night?"

I nodded. "Yeah, those were two of them."

"I see. Now that I know you've got the fated mates thing going on, I may need to meet them again. More officially."

"Uh, I'll see what I can do."

He smiled and set the clothing scraps on the bed. "I'll leave these for you to decide what to do with, but Makena, you don't need to keep anything from me. Thank you for telling me."

"So when I do end up shifting at night, you're not going to worry still?"

He let out a laugh and it sounded genuine. The strain that was in his voice was now gone. "Oh, I'm still going to worry. Even more so, and I might be checking your room every night to make sure you're safe. I'd be less worried, though, if you were out partying with people I didn't know, to be honest. This is a whole different ball game, and I have no idea how to handle anything." He pinched the bridge of his nose. "I can't believe all this time Mercaida was real. And all the stories she told."

With a sigh, he shoved a hand through his hair and stood up. "But do what you need to do. I'll always be here, and whenever you need anything, just ask."

"You got it." I bounded from the bed and threw my arms around him in a hug. "Thanks."

His hand rubbed my back. "You got it, kiddo."

Chapter Thirty-Two

Makena

*C*asen's heartbeat thudded beneath my cheek as I rested my head against his chest. His fingers glided up and down my arm as we laid on the ground and listened to the night life ending. The sunlight tried in vain to heat the frosted window, and not a single bird could be heard, all still nestled inside their nests. All was silent and peaceful, exactly how I wanted every morning to feel like.

We'd spent the night running, playing, and learning. I became more in tune with my wolf than ever before, and I was getting better and stronger by the day. I was convinced that by the time I went to Mercaida, I could blend in like a normal born and raised wolf.

Going to Mercaida was something I still needed to bring up with the guys. Things had been a little crazy around here, and our attention had been constantly split between so many crises that needed our attention. We hadn't had time for all of us to spend together, like we were doing now, even if the rest of them were asleep.

Casen wasn't though. He was a cuddler and refused to go to sleep until I did, but my brain was too wired with all the thoughts that kept running through my mind, and I was looking forward to what the next day might bring.

"What's going through your head?" Casen whispered, his lips against the top of my head. A blanket was draped over us, plus there were blankets beneath us and the hoodie I was wearing, but his voice still sent a shiver through me despite how warm I was.

"A lot of things." I maneuvered my finger so I was drawing invisible objects across his chest.

"Anything you want to talk through?"

I smiled. He was so sweet. I thought back to the first time I met him when he brought my clothes back to me and I shoved drinks in his hands. Good times. "I've been thinking about things lately. My friends found out what I am, but one of them moved away."

"And the other?"

"She's still here. Always busy with work, of course, but she won't say anything."

"That's good. I'm glad you have some people you can talk about it with. It's a big change, what you're going through."

"I also told my dad a few nights ago." My finger paused as it hovered over the blanket and I looked into his eyes. "I didn't have much of a choice, but he really didn't know anything about my mom being a wolf, so he was pretty surprised when I told him about me."

"I can imagine that must've been a big shock."

"It was, but I think he handled it well." I chuckled. "He honestly handled it better than I did."

"That's good to hear." There was a pause, and then he continued, "Is there anything else on your mind?"

"You guys have stayed here for me." I said it as a statement, since there was no question about it. They'd all admitted it, saying that finding their mate was always a wolf's top priority, even with everything Mercaida was going through.

"Mm-hmm," he mumbled. "And it's been worth it."

"I think we should continue on."

His fingers paused in their stroking. "What do you mean?"

"I'm ready to leave. I want to help. Continue on the journey you were on before, searching for allies, and then go back to Mercaida."

I waited for him to speak, biting my lip, but silence surrounded us. Birds above sang their morning song, but it wasn't the sound I was waiting for.

"Okay."

"What?" I lifted my head to look at him.

"We'd need to go over it with the others first, but I don't see why we'd have to stay here forever. We may need to stay a little longer until we're all convinced you're ready, but it could happen."

A smile lit up my face, and I lifted my arm to thread my fingers through his hair. The way the light was shining through the bare treetops and landing on his face made it look almost like he was glowing.

A sharp sound abruptly cut through the air, rousing all of my wolves who crouched low to the ground. A second blast went off, and Liam and Axel threw bags around for the guys who hadn't dressed after our nighttime wolf run. We hunched down, afraid to move. With my back to a tree, I wrapped my arms around my middle, grateful for my hoodie. The simple fabric wouldn't be able to shield me from a bullet, but it gave the false sense of security I needed. Once we were all clothed, we huddled closer together when a third gunshot sounded.

"What are they shooting at?" I whispered, as my breathing turned erratic.

"I don't know, but it's not us. Otherwise they would've hit us at least one of those times, it wasn't like we were moving," Denver murmured, as he kept his gaze on the forest around us.

When another gunshot didn't follow, we ran from tree to tree until we reached the town again. A car stopped in front of us on the road, and my dad hung his head out of the window. "Get in."

We piled into the car. I had no idea how we managed to fit five grown men in the back seat with me in the passenger seat, but somehow it worked.

"I was so worried. When I heard the shots, I went looking for you," my dad explained, as he turned the car toward the house.

"I'm sorry." I absentmindedly lifted my hand and played with the frayed ends on a few strands of my hair. "It wasn't at us, we don't know what happened."

"They could be shooting at whatever is responsible for the attacks," he suggested, and turned into our driveway. "As long as it wasn't you, though, it doesn't matter."

He cut off the engine and let out a long breath.

"After losing her, I couldn't bear the thought of losing you too."

I met his gaze with a smile. "Me too. Don't worry, I'll always be around." I swallowed hard when I realized what I'd just said.

"You don't need to stay in Carlisle forever though, you know that, right?"

"What?"

"If you ever want to leave, just let me know. And be careful. I'll always be a phone call away."

The back seat was silent as I took in his words. I guessed it was time to have a conversation with them.

———

A TAPPING on my window startled me out of my research, and I spun around in my chair. Kira was at my window, and she waited patiently for me to open it and let her in.

"What are you doing here?" I whispered. "Not that I'm not happy to see you," I quickly added.

"Nice to see you too," she said, as she plopped onto my bed and sank into the pillows. "I forgot how amazing a bed could feel." She sat upright before she could get too comfortable and crossed her legs as she fixed me with a serious expression. "I have some news."

"What kind of news?" I perched in my chair with my knees pulled to my chest.

"I don't know, but something isn't right."

"Things haven't been right for a while, Kira," I pointed out.

"This is different. I saw something."

I nodded for her to continue. She had my full attention.

"I was running around in the forest like every other day, minding my own business, when there were creatures there that didn't belong."

"Do you mean like more wolves?" I pressed. "They seem to be popping up everywhere nowadays. I'm not even kidding."

She shook her head. "Not necessarily. I mean, kinda, probably, but also no. They were something different."

"Well, what did they look like?"

"I don't know."

"That narrows it down." I glanced down at my notes and finished the sentence I'd been writing.

"They wore these dark cloaks so I couldn't see them and they walked kinda funny, but I can't really explain how. I never saw their faces with the hoods covering them. They looked human from the general shape, but they were definitely not fully human, if at all."

"There are a lot of creatures out there. I didn't even know about wolves until recently. Maybe it's something new?"

She shook her head. "I'm telling you, this is different. I haven't felt something like this before." She shivered. "They felt cold and evil. I think they probably knew I was there, but they let me go. I don't know. But with everything that's been going on, I figured I'd warn you."

"Thanks, I appreciate it and will keep a lookout."

She sniffed the air. "Do you have cheese?"

I chuckled and tossed her the bag of cheddar potato chips. "Help yourself, I need to find some real food anyway."

We passed the next few hours talking by going over some of my schoolwork. She was fascinated with the assignments I had, and what the humans were teaching other humans about animals. She muttered objections and rolled her eyes at some of the things humans claimed to know. We made it through a good portion of my schoolwork in a short amount of time, and I was pretty sure she even learned more about humans than I did about the assignment. I was so close to graduating now, I could practically taste it. Only a few weeks left to get through.

It was dark by the time she got up to leave, and even though the house was empty and she could use the front door, she insisted on using the window and climbing down the tree. She said it was more exciting that way. I didn't argue. Apparently my idea of exciting—before discovering wolves, of course—was a slow night at the diner.

Her back stiffened and she paused with one foot on a branch and the other one still inside the window. She looked out into the darkness, first at the broken street lamp, and then surveyed the area

"What is it?" I peered over her shoulder. Her nose twitched as she sniffed the air. I squinted, but I couldn't see anything.

"It's nothing, I guess. I thought I sensed something, but now it's gone." After a few more moments of scanning the darkness, she pushed herself the rest of the way out. "I'll do a round anyway to make sure."

As she lowered herself to the ground, I noticed a pair of yellow eyes across the street. They locked on me for a brief second before disappearing into a rustle of leaves in the bushes nearby. It could have been anything, but I didn't like the chill that ran down my back.

"Hey, do wolves have yellow eyes?" I asked, as she started to climb down. Perhaps I only imagined it.

"Some of them do, but if so then it's not a good sign. If you ever see a wolf with yellow eyes, run." She reached the bottom, stuck her hands in her coat pockets, and walked the length of the street. Each step she took was carefully placed as she studied her surroundings.

I watched the area for a while after she left, but I didn't see anything again. Instead, I convinced myself it wasn't anything to worry about, that I was seeing things. Perhaps the moonlight reflected wrong in the animal's glassy orbs. I came up with a long list of excuses to set my mind at ease, because one more puzzle piece to figure out would send me spiraling.

Chapter Thirty-Three

Makena

The door was unlocked when I tested the handle and then pushed my way into the diner. The only light inside was the glow filtering in through the windows. "Hello?" I called out. A cool blast of air hit me as the door shut, and I rubbed my hands against my arms, shivering. I wondered why the heat wasn't on in here. We wouldn't get busy until tonight when all the patrons would pile in and add their warmth.

"Oh, good, you're here." Rodge burst through the swinging doors and greeted me with a smile as he wiped his hands with a rag. "Perfect timing, it's almost ready."

"I'm glad I could help out. What is it you need me to do exactly?"

"Follow me and I'll show you." He waved for me to join him as he pushed through the swinging door again, and I did the same. Turning into the kitchen and the only place with a light on, I looked around and noticed various pots and pans with steam rising from them on the stove. It didn't smell like anything I recognized, which surprised me since I'd eaten everything that had been served here.

"Sit, sit." He gestured to a stool at the end of the long counter in the middle, and as he did so, his sleeve rose up his arm, exposing a long bandage.

"A cooking accident?" I asked, nodding at his arm.

He chuckled. "Something like that, you could say. Sit down, I'm eager to get started."

I did as he asked and waited while he added contents from the various pots and pans into a bowl and set it in front of me. And unfamiliar odorless steam wafted up.

"What is this?" I eyed the food before me. I couldn't figure out exactly what it was, but something felt off about it. My stomach, which would normally welcome every morsel I could get my paws on, revolted at the thought of even touching this food. The hopeful grin on his face was the only thing that kept me in the seat.

"It's a new recipe I'm testing out, and I wanted to get your opinion on it." He leaned inward with his hands braced against the edge of the countertop about a foot from me. His eyes were lit with an anticipation I hadn't seen in him before. This was the largest I'd ever seen his smile, and it looked like a genuine one. "I'm really eager to see what you think."

Not wanting to let him down, I picked up the spoon and paused before dipping it into the bowl. "What did you say was in this again?"

His smile widened. "I didn't say. It's a new recipe I'm trying out and want to get an opinion on. It's a secret surprise, if you will."

Deciding to get it over with so I could get back outside, I dipped the spoon into the bowl and lifted it toward my mouth, but I paused before it touched my lips.

Alarm bells were ringing in my head, but I didn't know why. The soup looked to be a normal red color, but I couldn't make out what it was made of or what the solid chunks were. I'd never failed a food test before. I could always tell exactly what it was just by the smell, so I couldn't stop myself from hesitating. I worked in a diner for crying out loud, food was something I knew rather well.

"I'm so excited for someone to try it," he urged.

"Did you talk to Justine about it?" I inquired, stalling for time. "She might be interested in a new recipe. Anything to keep the overflow of customers beyond maximum capacity."

"I wanted to surprise her. I thought it would go over better if I had a taste tester to back me up first."

My hand shook as I tried to force the food between my lips, and I finally gave up. The spoon clinked against the porcelain bowl when I dumped it back in, soup and mystery chunks splattering the countertop. "I'm sorry, I can't seem to eat it. Maybe have someone else try it?"

His eyes hardened, sending a chill down my spine. "There is no one else."

"It won't be long before the waitstaff scheduled for today will be here. They'd love to try it out, they don't need any excuse for free food. I believe Maribel should be showing up first along with Justine." I knew I was rambling, but I couldn't stop the word vomit of excuses from spilling out. "You could probably get her in here while Justine is setting up the diner." I pushed against the counter as I tried to stand, but his hand shot out and wrapped around my wrist, holding me in place as he squeezed. I swallowed a yelp, frozen in place as the pressure on my bones turned painful. His shirt rose up, exposing even more of the bandage, and I saw a small circle of blood at the top.

My eyes widened with surprise. He'd never done anything like this before in the time I'd known him, and his eyes had never looked this hard.

"Stay. Eat the food, Makena." His voice was sharp, leaving no room for disagreement.

I swallowed hard, unable to take my gaze off his arm. That was no kitchen accident. "I'm sorry to disappoint you, but I can't. I really do have to go."

"Go where?" he snarled. "Running off to those wolves of yours?"

His words were like a punch to my gut. "How did you—"

"What? How did I know?" He chuckled. "Why do you think I stayed in this crap shoot of a town instead of going somewhere better? I know who you are, Makena. I know *what* you are." He tilted his head toward his arm. "I even got riddled with bullets the other morning when I was trying to spy on you and your little wolf friends, waiting for the perfect moment to take you out one by one while you slumbered."

My heart pounded and I couldn't hear beyond the ringing that filled my ears. This didn't make sense, none of it did. Then I thought back to the strange occurrences in the dark hallway here, and my spine turned to steel.

He was the threat I'd been looking for.

Another piece fit into the jigsaw puzzle in my mind, but for once I wasn't thrilled. This wasn't the kind of situation I wanted to fill a spot in my puzzle. This wasn't something I wanted to deal with. Unfortunately, I didn't get to pick my battles.

The ringing subsided as my body hardened, preparing for an inevitable fight.

When my words failed me, he kept talking. "I need you to eat this food."

"No."

His eyes turned yellow, and his black hair that was tinged with gray grew out into a mane that covered his body. He snarled as his mouth elongated into a snout, shifting until a scraggly black and gray wolf was standing on the counter in front of me. Where my fur was silken, his was dried out and ratty. I could visibly see the fleas jumping up from around his mane and clear down to his paws. His breath wheezed as he growled. The whole sight repulsed me.

Unlike my beautiful wolves, he looked like a whole other breed. His white chef's coat hung from his thin body, and he had to shake it off since his wolf didn't fill it out enough to fully rip it to shreds with his shift.

A howl erupted as he threw his head back, and I turned to run, but the door shut before I could reach it, and I heard something heavy fall against the door from the outside. I grabbed the handle anyway, but the door still wouldn't budge. Someone was on the other side, fighting me on the handle.

"Help!" I pounded on the door, denting it slightly with a strength I didn't realize I had. "Let me out, please."

However, whoever was on the other side only snickered in response, and I accepted he wasn't going to help me after all. He was only helping Rodge. This was a bigger setup than I realized.

"Son of a—" I turned to face the beast who was salivating as he watched me from the counter. His growls shook his frail body, which I had no doubt was much stronger than it actually looked. My senses were on high alert, and I was angry with myself for not sensing he was a wolf much sooner. I felt sick at the thought that he'd known about me this whole time when I never once looked in his direction.

Without any other choice, I focused on calming my breathing. I needed to shift in order to protect myself, and it would go much better if I wasn't stuck in the middle of some messed up transformation because I couldn't get myself together.

My bones cracked and my body morphed until I was

glaring up at him from all fours. My paws kneaded the greasy linoleum and my back arched as I bared my teeth. He wasn't the only pup in town with a bite to match his bark. I might be new to shifter society, but underestimating me wouldn't bode well for him. Being backed into a corner only made me more ferocious, and I'd fight my way out as much as necessary.

He lunged toward me and I jumped, my teeth gnashing with his in midair as I aimed for his neck. I made contact with his shoulder, and we crashed to the floor and continued our fight as we slid around on the grease.

I didn't know how much time had passed before I heard a howl outside the door. It caused the split-second distraction I needed, so I took advantage of his misstep and used my full body weight to slam him against the nearest counter.

The force of the action sent vibrations upward, rattling the kitchen utensils above, and I jumped out of the way as a shower of knives and forks rained down. I heard a yelp as the metal blades made their landfall and the wolf stilled, with a growing puddle of red seeping out around him. I turned my head from the sight, averting my eyes elsewhere. Even though I couldn't sense his wolf earlier on, I could still feel the life force draining out of him at a rapid pace.

I knew it was life or death. The only choice I had was to kill or be killed. That still didn't make the situation any better. My body hunched over as I began to dry heave.

This was the only way. I was a caged animal, forced to fight for my survival. I'd never taken a life before, and the situation didn't do anything to calm my mind. I filled my head with excuses for why his death needed to happen, but my breathing only grew more ragged as I tried in vain to wrap my mind around it all. To connect the dots and understand the purpose of each one.

Something heavy was thrown around the hallway, and

the door busted from its hinges as wolves piled in. They were growling and menacing, ready for a fight, but they relaxed their stances when they spotted me and the motionless wolf on the floor at my back.

Casen was the first one to shift back into his human form. Kneeling down, he wrapped his arms around my shaking body and pulled me in close. I nuzzled him with my nose and hid my face in the crook of his neck. A Casen cuddle was exactly what I needed to calm me down and gather my thoughts before I figured out what just happened.

As my rapid heartbeat settled into a steady thrum, my body shifted back into human form. A shirt was placed over my head, and I was helped into it. I glanced up and saw Axel's bare chest as he stepped back and watched me with careful eyes. He had on pants and Casen was fully clothed. I didn't even notice when they had put on clothes. The sweats and t-shirt Casen was wearing looked oddly similar to the ones Julian kept hidden in a crate at the end of the back hallway. My brain struggled to process why he was wearing them, and my mouth couldn't form the words to ask such an odd question. It was strange how my mind zeroed in on something so small when I should be dealing with a much bigger issue.

"What happened here?" Casen questioned, as I sat up slightly and looked around.

The other three wolves were sniffing at Rodge's wolf body, which was now changing back into his human form, and the sight became even more gruesome. The sight of him in that form brought my anger bubbling to the surface, and I stood up on shaky legs.

"He's dead," Denver stated, as he shifted and reached for a chef's coat from the nearby rack.

I opened my mouth but nothing came out. Swallowing hard, I cleared my throat and tried again. "He tried to force me to eat something I didn't want to." *That's good, keep talking,*

I urged myself. "He said it was a new recipe he was trying, but I didn't want to touch it. I couldn't tell what it was, but something felt off, and I refused to eat it." My nose scrunched up as I recalled how hard it was to eat something so simple. "I literally couldn't get my hand to shove the spoon into my mouth when I tried. Then when I tried to leave, he attacked."

Axel picked the spoon up from the bowl on the countertop and sniffed it. "Poison," he announced, as he watched the chunky stream of cold soup fall from the spoon and back into the bowl. "It's laced with wolfsbane. It would've hurt you and most likely killed you."

"Why would he want to hurt me, and how is it he's a wolf and I had no idea?"

"You're a wolf and no one else had any idea," Julian replied, as he closed a button on the chef's coat he pulled on. His eyes were cold, and his fingernails dug into his palm with such force, I expected the simple act to draw blood. "Well, no one else did. I have no idea how he found out. This explains why I've never seen him. He always disappears every time I went into the kitchen, probably aware I would sniff him out. Did he say anything else to you?"

"He said he knew who and what I am, but didn't tell me how. I think he was working with someone else. Someone closed that door from the outside and blocked me in."

"We took care of it," Liam told me, sporting a matching chef's coat. "It was one of those new waiter kids. Mack. Turns out he was no high schooler, but an older adult. He looked really good for his age, fooled us all. I'm assuming this might explain the voices you heard talking in the hall, and might also explain some other things in general."

"Plus the yellow eyes," I mumbled.

"What was that?" Denver turned his dark gaze on me.

"I'd seen a pair of yellow eyes here and there. I always

thought it was nothing, since nothing ever happened. But now I realize he was spying on me. But then why not attack sooner, when I was more vulnerable? Why wait until here and now?"

"Because here and now is when you've been the most vulnerable," Casen answered.

"I don't understand."

Denver spoke up next. "At least one or more of us have been camped outside your house nearly every night and most days. Even in our human form, one of us was almost always with you when our wolves weren't. This was his chance to get you away from us, even from Julian. He wasn't scheduled to work until tonight."

"Then what about yesterday?" I asked.

"What about yesterday?" Denver questioned.

"Kira came to see me, and when she was leaving, I saw those yellow eyes again, but only for a split second before they disappeared, and I didn't see them again until now."

"Easy," Denver said. "You were still with a wolf. Even though she's a lone wolf, she likes you. I can't blame her. She would have most likely protected you if he was to attack right then, just like you would protect her and anyone else he attacks."

His explanation made sense. I didn't like it, but it sounded right.

"We really were being spied on," I muttered. My eyes caught on a pair of legs out in the hall. They weren't moving.

"He's alive, although I say he shouldn't be," Liam grumbled when he noticed my gaze.

"Let's take him and get out of here before anyone else arrives," Denver suggested, and Julian hoisted Rodge's body over his shoulder.

"Are we really going to walk out of here like this? It's broad daylight," I pointed out.

"We'll head out to the alley, dump the body, and then move it at night," Denver explained, as he led the way out of the kitchen. "My focus is more on the other one."

Liam picked up Mack, tossing him over his shoulder like he was trying to add to the bruises already forming, and we all followed Denver down the dark hall and out into the alley. Julian dumped Rodge into the dumpster, scrunching his nose as he did so, and then maneuvered the garbage bags to hide him from sight until we could get him later.

"There's something off about him," Julian observed. "He wasn't born a wolf."

Before I could ask what he meant, a scream sounded from inside and we all turned our attention to the still open door.

"We didn't clean up the blood," Axel said. "Run while we still have a chance."

Axel grabbed my hand and pulled me along as we darted off. Sticks and rocks cut into my feet, and my soles nearly froze on the icy asphalt, but I ran as hard and as fast as I could.

I didn't know how long we ran for, and I didn't pay much attention to where we were going, all I did was follow them until they stopped.

We ended up at the house they were staying in, and I realized it was the first time I'd actually been inside while they'd been here. Every other time, they'd been climbing through my window like everyone else in the world.

A blast of warm air greeted me when I slipped inside, and I fell onto the couch, taking my weight off my poor worn feet.

"What in the world, Makena?" Denver's eyes focused on the drops of blood that were trailing out from my feet and onto the carpet.

"Crap! I'm sorry, I wasn't thinking. I'll clean it up." I hopped up to find the bathroom, but Denver stopped me with his hands on my arms. I looked up at him, ready to apologize some more, but he began talking.

"That's not what I meant. I was talking about your feet. If I would have realized you weren't wearing shoes, then I would've carried you."

"Then your feet would be more messed up with having to carry me, too."

"They're used to the most rugged terrain. I don't actually need shoes, they're more for show and comfort. They ended up torn apart when we realized you were in danger and we jumped into action." His eyes were full of regret.

"Yeah, mine got messed up when I shifted. Honestly, though, I'd rather have my body still intact as opposed to a pair of shoes."

Axel appeared from the hallway carrying two tubs, one with first aid supplies and the other with some water. "Sit down, we got you."

Denver lightly pushed me to sit back down on the couch and I obliged. Axel sat on the coffee table across from me, set the tubs down, and dipped my feet into the water, while the others ran around getting supplies to tie Mack to a wooden chair. His head lolled to the side since he was still passed out, but ropes bound him to the chair at the chest, thighs, and calves, with his hands bound behind him.

Axel cleaned me up and treated my wounds. The water was a solid shade of pink by the time he set one foot back onto the carpet, nearly good as new, and the other was in his lap so he could massage my calf. I wanted to tell him he didn't have to, but it felt so good that I couldn't get the words out. My head fell back against the cushion as the tension left my legs. It was only when his hands traveled up to massage beneath my knee that I realized I wasn't wearing anything other than a shirt that fell to the top of my thighs.

He grinned as my cheeks heated. "Don't worry, I'm not up

to anything. We have some extra clothes here, and Casen should be coming back with some sweats."

As he finished speaking, Casen appeared in the living room carrying a pair of navy blue sweats, which he placed on the couch next to me. "There they are." Axel set my leg down and adjusted himself as he stood to turn his attention to their hostage, who was now beginning to wake up. He crossed his arms as a fire lit in his eyes.

"What did you do to me?" Mack struggled against the ropes to no avail, but I had to give him props for not giving up so easily. A bump was beginning to form on his head, and there was no blood that I could see, so they must have only knocked him out quickly and then busted through the door to get to me.

"Who are you and where are you from?" Denver stood in front of him with his hands in his pockets, and his posture was so relaxed, I could have forgotten he was questioning a hostage.

"I'm Mack, and I was taken from the diner. Release me."

"Not the answer I'm looking for. Who sent you?" Denver's eyes grew colder with every question he asked, and it sent a chill through me. He was fair and calm, but what bubbled below the surface when someone he cared about was in danger could become quite alarming if this guy didn't give him the answers he wanted.

"You did, when you dragged me here," Mack gritted out through clenched teeth. His skin rippled as he tried to shift, but the ropes were too tight, causing him pain, so he remained in his human form.

"So you're a wolf," Denver stated as he watched him. He didn't flinch or act surprised with Mack's attempted transformation.

Since when did Carlisle have all these wolves? Had they always been here, blending into everyday human society, or was there a current hotspot going on that I wasn't aware of?

"A wolf who isn't supposed to be, on top of that. Who turned you?"

Mack's head flew forward as he spit, the little ball of saliva landing on Denver's chef's coat. He didn't flinch at the action, instead he stared him down, and Mack sank into his binds like a wounded pup.

"It's why we weren't able to sense the wolf in them," Julian whispered when he noticed me hanging on to every word. "When wolves are created, their scents are more difficult to detect. It's another one of the many reasons they're so dangerous. That Rodge guy was probably close to going feral."

"We may need to get the tools," Denver mused, and Mack's eyes widened. Julian moved to stand in front of him with a fire in his gaze, matching the inferno in the others'.

"W-What tools?" he sputtered.

"To make you talk." Liam walked toward the hallway, but before he could get far, Mack screamed for help at the top of his lungs. A loud *smack* cracked through the air as Julian left a red handprint on his cheek.

"Your attempt is futile," Julian warned. "If you're of no use to us, then we may as well dispose of you like we did the other."

Mack paled, every ounce of color draining from him like an old-time TV show as the words registered in his head. "The other? What happened?"

"He's dead, Mack. Lying in a dumpster in an alley. If you want to join him, that could save us a lot of trouble, but it would really be much easier if you talked." Denver's glare was unwavering, taunting him with his calmness.

Mack gulped. "Okay, fine." He slouched in the chair as much as the binds would allow. "I don't know who sent me, they didn't let me see their faces, but they paid a pretty penny for Rodge, Griffin, and me to place ourselves here. They said something was going to change here, that there would be a new female wolf we'd need to take out. We weren't given any more information, and for a while we thought it was a setup. They paid us half up front and then would pay the other half when the job was completed. It wasn't until a few months later when I spotted this one here" —he nodded in my direction— "running from bush to bush without a lick of clothing. The only reason that would've happened was if she either had a wild night or shifted and had no clothes to change back into. I asked around about her, and she didn't seem to be one for a wild night with how tight-ass she was about school and work. So, Rodge and I placed ourselves at the diner, and Griffin joined her class even though she never acknowledged him," his face scrunched up, disgusted with me. "And now here we are. Please don't kill me."

Everyone was silent for a while as they digested the new information.

"First off, who's Griffin?" Julian asked.

"Wasn't he in class with us?" Axel whispered to Liam.

Mack tried to shrug, but the ropes prevented him from doing so successfully. "Some other guy who wanted in on it. He'd been turned around the same time I was, but I haven't seen him in the last week or so."

Liam smirked. "Oh, that guy." Mack paled when the thought of what happened to him ran through his mind.

"Do you have a pack?" Denver inquired, and Mack shook his head. "You're a lone wolf then. Seem to be running into quite a few of those lately," he grumbled.

Mack looked confused. "What do you mean? As far as I'm aware, it's only been me, Rodge, and Griffin. I didn't even know the guys until a few months ago."

"Were they lone wolves too?" Denver questioned.

Mack nodded. "We had a theory that they may be trying to bring lone wolves together into some messed up pack, but I guess it didn't work out that way after all." He looked so defeated, and for a moment I felt sorry for him. Until I remembered what he'd done to put me through all of this, then I no longer felt any pity for him.

"Was the money worth it?" I asked.

He turned his head to look at me. His eyes hardened and sent a chill through my body. "I guess not, since I won't be able to finish the job and will most likely lose my life."

"You remember that. Because you're not going anywhere alive," Denver growled before turning away. "Gag him and lock him in the closet." He sat down on the other end of the couch, leaned into the cushions with his head hung back, and pinched the bridge of his nose. The others shoved a sock into Mack's mouth and ushered him into the nearest closet, where we could no longer hear anything other than his mumbles.

The rest of the day passed exactly like that. We turned on the TV to drown out the noise while doing research. They took turns scouting around town looking for clues, then coming back empty handed and more frustrated than before. I found myself buried in our schoolbooks and on the computer, searching for anything that could be even the slightest hint about what we were up against.

That night I found myself lying across Casen's lap with his arm draped over me, while Julian stroked my hair. Liam and Axel took seats in the nearby chairs, their fingers flying across their keyboards as though in a race, and they jotted notes down in a worn notebook I hadn't seen them take out in class. It was dark and secured with a lock that only unlatched with a small key they each kept in their pockets. More secrets about their lives that I wanted to unearth.

"They're the best hackers I know. If there's something to

be found, they'll find it," Casen assured me, squeezing my hand. I smiled up at him. They ran through every theory they could think of, trying to figure out who the mysterious men were who sent Rodge, Griffin, and Mack into my life. Their brows were scrunched in such determination, I was afraid to break it by pointing out the odds that these guys were recruiting online was slim. According to Mack's story, we might have a better chance just by running around in the woods.

Warmth enveloped me as I snuggled against the men next to me. Casen's head drooped and light snores sounded as he fell asleep. My head rested against his shoulder as I drifted off next.

Fingers continued to stroke the curls of my hair and I heard Julian's voice whisper in my ear when I didn't move. "We'll keep you safe, Love."

Chapter Thirty-Four

Makena

A loud *smack* cut through my consciousness and I startled awake. I clutched the blanket to my chest as I sat up and looked around.

Mack was lying on the floor, still bound to the chair, with blood pooling around his mouth. Liam stood above him, shaking his hand in the air as though the tied and injured man had hurt him.

"What's going on?" I asked. Sunlight streamed in through the window behind me. When did morning happen?

"After the things he was saying, he's lucky he's still alive for now," Liam growled. "We have a problem."

"What's the problem?" Axel sat bolt upright.

"He's not bleeding enough."

"Dude, what did he say?" Axel asked as he got off the couch, and Casen took his spot on the cushion next to me and pulled me into his side.

"What's going on in here?" Denver questioned, as he appeared from somewhere down the hall.

"He was mumbling. He probably didn't realize anyone was listening, but I heard him." Liam was shaking with rage as he spoke. "He said he was going to kill her. He was debating if he should kill her slowly and make us watch, or kill us first and make her watch. He didn't know which way would cause more pain." His fists clenched at his sides, ready to swing again once given a target.

Denver looked at the man coughing on the floor. Blood spilled out of his mouth, dying the hardwood floor a cherry color. "Is this true?"

"Does it matter? Even if you kill me, it won't be enough. They'll still come after her. There are others."

Denver knelt beside him. "Why? Why does anyone want her dead?"

"Because she doesn't fully belong in either world and they don't want her."

"What's that supposed to mean?" he growled.

"I don't know, honestly, that's all they would tell me. That she would be a problem, but they weren't too keen on elaborating. I took the money and came here." Mack lifted his eyes to me and his teeth shined a bright red as he grinned. "Only a matter of time now, sweet cheeks."

The man keeled over and coughed up blood when Denver delivered a punch to his gut. He leaned in to whisper to him, but it was so quiet in here that I could still hear him clear as day. "If you touch one hair on her, I will personally skin you alive myself and make anyone you care about watch. If you want to live, then you should do as we say."

Mack nodded, and they left him to lie on the floor as they washed up. "It's a good thing I don't have anyone I care about." His words were so low, I wasn't sure if the others had heard him, despite how quiet it was. Lines appeared on his face that weren't there a few days ago. He was aging before my eyes and looked as though he wouldn't hold on much longer. I'd be surprised if he made it through another day.

Julian appeared in front of me with a tray filled with fruit and various breakfast bars. His knuckles were white as he held the tray with a death grip and watched the bound man while I perused the small selection. "This is a little bit of everything we have, so take your pick."

My stomach grumbled as I reached for an apple and a breakfast bar and then set them on the table. "I'll be right back. Going to the restroom."

I hurried down the hall. In the bathroom I stood with my hands gripping either side of the sink, looking at myself in the mirror. I looked worse than ever before. Not only with general life wearing me down, but all of this life and death stuff. Who knew that finding out who I was would be so wild?

My face blurred slightly as a transparent image of my wolf appeared then disappeared before I could realize what was going on. She was always with me. She was a part of me, and she'd tried to warn me about who I was long before the change began taking place.

I recalled running around the playground with Austin and Leah. They wanted to play cops and robbers, but I invented a wolf character. I was very convincing.

When I was young, I went weeks without sleeping because I couldn't stop dreaming about being chased through the woods, and large creatures in scary masks.

In a way, I guessed I'd always known this was going to happen. It only took me a long time to answer the call.

WE DROVE to the diner later that morning with Mack in the trunk of the car. Justine was frantic over the phone. Cops wanted Julian and me to come in and give character statements along with the rest of the employees, but the guys refused to let us split up. They also wouldn't leave Mack alone at the house, so he was now tied up, gagged, and passed out in the trunk. My stomach was in knots the whole drive there, wondering what I was going to say to her. We all agreed it would be best to act like we didn't know anything about what went down yesterday, as it would raise too many questions that we wouldn't be able to answer.

Well, if we did answer them accurately, no one would believe us anyway.

I pushed my way through the front door of the diner, like I had nearly every other day for the last couple years. The inside was somber. It had a darkened feel to it even with the fluorescent lights illuminating the crowded space. Tears and sniffles were like a music track on repeat. The diner was closed for business today and the place looked like a crime scene. The once vibrant place I'd spent most of my time when I wasn't studying now sent chills through my body. Memories from the night before haunted me, and I couldn't even tell the one person who relied on me the most, why I didn't want to be here. Yellow tape blocked off the kitchen, which I could see through the swinging doors that were now propped open on either side to keep them open while cops and detectives filed through to do their jobs. Shivering at the memory of Rodge's yellow eyes and hard stare as I refused to eat his poison, I averted my gaze.

Cops roamed around talking with people. I swallowed hard, reminding myself that I knew absolutely nothing and was going to be as surprised as everyone else. Julian stood with a hand against my lower back, and the other guys wandered around outside, keeping an eye on everything. At the earliest sign of trouble, they would be the first to know, and we'd have a split-second heads-up to prepare ourselves.

Justine's tear-streaked face glistened in the overhead lights, and when she spotted me, she pushed up from where she was sitting at a table and ran over to me. I braced myself for an onslaught of questions, but she surprised me by throwing her arms around my waist, forcing Julian's hand to leave my back to make room for her fumbling fingers to grip the back of my shirt.

"I'm so glad you're okay," she cried into the oversized shirt I was still wearing from the day before.

I returned the hug and patted her back. "What's happened, Justine?" The question nearly caught in my throat as I feigned ignorance, and guilt ate at me that I couldn't give her the answers to make everything alright. I couldn't be truthful with the person who always worked so hard to serve others, and was no doubt feeling like something heinous happened to a beloved employee and a hard worker. If she only knew the truth, her tears would shed for a different reason.

"Oh, it's so horrible." She continued to sob for a few more minutes then pulled away. Her eyes were puffy from hours of crying, and she wasn't even bothering to wipe the tears away. They left streaks down her swollen cheeks and created small puddles on the diner floor. "It's Rodge."

My body stiffened at the mention of his name. Not because I was concerned with what she was about to say, but because I could still see his teeth filling my vision as he smiled and urged me to eat his poison. The fleas that were jumping from his matted fur were still seared into my mind. I forced my face into an expression of concern and cleared my throat. "What about him?"

"He's dead, Makena."

"What do you mean?" Her confirmation gave me comfort while I consoled her.

"I don't know, but that's not what matters." She lifted

some wadded-up tissues that she had clutched in her hand and blew her nose.

I furrowed my brow, confused. "I'm afraid I don't understand." Why wouldn't his death be what mattered right now? I felt like I was missing something.

"I'm just glad you're okay." She tightened her grip around me and my mind swirled. There was no way she could know I was involved. Even if she did, she would know about wolves, and that would raise a whole other issue.

"Ma'am, if I could have a word with you."

I turned my attention to the man who had spoken—a cop. He looked rather young and had a serious expression painted across his face.

"Can someone tell me what's going on here?" I knew more than anyone else present, I was sure of that, but for some reason I felt as though I was out of the loop. Even Julian had stiffened his spine at the curious tone in his voice and turned his ear toward us, his full attention on what the cop was saying.

"How well did you know Rodge Callister?"

"I don't know. He worked in the kitchen and I'm a waitress. I put in orders for food, he made the food, I took the food out. Those are literally the only interactions I've ever had with him."

"We have reason to believe he was stalking you."

My heart pounded. My mind filled with questions I couldn't outright ask. "Come again?"

He handed me an envelope, and I pulled out the contents. There were pictures of me with little notes with short written descriptions about what I looked like and what I did with my life. On the backs of the pictures were scribbles of what I was doing that day.

Rodge was watching when I overslept and drove to class in a panic.

He was there when I was with Kira in the park walking the dogs.

He saw me running home the day I was shot at, and his picture caught the shortened lock of hair, which was still uneven. My hand reached up to touch the damaged curl, as if to be sure.

"This is unbelievable," I whispered, as I flipped through every picture. Bile rose in the throat. "I think I'm going to be sick."

The cop took the pictures from my hands and gave me a pitiful look. "We don't know what exactly happened to him. The cameras in the kitchen and all around the diner were conveniently disabled during the incident. It is unknown at this time if it was an accident or murder."

"How did he…" My voice trailed off. I knew exactly how he died, but they weren't aware of that.

"Pierced by kitchen utensils. Another employee found him in the trash. I was hoping you had some sort of connection that could help this case, but as it stands, we really have no idea what's going on here, or your involvement in this case."

My blood turned cold as I looked down at the pictures that were now in his hand, wondering if they suspected me for murder. A voice told me of course they did, I wouldn't be standing here talking to him at this moment if I wasn't a suspect. We were all suspects, and it was my fault this was happening. I hated how these good, innocent people were dragged into something I couldn't quite handle on my own.

"I'm sorry this has happened to you," he continued, his voice softening as my face drained of color, "but I have to tell you to watch your back. There's no guarantee that he was alone in his interest of you."

He had no idea how right he was. Rodge wasn't alone in this at all. His partner was tied up and knocked out in the trunk of the car I rode here in, but I wasn't about to admit that to a room full of cops. Shifters remained hidden for a reason, and I wasn't going to expose them because of my desire to help.

"Thanks for letting me know, I'll be sure to keep an eye out."

After answering every question that was thrown at Julian and me, consoling a weeping Justine and a freaked out Maribel, while trying to keep the whole story straight for them, we headed back outside. However, when we reached the car, the trunk was wide open and nobody was anywhere to be found.

We immediately went on the defensive. Our backs pressed together as we looked around at our surroundings. I listened for every noise I could hear, even the faintest whisper of butterfly wings in the wind. Then I heard it.

Muffled noises sounded from nearby, and we rushed toward them until we found our guys kneeling on top of Mack.

"He tried to get away," Liam informed us as we approached, without taking his eyes off the man. They were darker than I'd ever seen them before and filled with a coldness that made me take a step back.

"We heard him talking, so we opened the trunk," Denver said. "Don't know if it was a ruse to get us to let him out, or if he has a way to communicate with someone."

I knelt on the ground and gripped Mack's chin between my thumb and forefinger, turning his head to face me. "You had one job, and you failed. You have no power over me. I just came from the diner. It's a crime scene right now, and all I have to do is drag you back there. Do you want that? Do you really want to be handed over to the police to explain your involvement? You're not exactly innocent." His eyes widened and I smiled. "Didn't think so. Now let's go."

"What are we going to do?" Casen asked.

"Take him back to the diner, let the cops deal with him. He can rot in jail. If he tries to tell anyone the truth, they won't believe him. His mouth will cause him more issues than we could inflict. On top of that, if these mysterious beings get mad that he didn't fulfill his end of the bargain, they can take care of him. He's someone else's problem now." I walked back toward the diner. I was tired of dealing with things that caused me nothing but stress.

Liam hoisted Mack over his shoulder and followed me. Axel was a lookout, using his camera to focus in and make sure the coast was clear before we dumped him. Liam gave him one final knock into unconsciousness, and we left him slumped against the driver's side door of a police car.

"Where do you want to get lunch?" I inquired, as we headed back to the car. "I'm thinking somewhere outside of town."

Chapter Thirty-Five

Makena

"Come on, we're going to be late," Leah said, as she urged me from my room. "You look perfect, now let's celebrate already."

I'd passed all my tests and was ready to embark on some new adventures. I had no idea what the future held for me, but I was excited to find out. First, I was going to take some time off, and travel around and help in the search for allies for Mercaida, before heading to the one place that could answer any of my lingering questions. It wasn't easy to get Denver and Liam to agree, but they eventually caved when they realized how much progress I was making connecting with my wolf. I hadn't destroyed my clothing in weeks, and all my shifts came with ease.

A thrill filled me when I thought about the adventure ahead. I was practically dying to find out more about myself.

We followed every lead we could find but always came up empty when it came to the strange creatures in the woods.

My wolf and I were now in sync, and when I felt like

something might be off, I listened to it. Hearing your instincts is one thing, but actually listening is entirely different. I couldn't become the shifter I was born to be if I ignored half of who I was.

I climbed into Leah's car with Liam and Casen in the back. The other guys were there early to help setup.

As we pulled into the diner, it became impossible to keep the excitement off my face. I unbuckled my seatbelt and was opening the door before Leah even put the car in park.

"Whoa there, wolf girl. I wouldn't recommend jumping out of a moving vehicle no matter what form you're in," she teased.

The diner was decorated with white and silver, the only color combination I requested, along with hints of blue. Very few people knew that reason was because it matched my wolf.

Everything was perfect. All my favorite people in the world were here, all except for one who was currently off adding adventure to his life, but the amount of people who willingly showed up to celebrate with me was more than I could've hoped for. I supposed I had more friends in this world than I thought.

Even Trischa greeted me with a smile while avoiding eye contact with Leah. I'd found out the reason Trischa left Austin was because she felt like there was something more with him and Leah. Despite denying her accusations, he still proved her right a few weeks later when he and Leah started to explore the spark between them. Even with him gone, the two girls still couldn't look at one another. Trischa was counting down the days until it was her turn to leave.

I still didn't know why she kept my secret. The warmest conversation we'd ever had was at my birthday party, and this was the first time we'd seen each other since. Whatever her reason was, I was grateful.

Even the cops from the incident a few weeks ago had come. Memories from that time sent a shiver down my spine, but I took comfort in knowing that Rodge was gone and Mack was rotting in jail. They found evidence that he was there when Rodge was killed, and he became the prime suspect. I assumed my wolves might have helped with that, being as clever as they were, but I accepted it and chose to move forward. He wouldn't be in there forever. It was only a matter of time before he went feral, and that wouldn't do him any good. I only worried about the other prisoners who were in there with him, so I asked to be kept up-to-date on his happenings, no matter how strange of a request that might have been.

I went to visit him a couple of weeks ago out of curiosity, he looked worse for wear. His skin was peeling, his eyes were yellowing, and his hair fell in clumps around the table when he talked to me through the glass. His voice held a sneer that only increased in intensity the longer I sat there, until I finally walked away from him, his growls growing more strangled and distant with each step I took.

My teacher, Mr. Morrison, walked in carrying a cheese plate and said, "Congratulations," as he passed. My other three wolves each greeted me with a kiss, and I shook my head at the surprised looks of those around me. They could think what they want. Very few knew about our relationship, and I didn't feel like explaining it to a room full of people right this moment.

Everyone was here now, and I kept looking at the door, expecting something terrible to happen because that seemed to be how things worked in my life. Things went well, I got happy, and then everything blew up.

"Looks like all your wolves are here," Leah whispered to me.

I shook my head when I looked around. "Almost. All but one of them are."

She counted all five of my guys. "Who did I miss?"

"Kira."

"Oh. Is she going to show?"

"Maybe, maybe not, but she seemed excited when I told her about all the food that would be here. Plus cake." I wrung my fingers as I watched the door and the familiar feeling of dread returned. My thoughts repeated. *Things went well, I got happy, and then everything blew up.*

"Maybe she's just running late, or she wanted to see you later. There could be too many people for her to be around right now."

"That's true. I'm going to step outside for a moment, I'll be right back."

"Do you need company?"

I smiled. "Thanks, but I'm good."

The road was eerily empty as I went outside and my guys filed out around me. "It's so quiet out here," I commented. The grass was covered in a thin layer of ice and the sky held the promise of snow.

"Of course it is. Because everyone who lives in Carlisle is currently inside eating cake," Axel joked, but the muscles in his forearms tightened when he clenched his fists. He looked up and down the street. I couldn't tell if he was just picking up on my paranoia, or if there was something else going on.

"I think she's right to be concerned," Denver whispered. "Something's coming."

We walked down the street, our ears perked for the slightest of movements, but not even a bee could be heard buzzing around the flowers that lined the road.

Quick movements from somewhere off to the side distracted us, and we all spun around to face whatever was hurtling toward us.

A woman covered in cuts and mud, with a mess of matted brown hair flying around her, came sprinting through the brush and ran right into me. I let out a cry when my arm slammed into the pavement.

"Kira? What happened?" I moved to the side and rolled her onto her back. Fur lined the sides of her face and the backs of her hands from a partial shift. She trembled when she raised her hands. Her eyes were wide and filled with terror and pain. "Kira, can you hear me?"

Her mouth opened and closed as she looked around, but her eyes were unfocused. There was something in her gaze that iced the blood in my veins.

Finally her mouth opened and she spoke, her words quiet and cracked.

"They came for me," she whispered.

"I don't understand. Who? Kira, talk to me," I urged.

"I saw them."

To be continued in Fall of the Alpha.

THANK YOU

Thank you so much for reading! It would mean the world to me if you left a review to help other readers who are looking for their next book. Reviews help both readers and authors and every single one counts.

BOOKS BY MAYA RILEY

Wolves of Mercaida

Call of the Wolf

Fall of the Alpha

Rise of the Pack

Releasing the Magic Series

Infected

Salvaged

Reclaimed

Veiled

Released

Stories from the Apocalypse

Standalones

Where the Blue Thorns Grow

Fuck You

ACKNOWLEDGMENTS

This is my first new series since I started publishing, and to say I'm nervous is an understatement. If you're reading this then I appreciate you so damn much for either sticking with me throughout this journey, or for picking up the book and giving a new author a try. You're amazing and beautiful inside and out. Keep searching for those new worlds.

Thank you to my editor and my new beta team for helping to make this even better than it started out as. I don't know where I'd be without you: Jess Rousseau, Amanda, Amber, Ashley, Brandy, Claire, Danyelle, Izzy, Jessica, Kaitlyn, Kathryn, Katy, Kelly, Kimberly, Nedia, Sabrina, Tiffany.

My husband: thank you for the support and encouragement to keep going and improving. And for making sure I still eat occasionally when I can't pull myself away from the computer.

ABOUT THE AUTHOR

Maya Riley enjoys coffee, long walks on the beach, a little hair pulling and—oh… let's start over.

Currently living in the South with her husband and all the critters that frequent their lake life, Maya has been experiencing the journey of good ole Southern cuisine, humid summers, and sassy idioms. While she can't handle sweet tea, she more than makes up for it with her obsessive coffee consumption. When Maya is not writing or occupied by any of the millions of hobbies she has, she's working on her fixer-upper home, laying by the pool—or in the pool, most likely with a margarita or a floating wine glass—or plotting world domination.

To keep up-to-date on releases, teasers for upcoming projects, and all-around craziness, join her reading group—Maya's Maniacs – A Maya Riley Reading Group: https://www.facebook.com/groups/mayasmaniacs/

For even more updates and the first to see certain additional scenes or sneak peeks, sign up for the newsletter on her website here: www.mayariley.com

Printed in Great Britain
by Amazon